Poured with Passion

A Blossom Hills Romance, Volume 5

Kate Alexander

Published by Kate Alexander, 2025.

This is a work of fiction. Similarities to real people, places, or events are entirely coincidental.

POURED WITH PASSION

First edition. May 15, 2025.

Copyright © 2025 Kate Alexander.

Written by Kate Alexander.

This book is dedicated to Patrick. Every girl should have that guy best friend who makes her laugh and is willing to go to extremes to make sure that it really is all good and everything is freaking wonderful.

Chapter 1

Derek's heart raced as he tried to make a discreet but expeditious exit from the bar to the back room and his office. Maniac Marla was back in town, and he definitely did not want to see her. Sure, her body could stop a man in his tracks, but her mind did not like to stay in reality. Nobody warned him when he first met her that she tiptoed on the line of sanity. Oh no, they let him find out the hard way. Some friends he had. She had been in town for one of the weddings at the orchard and said she was looking to have some fun before she went back home. And boy, did they have some fun, but once the sun rose, that was when things got really weird.

Marla decided that they were in love. She started making him breakfast and told him all about her plans to move to town so they could be together. It was a small miracle he was able to get her out of his house and convince her that he was in love with someone else. Was it a big lie? Yup. Should he have used someone else's name other than his best friend, Zoey? Abso-freaking-lutely, but hindsight is twenty-twenty and all that.

He could hear a commotion and loud voices out at the bar and cringed. Marla's shrill, shrieking voice was asking where he was. Tiny calmly told her that he was not available, but she was having none of it. He really needed to give Tiny a raise. There were so many times he chased off women for him; it was kind of embarrassing. Derek poked his head out of the office trying to listen to what was happening, only to hear the voice of Zoey also rising above the crowd. Shit, when did she get here?

"You broke his heart," Marla exclaimed. "He loves you and he can't move on because of you!"

Fuck. The last thing he needs is the whole town spreading rumors that they are more than friends. They had to put up with that crap in college. Deciding to face the music, he pushed the door open to face Marla. He first met Zoey's wide, stunned eyes, and she tilted her head in a non-verbal command that said do something about this. So much for his free cupcakes.

"Marla!" he shouted.

Marla's blonde hair whipped through the air as she turned to look at him. With a breathy sigh, she said, "Derek!"

Before he could make any movement, she had her arms wrapped around him in what he thought was supposed to be a comforting gesture. "I was in town for another wedding, and I just found out that she married someone else, and now she is trying to have a baby with him. I can't believe it, even after you declared your love for her. She's so heartless."

Zoey put her hands on her hips. "You did what?"

If it wasn't for the death grip that Marla had on him, he would have shrugged. Normally, she didn't mind his little antics with women, but this one may have crossed a line. Just a little bit. When he threw Zoey's name out there, she wasn't married yet. He should have said he was in love with Josie or something. Marla wouldn't have dared to come within ten feet of her. Josie was well known for her skill with a gun and even taught self-defense courses.

Derek tried to wiggle out of Marla's death grip. "Marla, can you let me go?"

He struggled to find something to say to make everything magically better, but his mind was a complete blank. Normally, he was smooth with his words, but not today. Seeing the wild look in Marla's eyes had him speechless. He needed to figure something out, and fast.

She placed her hand on his arm while he was still thinking of what to say to get rid of her. "I told you that I was here for you if you needed anything. You needed me. Why didn't you call me?"

Derek desperately looked around the bar trying to come up with something but only found his friends and staff enjoying this train wreck. They were also not helping. Traitors. "Marla, I'm sorry. I know I said I would call if things didn't work out for me and Zoey, but my heart just isn't in it. I'm not ready to move on yet."

At the end of the bar, he heard someone say, "I heard you put something else in that red head last week."

Marla turned to look at Jed, who was wearing his worn-out trucker hat and a mischievous grin. She turned back to Derek and glared. "You told me that if you couldn't have Zoey, you didn't want anyone."

Now he heard Tiny snort, trying to hold in a laugh. They were all turning on him. "I know, but it was just something to distract me from..."

Marla pointed at Zoey accusingly. "From her rejecting you."

Zoey rolled her eyes. "Oh, yes. He begged and begged for me to love him, and I just couldn't do it."

Was that level of sarcasm really necessary? He tried to plead with his eyes to his best friend. First for her to go along with this ridiculous charade, and second, to forgive him. Tyler, Zoey's husband, was going to kick his ass later, or maybe hack his website and put up embarrassing pictures.

Marla turned back to him and slid her hand up his chest to rest on his shoulder. "I can help you forget her. We had that magical night, and I know that we would be fantastic together."

The sound of a chair scraping on the floor broke the awkward moment and Josie's loud voice filled the room. "Oh, for fuck's sake." She pulled Marla away from Derek and turned her to face her. "Look here, psycho Barbie, Derek doesn't want you. He lied to you just to get rid of you. You had sex like grownups, and you went all batshit crazy on him the next day, so he said what he said to ditch you. Nobody likes a clinger. Now take your scrawny ass out of here before I drag you out by your fake-ass extensions."

Marla didn't move for a minute. She just stared with her giant eyes at Josie, trying to make a decision. Derek hoped she would make the right one and leave. She finally turned her head and asked, "Is she right? Did you lie to me?"

Derek put his hands in his pocket and nodded his head.

Marla's face went from the sad rejected puppy look to crazy pissed off bitch in less than two seconds. Derek wanted to instinctively cover his balls. God, he really hoped she wasn't going to knee him in the balls. He was rather attached to them. Instead, she grabbed the beer that was in front of Josie's husband, Grayson, and launched the contents at his face. Yeah, that seemed fair.

"You're an asshole!" she screamed as she slammed down the mug and stormed out of the bar.

Breathing in a sigh of relief, Derek walked behind the bar and started to clean his face. He poured Grayson a new beer and felt the stares of his friends on him.

"What?"

Zoey stood on the rails of her barstool to appear a little taller and said, "Are you kidding me? You used me as your excuse?"

"It seemed like a good idea at the time. You had just moved here, and it would have been believable that I was in love with my best friend."

"We have spent half of our adult lives convincing everyone that we are just friends, and this was the best you had?"

Derek winced. "She started talking about moving in with me, getting married, and I freaked out. Going for the excuse that my heart belonged to someone else seemed like a good idea at the time."

Josie took a sip of her wine. "You do realize that you are going to be front and center on Penny's gossip page today. That flash you saw was from one of her spies."

Zoey pointed her finger at him. "You're going to tell Tyler what happened, *and* that it's all your fault."

"Yeah, okay."

"How many times has she texted you?"

Derek shrugged. "I dunno. Maybe once a month or so."

"If you slept with her when I first moved to town over two years ago, that didn't set off any alarm bells?"

"Maybe a couple, but she didn't live here, so I didn't think it was a big deal."

"You know, if you actually started dating like a normal person, things like this wouldn't happen to you," Grayson said.

"It's just one crazy woman."

Zoey huffed. "A crazy woman who knew I was trying to get pregnant. How did she know that anyway?"

"Probably from Penny's Facebook page. She blabbed all about your hormone treatments and how you have been crying into the caramel for the extra salt flavoring."

Zoey had been receiving hormone injections and trying to get pregnant for a while. They already had one in vitro session that was unsuccessful, and it broke Derek's heart to see his friend struggle so much. Zoey looked down at the bar and her eyes welled up with tears. "I still can't believe she posted about that."

Derek reached out over the bar and took Zoey's hand. "She wasn't thinking it would hurt your feelings. She even said that she wanted people to be aware so they would be nice and understanding when they saw you upset. She didn't do it to be mean."

"I know," she said in a small whisper.

Wanting to change the subject, Derek asked, "Are you guys ready for the dress shopping with Ariel next week?"

Zoey's mood brightened a bit, and she smiled. "Yup. All of the girls are going to have a weekend trip to Raleigh and do some shopping, visit the rose garden, and go to the art festival."

"Ariel has been packed for days. Kyle said that she is dying for the getaway."

Grayson laughed and nodded his head to Josie. "She is, too. She can't wait to get some time away from the kids."

"Hey. I deserve it. Between teenage twins, the energetic munchkin, and now Bryce has decided he loves to walk, and it is fun for me to chase him all over the house. I need a recharge. I don't know how my sister did it when the twins were younger. I just want to put Bryce in a hamster ball so he doesn't get hurt and can just roll around the house."

Derek was so impressed with Josie. She had been kidnapped with Stacey and Andrew when they were kids, and the cop who rescued them adopted all three of them. Stacey and Andrew had fallen in love and eventually married and had four kids before they died tragically in a car crash several months ago. "You know, I think they actually make those giant bubbles that people can get inside of, but I think they are meant for walking on water."

Grayson laughed. "Yeah, I've seen those. Nobody can walk in those things. They just spend the whole time taking a step or two and falling on their asses."

Derek grabbed a couple of empty glasses from the side and started washing them. "Are you going to be taking care of the kids while they are all gone?"

Grayson nodded. "Yeah, but I always have Josie's parents as back up if needed."

With a wolfish smile, Derek looked over to Zoey. "I can't wait to see what giant poofy dress my sister picks out for you all."

"I already reminded her that if it has too much material, Miss Graceful over there will just trip over it all night long," Josie said.

Zoey frowned. "Hey. I didn't trip on my wedding dress all night."

"Honey, that's only because Tyler barely put you down all night. Every time we turned around, he was lifting you up from under your ass so he could kiss you stupid."

Zoey's eyes grew soft. "Yeah. He knows how much I love it when he does that."

Josie shook her head and turned her focus to Derek. "You realize you're next, right?"

Derek flinched. "Me? God, no."

Zoey nodded her head in agreement. "Yeah. You need to stop sleeping with all the tourists and find someone who can give you everything you need."

Derek made a sweeping motion with his hand. "I have everything I need. I have my bar, I have my family, and I have you guys. I don't *need* anything else. Besides, if I went off the market, hearts everywhere would break."

"Uh-huh. It would also stop all the Marla's from popping out of the woodwork."

"I'm fine with how my life is now," he said in an all too confident tone. But the truth was, he wasn't fine. He found himself at home... alone... a lot. If he was really honest with himself, seeing all of his friends find true happiness and love was messing with his head. Zoey started the domino effect when she fell in love with Tyler. Then Chase got off of his ass and married Dixie, the woman he had been in love with since they were kids. Next, his sister, Ariel, and his childhood friend, Kyle, finally got their act together and were getting married. Josie and Grayson were just the latest to get married. Grayson proposed to her right in Derek's bar, and they were married a couple weeks later at Grayson's dad's ranch house just outside of town.

How did that old song go? The cheese stands alone. Well, here he was, the stinky old cheese, standing alone in his bar. But this cheese was never meant for love. He watched his dad cheat on his mom time and time again, and he had to watch his mom's heart break nightly after she kicked him out. It destroyed him seeing her devastated, and if that is what love did to you... no thanks. Then he became close friends with Zoey and her boyfriend, Trevor. But Trevor died from a brain aneurism, and he saw Zoey fade into a shadow of the person she used to be. Even after his death she found out she was pregnant and then lost the baby too. It took her years to finally return to the strong, independent woman that she was when she moved here a few years ago. Love could be amazing, but it could also shatter a person into a million pieces, and he didn't want to be on the receiving end of that, or God forbid be the cause of it, like his dad.

Before he could continue to defend his playboy ways to his friends, Dixie and Chase walked into the bar with their newborn son strapped to Chase's chest. Confused at seeing

Dixie, Derek said, "Hey. I thought you had a wedding shoot today."

Dixie plopped down her diaper bag and jumped onto the stool. "I did, but it got canceled. The whole thing was a mess."

Blossom Hills was a well-known destination in North Carolina for weddings, so hearing that a wedding got canceled on the big day was not uncommon. "That sucks. Runaway bride or groom?"

"Groom. The poor girl waited for an hour in her dress at the gazebo, looking as lost as I have ever seen someone. Then when she went to pay us for our time, there were some issues with her credit cards and she had to make arrangements for me, the pastor, and Phil."

Zoey's head popped up at the name of her part-timer, Phil. "Oh, poor Phil. This is the second time he has delivered for me at a canceled wedding. Did he take the cake back to the bakery?"

"Yeah. He told me that you guys would just slice it up and sell as single servings for the bakery."

Zoey nodded. "It wasn't a big cake. Just two tiers. They were going to freeze the top layer and use the bottom one today. I feel bad for Phil. This was his first solo decorated cake, and he was so proud of it. I should go call him; I'll be right back."

Derek shook his head. "See? This is why I will never tie myself down. Love leads to disappointment, but sex... sex never disappoints."

Grayson pulled out his wallet and held up a twenty. "I've got a twenty that says he falls head over heels within a year."

Chase put his hand in the air. "I've got nine months."

Grinning, Dixie added, "Six months!"

Everyone turned to Josie, who gave an evil grin. "Three months."

Within a minute, everyone had a pile of money on the bar. His friends were assholes.

"Who's the keeper of the bet?" Grayson asked. "I mean, who's going to hold the money and be the judge of when this guy is in love?"

A large hand reached between Josie and Dixie and covered the money. Derek looked up to see Tiny swipe the money and give a satisfied look to everyone. "I've got this."

Derek glared at his friend and employee. "Thanks."

Tiny shrugged. "It's only a matter of time. Your turn is comin', Bossman."

Needing to get away from this conversation, Derek pulled the garbage bag out from the can and tied up the top. "You're all wrong. I am not going to turn into you bunch of saps."

He heard their laughter as he walked towards the back exit door to the alley. Once he opened the back door, he took a deep breath and tossed the bag into the dumpster. When he walked back, he stopped just a few feet from the door and rested against the wall. He just needed a minute to compose himself before plastering on his good-natured smile for everyone.

Just as he thought about going back inside, he felt something fall into his hair. Thinking it was a bug, he ran his hand through his hair, but instead of some insect flying away, a small white flower petal fell out. He bent over to pick it up but noticed there were about half a dozen more scattered on the ground. He looked up to see a giant white fluffball and another petal falling through the grates of the fire escape landing and down to the ground. Fantastic. His friends were just taking bets on when he would fall in love and some woman was on his fire escape above his bar in a wedding dress, and if his ears weren't deceiving him, she was also crying.

He should just walk away, leave the crying woman alone to deal with whatever trauma was happening to her, and get back to his day. As he placed his hand on the doorknob, he could hear his mother's disapproving voice in his head. She would be disappointed if he didn't at least go check on the girl. Sighing in resignation, he let go of the knob and turned to the stairs to go talk to her. Damn it.

Chapter 2

Mia felt her tears falling down her cheek and she just didn't have the energy to try and stop them anymore. Her grandpa would have disapproved of her crying over a man, but this was supposed to be her wedding day. She was allowed to cry today. Today was supposed to be picture perfect. They were going to get married in the charming gazebo in their new home town. Jack had been so excited about their fresh start in Blossom Hills; she never thought that he wouldn't show up on their wedding day. But not only did he not show up, oh no... he'd cleared out their bank account and even disconnected his phone.

When Mia tried to pay the vendors for their time today, all of her cards were declined. Jack had always taken care of all the finances. He paid each monthly bill online and told her to just worry about taking care of her terminally ill grandpa. She had just deposited the large inheritance last week that she'd received from when his estate was finally settled. There shouldn't have been any issues with making payments today. When she finally resigned to the fact that Jack wasn't showing up, she tried to pay everyone and each card that was run was followed with that embarrassing declined message.

What a great first impression she was making on the town. *Did you hear about the new girl? She got stood up at the altar and she can't pay any of her bills.* At least she had this apartment. It was perfect for their needs. The woman who showed it to her said she would provide a discount if she paid all six months of the short-term lease up front. So that's what she did, two months ago, when she still had money.

She had been desperately trying to reach Jack ever since she got home. There wasn't much signal inside the apartment, so she had climbed out to the fire escape with her phone and the bouquet that she was clinging to like an anxiety blanket. Not having any luck reaching Jack, she tried calling his sister, Tabitha, who had also disconnected her phone. That was a little extreme. She kind of understood Jack disconnecting his number if he was ditching her like this, but his sister, too? When she decided to throw a small temper tantrum on the fire escape, the window that she had crawled out of fell down and locked her out. That was how she ended up stuck outside in her wedding dress, pulling out the petals from her bouquet and ugly crying. And that is what this truly was, ugly crying. There was no way that the waterproof mascara was going to hold up to the flood of tears falling down her cheeks. Maybe she would just make this fire escape her new home. She could live out here. She already stole a pickle bucket from the bar downstairs. Maybe she would get lucky, and someone would lose their fluffy sweater that she could use as a pillow.

Just as she plucked another petal to toss to the ground, she heard heavy footsteps coming up the stairs. Oh, God, someone was going to see the hot mess express that she was.

While she was looking for somewhere to hide, she heard a deep masculine voice ask, "Hello, are you okay up there?"

Crap. No. No, she was not okay, but really, was she going to say that to a strange man coming up the stairs? "I'm fine," she squeaked. Great, real convincing Mia.

Hearing that he was almost at the top, she quickly thrusted what was left of her bouquet in front of her face. Maybe she could hide behind it, and he wouldn't notice what a disaster she was.

When she could see his feet in front of her, she buried her head even further in the flowers. "Totally fine. Nothing to see here."

She heard him lean against the railing before he said, "Really? Because it was raining flowers a few minutes ago down there and people don't typically do that to their wedding bouquets. And then there were the tears and that quiet, hiccupping sob I heard while walking up the stairs. Was that coming from you?"

Mia narrowed her eyes, not that he could see that behind the flowers. "Nope. It wasn't me. It was the magical fairy living in my flowers. She was having a bad day."

"Hmmm. Even worse than the girl who was stood up at the altar today?"

Mia lowered the bouquet only to see the most handsome man she had ever seen. His skin was a golden tan, and his perfectly styled brown hair matched his deep brown eyes. Before she got too lost looking at his muscular chest that was wearing a t-shirt with the logo of the bar downstairs, she whispered, "You heard about that?"

The way too beautiful man gave a small shrug. "I did. One of my good friends was the photographer. She came in for a visit and told me about it. So, this magical fairy... she was having a worse day than not getting married today."

Mia sighed. "She also had her bank accounts cleared out, can't get a hold of her fiancé... or maybe ex-fiancé... I don't know what to call him now... or even his sister, who was supposed to be her friend."

"Wow. She *is* having a bad day."

Mia shook her head. "But it doesn't stop there."

"No?"

"No. She also doesn't have a job, has about three days' worth of food in her apartment, only a suitcase full of clothes, got locked out from her new apartment, and she may have stolen a pickle bucket from the bar downstairs to use as a chair."

"You stole a pickle bucket?"

Mia proceeded to close her eyes and lift the bundle of the dress that was covering the stolen goods. "It's empty, I promise." She sighed. "Please don't call the cops on me. Me and the fairy are having a really bad day."

The man started laughing and sat on the top step. He stopped for a minute, only to start laughing again.

Glaring, Mia said, "This isn't funny."

He cleared his throat. "It's kind of funny, but you should know that the sheriff is in the bar downstairs, with his wife, your photographer."

Mia buried her face in her hands. "Of course he is. I promise I'm not normally this much of a hot mess."

"I think I should introduce myself. I'm Derek McKenna."

Little lightning bolts of recognition went off in her head. She was living above McKenna's bar, and the woman who leased the apartment to her said her son owned the building. Lovely. She was making a fool of herself to her new landlord.

She was still berating herself when he continued, "You mentioned that you were locked out."

Mia nodded and pointed to the window. "The window fell down after I crawled out here and it slammed so hard that it triggered the lock."

Derek shook his head. "Sorry. Mom should have warned you about that. We're going to replace the windows, but I just haven't gotten around to it yet." He extended his hand out to her. "Come on. I have a spare key in my office at the bar. We can get you some food and have you back in the apartment in no time."

Mia's lip quivered. "I don't have any money for food."

Derek shook his head. "Don't worry about it. All jilted brides and grooms get free food on the intended day of nuptials."

"You're lying just to make me feel better."

With a self-deprecating laugh, he replied, "No. It's true. My friend, Kyle, even did a feature in our paper about how we're the bar with a heart. Jilted people eat free, and fire and police officers eat at a discount."

Mia was going to decline the invitation for the free food, but her stomach grumbled in protest.

"See? Even your stomach thinks it's a good idea." He extended his hand in invitation to help her up again, and she finally took his hand. A warm tingle shot up her hand when their skin touched. Did he feel that? She could have sworn that he did. Looking into his eyes that slightly widened with the touch, she saw that he did feel it, but with her sitting in her wedding dress, now was not the time to try and figure out what that was.

She gathered up her outrageously large fluffy wedding dress and started to follow Derek down the stairs. When he turned around to check on her progress of getting down the stairs, he shook his head. "That's a lot of dress."

She blew a loose section of hair away from her face. "It was Tabitha's idea."

Derek stopped and turned around with a frown on his face. "Who's Tabitha?"

"My fian—ex-fiancé's sister."

"You let your fiancé's sister pick out your wedding dress?"

Feeling a little defensive, Mia said, "We picked it out together."

Derek tilted his head in thought. "But it wasn't the one you wanted?"

Mia thought back to that day in the bridal shop and how Tabitha had been so excited about this dress. Mia liked the simpler empire-waisted dress with a lace overlay. This Cinderella gown with nine hundred layers wasn't her idea, but Tabitha loved it on her. Mia wanted her future husband's sister to like her, so she bought the fluffy monstrosity of a dress. In the grand scheme of things, her wedding dress wasn't that big of a deal to her. "It was my second choice."

She heard him huff in disbelief. "If you say so."

Once they reached the bottom of the stairs, she followed him to the back door. He entered with all the confidence in the world while she peeked her head in like someone may jump out and attack her.

Derek took her by the hand and pulled her in. "Come on. You're going to let all the snakes in."

She immediately sprinted through the door and slammed it shut behind her. "You have snakes!?!"

Laughing, he said, "No, but it was the best way I could think of to get you inside the doorway."

Putting her hands on her hips, she scowled at him. "That was mean."

"But effective."

She followed him into his office and looked at herself in the small mirror on the wall that said, "People can hear your smile." She gasped in horror as she saw what was left of her make-up that made her look like a creepy clown. "Oh my God. You let me come down here like this?"

She lifted the top layer of her dress and frantically started wiping at her mascara tracks. It wasn't helping. Actually, it was making things worse. "I don't suppose you have any make-up remover, do you?"

With that blank expression men always seemed to get when women talked about anything feminine, he said, "Uh... no." But then, as if a light switch went off, he said, "Oh, wait!"

Before she could ask wait for what, he disappeared towards the door that she assumed led to the bar.

She wanted out of this damn dress. Or at least peel a few layers like an onion to make it more reasonable to sit or even walk in. Seeing a pair of scissors on the desk, she pulled them out of the pencil holder, held them aloft like a conquering hero, and viciously started cutting the top layers of the dress. Six layers. There were six layers to this God-awful dress. Now she was down to two. With the other layers on the ground, she was contemplating making it a mini dress instead of the floor-length disaster just as Derek returned brandishing a small bottle in his hand. "I got the—"

She looked at the ground and then back to the sexy man's confused face. Helplessly, she held up the scissors and gave a weak smile. "I borrowed your scissors."

He started to respond, but then heard a commotion coming from the door to the bar. "Josie, you can't just—" one woman's voice said.

"Like hell I can't," another woman's voice said as she approached the office and gasped as she saw Mia sitting still holding the scissors, wearing her jaggedly cut dress and her face still sporting the awesome creepy clown makeup.

The other woman reached the door and dropped her face in sympathy. "Oh, sweetie."

Mia looked at the two women who had pushed Derek aside like he didn't own the place and stepped inside. The super polished woman with perfect hair and a buttoned-down blouse took the bottle from Derek's hand. "Get back to the bar. This is out of your pay grade."

Derek crossed his arms. "Josie, I can handle—"

The woman, who Mia assumed was Josie, placed a hand on his chest and gently pushed him out of the office. "This isn't the playground where you get to claim that you saw her first. Go take care of your customers and let us take care of the poor girl."

Did she get a say in this? Looking at the obviously headstrong woman, she didn't think so, but Derek didn't budge until the second woman with strawberry blonde curls placed a gentle hand on his arm and softly said, "Go on. I promise we'll take good care of her."

Derek looked at Mia and then back at the other woman. "Zoe."

"It's okay."

His face softened, and he nodded. Who was the second woman? His wife? Girlfriend? She certainly had an effect on him. Mia felt the calming hand of the second woman on her hand that was still holding the scissors. "Can I have those?"

Mia looked down at the scissors and nodded.

The woman smiled and said, "I'm Zoey, and this is Josie. She is our resident make-up expert. She can apply and take off the most stubborn makeup."

Josie wiggled the little bottle in her hands and said, "It helps when you have the right tools for the task."

Mia didn't quite know what to say. If she tried to deny the help, she was pretty sure the bossy one would just wave her off and keep doing whatever she wanted. She watched as Zoey opened a cabinet and pulled out a box of tissues, handing them to Josie.

Josie used a tissue with the makeup remover and started to wipe away the layers covering Mia's face. Honestly, it felt good to have her face feel clean of the gunk and tears. She closed her eyes at Josie's orders and allowed the woman to wipe away the last of the mascara.

Tossing the tissue into the can, Josie declared. "There, that's so much better. Now about that dress. What exactly were you trying to do?"

Mia lifted one shoulder. "Get rid of the giant poofiness. I got rid of some of the layers, and I was going to make it shorter when Derek walked back in."

Josie nodded. "I can help with that. Stand up."

Mia obeyed without a second thought. She wondered if everyone did whatever this woman commanded. Josie took the scissors and cut the dress to just above Mia's knees.

Zoey's smile brightened as she saw Mia's white bedazzled sneakers. "I love your shoes."

Mia blushed. She knew they were ridiculous, but those shoes were the last thing her grandpa bought her before he passed, and she thought making them pretty and wearing them for her big day was a good way to have her grandpa walk down the aisle with her. She guardedly looked at Zoey for any sarcasm but was pleasantly surprised when she found her smile to be genuine. "Thanks."

Josie finished her last snip and nodded her head in approval. "We just need one more thing."

She turned around to the shelf behind her and grabbed a similar t-shirt to the one Derek was wearing only it was definitely designed for a woman's curves and low V-neck. Josie looked at the tag and handed it over to Mia.

Mia looked at the shirt and back up to the two women. "I can't take this. I don't have any—"

Zoey tilted her head but had a knowing look to her smile. "It's okay. My treat. If you put on the shirt, it will just look like you are wearing a skirt and shirt and not look like the runaway bride."

Mia frowned. "I wasn't the one who ran away."

Zoey waved her hand in dismissal. "Doesn't matter. Come on. Let's get your free dinner. Tiny makes an awesome jilted special."

Only flinching a little Mia asked, "Derek was serious about the free food for jilted brides and grooms?"

"Oh, yeah. It's a whole big thing. We get at least one a month."

"That seems like a lot."

Josie chuckled. "Not nearly as many as Daisy's Diner sees for the annulment special."

Mia gave a slow blink. "Annulment special?"

Zoey laughed. "Our little town is also starting to get known for spontaneous marriages. Our mayor decided to open the clerk's office twenty-four hours a day to help with tourism, and since there is no waiting period for North Carolina, people can get married right away. Quite a few townspeople are making good side money performing marriage ceremonies in the middle of the night."

Understanding a little better Mia said, "And thus the annulment special."

"Yup. A complete breakfast and attorney referral for three ninety-nine. Daisy gets a nice bonus from the attorneys she sends them, too."

Mia looked back down at the shirt and then to the tag that read large. Mia sighed. "I need an extra-large."

Josie looked at Mia and shook her head. "No you don't. This will fit you perfectly."

No. Actually, it wouldn't. It would cling too tightly to her stomach that was not as flat as she wanted because she loved carbs too much. Well, that and she hated going to the gym. Who wants to run on a treadmill and never get anywhere, or even worse a bike that doesn't go anywhere? Realizing that arguing with the woman wouldn't work Mia pulled it over her head and looked down at her new outfit. Mia tugged at the bottom trying to pull the material away from her stomach and stopped when she saw Josie frowning.

"You look great. Let's go get some food and some fruit-flavored happy drinks."

Josie turned to leave and stopped a few steps away from the door when Mia didn't immediately follow her. "I meant now. Come on."

Not wanting to argue, Mia started to follow and glanced back at Zoey who shut Derek's door. Careful to whisper she asked Zoey, "Is she always this bossy?"

Zoey pressed her lips together looking as if she was holding back a laugh and said, "No."

"Oh, good."

"Usually, she's much worse."

Chapter 3

Derek was serving a drink to Chase when Zoey and Josie returned to the bar with Mia in tow. She looked so much better now. Gone were the dark lines on her face from the mascara, and she turned the gigantic gown into a mini dress and was wearing one of the t-shirts with the bar logo. She did look a little uneasy with the women as she walked up the bar though. The poor girl probably hadn't met anyone like Josie before. Josie could be pretty intimidating, but once she became your friend, she was also your fiercest protector. If Zoey hadn't gone back there with her, Derek would have stayed to make sure everything went okay.

Zoey sat down next to Dixie and gave a wink to Derek letting him know that everything was good. He let out a breath of relief and leaned over to Mia who sat next to Zoey. "Okay, so what will it be? We have the Bastard Burger, the Son of a Bitch Salad, Caribbean Jerk Wings, or the Clueless Chicken Fingers?"

Mia tilted her lips. "So many great choices. I think I'll have the Clueless Chicken Fingers."

Zoey gave a little moan of appreciation. "Make that two, please."

Derek pointed his finger at his friend. "Yours is not free."

Zoey frowned. "But you love me."

"I do, but you cut me off from donuts this morning."

"I only did it because I care. Nobody should eat five donuts for breakfast."

Derek rolled his eyes. "Uh-huh."

Pushing the door open, he yelled out the order for the girls. Tiny's bald head appeared over the counter when he heard the title of the order. "We got the jilted bride from Dixie's wedding today?"

Derek rubbed the back of his head. "Yeah, and she's the new tenant upstairs."

Tiny loudly set down the stainless-steel bowl he was using to season the wings. "Dude, you've gotta stop renting that place out. I'm telling you it's cursed."

"It's not cursed. Its just had a little bit of bad luck and we haven't found the right tenant."

"Even your mom says it's cursed. That's why she doesn't want to rent it out longer than six months."

"Not cursed." Yeah, okay, it might be a little cursed, but he wasn't giving anyone else the satisfaction of knowing that. When he bought the building, he had every intention of living there himself, but after a few weeks of living and working in the same building, he'd decided he would rent it out and buy a house. And that worked out well because he bought a two-family home and his sister, Ariel, lived in the upstairs unit until she moved in with Kyle.

After Derek moved out of the apartment, the first guy he rented to was an old man who'd died from a heart attack, but to be fair he was eighty years old and ate bacon every day since he was nineteen. Then there was that one girl who lived there until she lost her job and had to move to Raleigh, but she got a better job out there and was probably better off. Then there was that park ranger who moved out after because of a bear attack, but it was more of a bear hug. The bear liked him and wanted to snuggle with his giant body on top of the guy. Oddly it happened a few times, and he had to be transferred. Then there was that cute couple, but they got divorced two months after moving in. Okay... it was a lot of bad luck, but he didn't believe in curses, ghosts, fate, or any of that other nonsense.

Tiny continued shaking the bowl with the wings and asked, "Is she going to move out now?"

Derek looked back at the door as if he could see her and shook his head. "I don't think so. She paid Mom the full six months up front. She said she doesn't have any money, so I doubt it. It sounds like the jerk cleared out her bank accounts before he stood her up today."

"Fucking asshole."

"Yup."

Derek grabbed the wings once Tiny plated them and gave a nod as he walked back out to the floor. He dropped off the wings to the obvious tourists sitting in the back and returned to his friends at the bar. Mia was now playing with Dixie and Chase's son and had a brilliant smile lighting up her face. Damn she was beautiful. Shaking that thought off, he refilled Dixie's soda. "Good idea using the kid to cheer her up."

"Babies make everything better and Eli is perfect for that. He is so good with new people."

He looked over to Zoey who was watching with a wistful expression. He knew that she was happy for her friends, but still struggled with the difficulties that her and Tyler were experiencing with having their own child. He caught her attention and mouthed the words, "You okay?"

She only responded with a small smile and nodded her head. Damn it. He wanted to give her a big hug and tell her everything would be okay, but he knew that bringing attention to her hurt would only make it worse. She was still on hormones and shaky ground from the last failed in vitro attempt.

He felt eyes on him and turned to see Mia watching the interaction between him and Zoey. Wanting to take the attention off his friend, he held out his arms and said, "Give me that baby."

Mia readily handed over Eli and Derek lifted him above his head and began making airplane noises. Heavy breaths like laughter came out from the baby and everyone laughed as Derek blew raspberries on his chubby little cheeks. "I'm going to teach you how to woo all the women."

Chase held out his arms for his son. "You will not. Gimme my kid. There will be no playboy antics for my son."

Derek passed Eli over to Chase and said, "Let the kid have some fun before he turns into a boring rule follower like you."

"I'm not boring," Chase muttered.

Dixie cupped his cheek and smiled dreamily at him. "You definitely weren't boring last night."

Chase's eyes dropped in desire, and he growled, "Damn right, I wasn't boring."

Derek threw his towel at Chase's head. "No sex on the bar."

"Pfft. Is that right? Does that rule apply to everyone?"

"It sure as hell applies to everyone who doesn't own this bar."

Once Derek returned to the bar after serving more food he saw Josie, Grayson, Dixie, and Chase getting ready to leave. "You guys heading out already? That's a quick visit."

Grayson nodded. "Molly called. Bryce is having a meltdown, and she said that she thinks he has a fever."

"Poor little guy. Go home and rescue your teenager."

Grayson nodded and led Josie out of the bar with his hand falling to the small of her back. Derek was happy for them. Josie had been through hell her whole life and deserved a man like Grayson who could love her unconditionally.

Chase's voice broke his attention away from the retreating couple. "Yeah, we're going to put this guy down for a nap and take advantage of Dixie's early day off." Chase winced as he realized that their early day was at the expense of Mia. He looked over to her and said, "Sorry about that."

Mia was drinking and quickly set down her most recent blue alcoholic concoction. "No worries. Enjoy your day."

As Derek served his other customers, his gaze continued to drift over to Mia who was talking to Zoey. He tried to remind himself that Mia was in good hands with Zoey. He didn't need to go over and keep checking in on her, but his brain was being overruled by his body that was magnetically drawn to her.

When he returned to the kitchen Tiny had the girls' chicken fingers ready. As he picked up the second plate Tiny called out, "You're gonna get a kink in your neck if you keep turning your head to stare at her all night."

Turning to open the door with his ass Derek shouted back, "Fuck off, asshole."

He heard Tiny's booming laugh even after he was well away from the door. As he approached, he saw Mia's pale face now flushed pink, probably from the alcohol. At least it wasn't red from tears anymore. As he set down the food in front of the girls, Mia asked, "Were you really going to wear a dress for Zoey's wedding?"

He smiled and leaned in close. "Absolutely. It always gives me great pleasure to annoy Zoey's mom, and as the man of honor I was willing to wear the same dress as the others who were going to be standing with her."

Turning to Zoey, Mia asked, "Is your mom mean?"

Zoey shook her head. "No."

Derek raised one eyebrow at his friend.

"Well, it isn't intentional. She always had certain expectations of what her daughter was supposed to be like, and I didn't check any of those boxes. Sometimes she says things that are hurtful, and I just have to remind myself that she doesn't realize what she says, and she lives in her own little world. She loves me... she just drives me insane, but I think a lot of mothers and daughters are like that."

Mia picked up a french fry and before popping it in her mouth said, "Not mine."

Zoey smiled. "Oh, you got lucky and have one of the sweet supportive moms?"

"Ha! No. If I did, she would be here consoling her daughter on her missed wedding day."

Derek thought about it for a minute and realized that she was alone on her wedding day. No friends. No family. Before he could think better of it, he asked, "Where is your family? Shouldn't they have been here today?"

For a minute Derek thought she wouldn't answer, and to be honest he couldn't blame her. It wasn't really any of his business. She took one large gulp of her drink and said, "My parents are somewhere in Europe, and don't care about me at all, and my grandpa just died. Jack and his sister were going to be all the family I had."

Zoey placed a comforting hand on Mia's arm. "I'm so sorry. What about your friends?"

Mia lifted one shoulder. "I only had a couple before I met Jack, and when Grandpa got sick and Jack took more and more of my free time, my friends just pulled away. I didn't realize how isolated I was until today."

Derek looked at Zoey who must have had the same thoughts that he did. Zoey had left an abusive relationship before moving to Blossom Hills. Her ex, Shane, had isolated her from her friends and left her with nearly no one before she finally had the courage to leave him. He knew better than to ask now though. Today was definitely not the day to press for answers to the questions floating around in his head. Instead, he turned around and poured a refill for Mia. "I have news for you. Welcome to small-town life. You won't feel isolated anymore. Everyone will be showering you with attention within a week."

Mia's eyes widened. "What? I don't... I mean, I'm not..." She looked around the room and saw that some people were already showing interest in her with curious glances. "Oh, God." She buried her face in her hands.

Zoey placed a gentle hand on her back. "Nice going, dork. You're scaring the poor girl." Zoey leaned in and gentled her voice. "I promise it won't be too bad. People here are nice. Nosy, but nice."

A customer raised his hand for Derek's attention. "Sorry. I didn't mean to. It won't be too bad, I promise." The customer cleared his throat and raised his hand again. "Sorry, I'll be back."

Famous last words. Don't they say to never say I'll be back? Or is that only valid for scary movies? Things got crazy, and he didn't have time to talk to the girls like he wanted. Normally, a busy bar was kind of a rush for him. He basked in the craziness of running around refilling drinks and chatting it up with his patrons, but not today. Nope. His body wanted to scoop up the pretty jilted bride and take her in the back to make her forget about the asshole who took advantage of the sweet girl.

As he was cashing out a customer, he watched Zoey give her a hug and gave him a small wave goodbye. It was almost closing time, and Mia was picking at the lava cake that Tiny had dropped off. She looked so lost. He couldn't imagine not having a family that cared about you, or even a supportive network of friends.

Trying to refocus, he cleared a table of the dishes and walked into the back. He saw Tiny washing dishes and looked around for their new part timer who should have been helping clean the back. "Where's Joe?"

Tiny sprayed off a plate and huffed. "Joe decided that working in a kitchen was hard work and he didn't want to work here anymore."

"Great. Is that why Diane left early?" Diane was Derek's latest server who lusted over his now ex-employee.

"Probably. Did she say anything before she left to you?"

"Just that something came up, and she needed to leave." Tiny nodded towards his office. "Well, she left you something in the office before she bolted out the door."

Derek, dropping the last glass on the shelf a little too harshly, growled. "Fuuuuckkkkk. Think she quit too?"

Laughing Tiny said, "Oh, yeah."

"Dammit. Now I am going to owe Kyle twenty bucks."

"What was the bet?"

"Diane wouldn't last a month."

"Shit. You guys need to start cutting me in on this action. I would have won with two and a half weeks."

Derek walked towards his office and gave Tiny the one-finger salute. Sure enough, there on his desk was the server's apron, and a note dropped on top with two simple words. "I quit."

Looking at the clock he gave a sigh of relief that it was five minutes until closing. He started to walk up front and nearly knocked over Mia who was carrying a stack of dishes. "Shit. I'm sorry."

She hung her head with her face blushing another shade of pink. "Your last table left, so I thought I would help."

Derek carefully extracted the dishes from her hands and walked back to the washing station. "You don't have to help."

Mia shrugged one shoulder. "What else am I going to do?"

Grabbing the cleaning bottle and some rags Derek shook his head. "You should be unwinding on the couch or taking a nice soak in the tub." Derek's mind started to picture her naked in the tub with bubbles gently kissing her exposed skin. Nope. Stop that.

"Can't."

"What? Why not?"

Mia finally gave a small smile. Damn, she was cute. "I'm still locked out, remember?"

He almost started banging his head on the wall for being an idiot. "Shit. Right. I'm so sorry. Let me get you the key."

Mia started to fidget with her fingers. "Actually, I kind of don't want to go up there alone right now. Can I help you close up? It would keep my mind busy."

Derek looked into the big pleading brown eyes and couldn't say no. "Okay, but only if you let me get you breakfast tomorrow at Zoey's bakery. She's amazing with all things sweet."

"I can't let you buy me breakfast too. You already fed me today."

"Nope. That was the jilted bride special. Breakfast would be for helping me close tonight."

She bit on her bottom lip considering his offer. Finally, she grabbed the cleaning bottle from him and nodded her head. "Okay. Sounds good."

After locking up for the night it only took about forty minutes to clean and get everything prepped for the next day. He could tell that she must have worked in a restaurant before, because she completed side duties that most people wouldn't think about like topping off the salt and pepper shakers. After she rolled the last of the silverware Derek jokingly asked, "You want a job?"

Mia's eyes flew up to meet his. "Really? Are you serious? Because I could really use a job."

Derek was a little thrown by the slight desperation in her voice and he must have paused to long because she started rambling again.

"I'm sorry. You were probably joking. I mean, you don't have to hire me because you feel sorry for me. It's just that I found out I don't have any money and a girls gotta eat. Sorry."

Derek held up his hand and was trying not to laugh too much at her cute mini rant. "Whoa. Slow down. You don't have a job?"

Mia hung her head again and shook it slightly for confirmation.

"And you want to work here?"

With her eyes still looking at the ground she gave a weak reply. "Yes. But you don't have to hire me if you don't want to."

Derek was dying to wrap his arms around her, but it really wouldn't be appropriate. Especially if he was going to hire the girl. "I would love to hire you. That server you saw wandering around earlier quit on me today and I could really use the help."

Mia's head bounced back up to his. "Really?"

"Yes. Really. You already did more today than she did all week. Consider yourself employed."

Before he could register what she was doing, he found himself with her arms wrapped around his neck giving him an overly excited hug. "Thank you, thank you, thank you."

Giving in, he wrapped his arms around her and reveled in her warm body pressing against him. Before his dick could get too excited about the soft woman pressing against him, he released her and smiled. "Okay. How about we get you a couple more shirts and back into that apartment of yours?"

It was only a few minutes later when Derek found himself following her up the stairs to her apartment. Her hips swayed in front of him like the world's most tempting sexual dance. He was so fucked. When they reached the door, he pulled out the key and unlocked it. He wasn't sure why, but he followed her inside, like it was the most natural thing to do. Like he belonged there with her. Starting to panic he abruptly stopped his steps and asked, "Got your key?"

Mia picked up a small keychain with a tiny basketball on the end and gave it a little wiggle. "Got it. Thanks for letting me in... and dinner... and the job."

"You're welcome. Try to get some rest. It's been a big day for you."

Mia looked down at what was left of her wedding gown and frowned. "It was supposed to be a big day, but I never thought it would end like this."

Derek nodded over to the clock on the stove that said 2:24 a.m. "Look, the day is over already. You got through it. It's all good."

Mia rolled her eyes. "Clearly, you haven't seen my luck."

Thinking about Zoey and everything she had been through Derek said, "Believe me, I've seen worse. It will look better tomorrow."

"God, you're an optimist."

When his body reminded him that things were looking a little too up, Derek gave a nervous laugh. "I absolutely like to think the glass is half full. You moved to an awesome new town, you have this amazing new job and boss, and you made some new friends."

"Oh, I don't think they want to be my friend. They were just being—"

"Believe me, they just made you part of their circle. You won't have a choice. They will hunt you down and make you love them."

"Oh."

A small moment of silence fell between them and before he could do something stupid, he started walking back towards the door. "I'll pick you up in the morning for breakfast."

Playing with the key she was still holding she nodded her head. "Okay."

After reaching the hallway and listening for the solid click of Mia's lock, Derek bent over at the waist, put his hands on his knees, and expelled a long breath. "Fuck, I'm so screwed."

Chapter 4

Mia's head was pounding. It was like a persistent thump, thump, thump. She rolled over and grabbed the extra pillow to cover her head. Maybe it would stop if she could drown out all light and sound. She heard the thumping again and groaned. Why? Why did her body hate her so much? Oh wait, that's right. She drank like four, maybe five mixed drinks last night. The thumping was getting louder now. Then her head cleared. Oh, shit. Knocking. Derek.

She threw the covers off and sprinted to the door. Breakfast with Derek. Shit. He was going to think she was a flake.

"Mia, are you okay?"

Fumbling with the locks she finally managed to open the door. "Hi! Sorry, I overslept. Come on inside."

Derek didn't move. He just stood there in front of her with his mouth slightly open. "Uh, Mia?"

"Yeah?"

"Your uh…" He didn't finish his sentence; he just gave a general motion at her body.

Mia looked down and gasped. "Oh, my God!" Was she wearing normal pajamas? Oh, no. Last night she got a little depressed and decided to wear her wedding night lingerie to bed. She felt bad for the expensive scraps of silk and lace that wouldn't see the light of day for years, so she decided for this one night, she would wear them to bed and feel pretty.

Desperately trying to cover her chest, she turned around to escape back to the bedroom.

Derek must have collected himself because she heard him close the front door and call out to her. "If you want to wear that to breakfast, I think I'll order delivery."

"No, that's okay. I'll be ready in five minutes." *Does he have to be cute* and *funny?*

Mia started tossing clothes out of her suitcase trying to find something clean and casual. Finally finding jeans and a blue t-shirt, she changed and frantically pulled her hair up in a messy bun. She peeked out the door and saw Derek looking around the apartment. Well, jokes on him, he wouldn't find much that wasn't already supplied in the furnished apartment.

"Hi. Just a couple more minutes."

She popped into the bathroom to get rid of that horrid morning breath and took a look at herself in the mirror. No make-up, messy hair, and bags under her eyes. *Way to make a good impression, Mia.* She wouldn't be surprised if he went running and screaming out of the house. Mia tapped her temple. "Positive thoughts, Mia. You are *not* a disaster. Everything will be okay." Her grandfather always tried to make her realize that she was worth more than what she was dealt and not to dwell on the negative. She'd promised him before he died that she would make every effort to have more faith in herself. But, it was just kind of hard when you got stood up at the altar and your ex stole everything you had to your name.

This was going to be a good breakfast. She was going to see Zoey again. She was nice. Straightening her spine, she plastered on a bright smile. Looking in the mirror she winced. Maybe tone down the smile a smidge. She looked like some crazy girl who might get a little stabby. Damn, she really needed to get her shit together.

IT TOOK NEARLY THE whole walk over to the bakery for Derek to get his dick to calm down. Seeing Mia answer the door in that amazing bit of lace was the best thing he had ever seen. He nearly stormed in and fucked her against the door. Then when she ran back into her bedroom to change and he caught sight of her near perfect plump ass, he thought he would lose his mind. He had to recite basketball stats in his head to get his body to stop overheating.

Now she was trying to give him a heart attack. They ordered donuts, and she kept on licking and sucking on her finger to get all the powdered sugar off. Was she doing it on purpose? Oh, and let's not forget the slight moan as each finger got cleaned off. Yeah, that wasn't making his dick do a little happy dance in his pants.

Other men were starting to notice now too. He already had to glare at two of the firemen, Austin and Eric. Eric was kind of an asshole. No way he was going to let him near her. And Austin, well he was a nice guy, but... well, he couldn't think of a "but" other than Derek was feeling like a kid who didn't want to share his favorite new toy. This was going to be a problem.

Needing a distraction Derek asked, "I noticed you didn't have many boxes. Do you have a moving truck coming with the rest of your stuff?"

Mia's eyes welled with tears. "No."

"Oh. Do you need help getting it from your old place?"

Mia put down her donut. "No. I don't know where my stuff is."

"What?"

Mia looked down and bit her lower lip. "Yeah, one of those phone calls I made while I was stuck on the balcony was to the moving company we hired. Only the guy that I talked to said that Jack canceled the truck saying that we decided to go with someone else."

"So, it's all still at your old house?"

"Nope. I called my old landlord to ask about working out a deal to get my things out, but he said that it was empty, and he gave Jack the deposit check back when he turned in the keys."

"He didn't leave anything? Not even your clothes?"

Mia picked up her jug of chocolate milk and waved it around. "Not a single thing. He has it all. Clothes, jewelry, photos... my whole life is gone. Just like that... poof. I don't even know the moving company he used to take all of our stuff out of there."

Derek wanted to kill the guy. He knew that there were conmen out there that would clear bank accounts, but to take every possession? There was a special place in hell for him.

Mia continued when he didn't respond. "To be honest, I didn't have much. I always lived simply and just had the bare minimum, but what I did keep was important to me. I can replace most of it easily enough, except the few things I kept of Grandpa's." She started to play with the napkin folding it over and over while she looked down and said weakly, "I just wish that I would have gotten all the pictures digitized like I had planned."

Derek was at a loss. He knew that women valued tangible memories so much more than men did. His mom and sister had photographs everywhere in their houses. He only had a few, and nearly all of those were given to him by other people. "I'm so sorry. Do you know if anyone else might have some to help replace them?"

"Not really. My parents are not kind people, and couldn't care less about me, or each other to be honest. They love their money and their luxuries. They never took pictures of me as a kid. The only photos of my childhood were from my grandma and grandpa when I visited them. I had those and pictures of my grandparents. The ones from when they were dating and first got married were my favorites. Grandma was almost always laughing when they were together. Grandpa said her smiles could light up the whole world."

"They were lucky."

Mia nodded. "Yeah, they really were, but Grandma died when I was around ten. My parents brought me back to Grandpa's for the funeral, and then right after that I started living with Grandpa."

"Your parents just left you there?"

"Yeah, the only reason they came was to see if they would get any more money. They did, but only if I got to live with Grandpa."

"He forced your parents to leave you behind?"

"They had left me a long time before that. Believe me, it was for the best."

Derek was confused. How could a parent just leave their child behind? And it was for the best?

Mia gave him a small smile. "I can hear your gears grinding in your brain."

"I'm just trying to understand."

"I got to spend a lot of time with Grandpa during the couple days before the funeral. He asked me what it was like living in Europe and just like any other kid I was very blunt with the truth. My parents dumped me at a school, and I hadn't seen them for three years until that week when they pulled me out of school to come back with them. They never called or wrote. The school would send them updates and I stopped asking for them. I was considered a burden and a reminder that my mom's perfect body was ruined by having a child."

Derek could feel his mouth drop open. He wanted to give comfort, but she really didn't look like she needed it. This appeared to be something that she dealt with a long time ago and had completely moved on. "I couldn't even imagine my parents being like that."

"You've got good parents?"

Derek felt his smile as he thought about his mom. "My mom is the best. She's one of those people who loves with her whole heart. Mom has adopted all of our friends as her bonus kids."

"That's amazing. What about your dad?"

Derek slightly adjusted in his seat. This is where he kind of looked like an ass. Actually, they both did, but they had been working on it. "My parents are divorced. Dad didn't know how to stay faithful, and Mom kicked him out after hearing about the second affair."

"I'm sorry."

Derek gave a tight smile. "Thanks. It was all a big mess at the time. It nearly broke Mom, and seeing her upset drove me insane. My dad isn't a horrible person though. He was a good dad to us. He came to all the games, school plays, and did everything a dad was supposed to do."

Mia showed an understanding in her eyes. "Except knowing how not to hurt your mom."

"Exactly."

"Are you guys still close?"

Derek sighed. "We're working on it. I didn't really talk to him for years, and we have only just begun to rebuild our relationship. He recently got married to a nice woman."

"That's good."

"Yeah, but I kind of acted like a jerk when they first told us. I'm kind of a work in progress too."

Mia looked him up and down and gave a small smirk. "I knew you couldn't be all perfection."

Derek leaned in and whispered, "You like what you see, huh?"

Before Mia could respond the scraping sound of the chair moving next to them echoed in the air. Derek turned to see his sister sitting down next to them. She looked from Mia and back to Derek before asking, "Hey, big brother, whatcha doing?"

Moving slowly away from Mia he said, "Having breakfast."

"Obviously." Derek watched as a sly smile went across Ariel's lips as she turned to Mia. "Hi, I'm Ariel, this big idiot's sister."

Mia was looking slightly overwhelmed. "Oh. Uh, I'm Mia, it's nice to meet you."

Ariel nodded. "I heard about what happened to you yesterday. I'm so sorry. I couldn't imagine going through what you did."

Mia looked slightly horrified. "You heard about it?"

Ariel placed a gentle hand on Mia's arm. "Yeah, news travels fast around here. I talked to Zoey earlier this morning while she was doing prep."

Derek quirked an eyebrow at his sister. "You were here before six?"

"Yes," she replied a little defensively. "Kyle was traveling to Raleigh this morning for an interview with that state senator who wants to allocate some funding for improvements here. He had to be there by seven. He's never quiet when he gets ready in the morning and I couldn't sleep; so, I thought I would load up on carbs and sugar."

"You working today?"

Ariel shrugged. "I thought about going in for an hour or so to get some paperwork done. Lana and Myrna are both there today though."

When Mia looked a little confused, Derek clarified. "My sister owns the card and gift shop next door."

Mia smiled. "Oh, I love that shop. The girl that helped me there was really nice."

Ariel smiled. "That was probably Lana. She's the best. It's going to hurt when she leaves me after graduating this winter, but she's worked so hard and deserves to have her dream job."

"What is her degree going to be in?" Derek asked.

"Physical therapy. She has been interning at the NC Core Center just a few miles from Grayson's shop and they seem to really like her. She really likes it here and hopes to move here permanently. The thought of moving back in with her parents nearly gives her a panic attack."

Mia nodded her head and said, "I can relate to that."

"Oh, they drive you crazy too?"

Mia just lifted one shoulder. "Not really. I mean they can't drive you crazy when they live over an ocean away and never talk to you."

Ariel looked like she didn't know quite what to say. Mia waved her hand in a dismissive gesture. "It's okay. Really. I dealt with my mommy and daddy issues a long time ago. They suck. I'm worth more. You know all that good stuff that the therapist taught me."

Jesus she was blunt. Derek really had to appreciate that. He knew so many women who used to try to manipulate him into a relationship by telling their stories. Some were true, and some were greatly exaggerated to gain his sympathy. That was one of the reasons he stopped dating townies. He knew most of the stories and got tired of knowing when someone was lying to him just for attention. Wanting to redirect the conversation Derek said, "Mia is going to work as my server at the bar."

Ariel winced a little. "Really?"

Derek sat up straighter. "What's that supposed to mean?"

Ariel's cheeks pinkened with embarrassment. "Sorry, I didn't mean anything bad against you, but we are in the height of tourist season."

"Yeah, and I am short staffed."

"And some of the men from out of town can be assholes."

Mia smiled. "I can handle rude drunk men. I used to work at a bar a few blocks from Frat Row in college. Believe me, there is nothing worse than when you gather a bunch of guys who have recently had their first taste of freedom from home, or the ones who were pledging into a house."

"Yeah, but all those hot guys in one place had to be fun."

"Sure, if you liked all that machismo crap and dick-measuring BS."

"The dick-measuring crap sometimes doesn't stop with college."

Mia laughed. "Oh, no, I meant literal dick measuring."

Derek nearly choked on his coffee. "Like they took out a ruler and measured?"

"Actually, I heard it was a measuring tape because they had issues measuring with rulers due to some curvature issues." She helpfully crooked her finger into a hook shape to demonstrate.

Ariel's laugh was causing others to turn their focus to their little discussion. "Did you know who had the biggest and smallest dick?"

"The whole campus did. The frat house made them all wear numbers on their backs like runners in a race during hell week. If you didn't wear your number you were out. They were numbered from largest who was number one, to the smallest who was number thirty-seven."

Derek shifted uncomfortably in his seat. He knew he wasn't small, but also from his locker room days he knew he wasn't the biggest either. One of his teammates had even had issues with some women turning him down because they thought he was too big. Suddenly feeling sorry for number thirty-seven Derek asked, "Did the smallest guy at least make it in?"

Mia nodded. "He did. He was a legacy, so he was pretty much guaranteed a spot anyway. I heard he was under a lot of pressure to join and didn't have much of a choice." Looking at Derek, Mia asked, "Did you join a frat?"

"No. It never really interested me. I went to college for my education and basketball. The team gave me the brotherhood that a fraternity might have given, and I really liked the guys I roomed with in our townhouse. I went to a few frat parties the first couple of months, but it wasn't my scene."

"You're lucky. I lived in the dorm with a girl who played on her computer all day and barely said five words a day to me."

"Where did you go?"

"George Mason in Virginia."

"Is that where you are from?" asked Ariel.

Mia nodded. "Yeah, I lived with my grandpa in Falls Church. When I went to college, I wanted to be close to home, but he insisted I have the full college experience. Only my junior year I left to take care of him when he got sick."

"Did you ever go back and finish?"

"No. I was going to do that after the wedding, but I guess I need to figure some things out first. My head is definitely not in the right place to concentrate on school again."

Derek had to admire her for how well she was taking everything. She had a lot of strength under her soft-spoken manner and sweet smile.

Ariel and Mia continued to talk like they were old friends. Derek sat back and enjoyed listening to the two of them share their stories. Occasionally, he noticed curious glances their way at the obvious new person, but nothing that would made it to where she felt uncomfortable. He only had to restrain himself a few times from wrapping a possessive arm around her when a couple men took notice of her curves that Derek desperately wanted to explore.

Ariel was looking at him with an eyebrow raised. "Are you planning on answering my question today?"

"Huh? Sorry." Derek winced. "What was the question?"

"Are you hosting poker night this week or do I need to clean the house?"

"Oh. Yeah. My place. It was supposed to be Ty's turn, but he is flying back in that day, so I offered to host this time."

Mia smiled. "That was nice of you. I bet it is fun having a guy's night."

Ariel laughed. "Well, mostly guy's night. Zoey goes too, and she usually cleans them all out. She may be a klutz, but her card skills are no joke."

"I never really got the hang of poker. I mean, I played on some slot machines, but playing in person was just too intimidating."

"I could teach you," Derek offered.

Ariel shook her head. "No way. Zoey was a lost cause long before she moved here, but you are not dragging another one to the dark side."

Derek rolled his eyes. "The dark side."

Ariel shrugged. "I said what I said."

Chapter 5

For a small-town bar, McKenna's was busy. Mia thought her feet might actually fall off at the end of the night. Half of the residents of town must have come in for a drink today.

Leaning her tray and body against the bar she waited for Derek to pour her latest round of beers for the four old men who bragged about their escape from the retirement home. "Is it always this busy on a Sunday?"

Derek nodded. "Yup. You have to remember most of this town's business is focused on weddings, so our Sundays are kind of our version of Fridays in a normal town."

"Huh. I didn't think about it like that. Makes sense though."

Setting down the second beer, Derek gave her a wide smile. "You're doing great with all the craziness."

"It helps that your POS is the easiest system I've ever seen."

"You can thank Tyler for that. He completely wrote the program so that anyone without bar experience could at least put in the orders for the drinks."

Mia thought back to all the names that had been floating around all day and asked, "Zoey's husband, right?"

"Yup. That's him."

"Great. One down and only a million more to go."

Derek set down the last beer. "Nah. Just a couple thousand."

Mia rolled her eyes. "Yeah, that's all."

She was skillfully walking to the older men and nodding to other customers when she saw Zoey settle into the bar and talk to Derek. Focusing back on her customers she set down the beers and gave a sly wink to the flirtatious octogenarians. "Now, gentlemen, is there anything else I can get for you today?"

The youngest one of the group, who still had to be nearly eighty, smiled and asked, "How about your phone number?"

"Didn't you hear? I am still mending my broken heart. Let a girl have at least a week of giant bowls of ice cream and a steady stream of romcoms before you ask her out."

With an exaggerated droop to his face, he clutched his chest. "But, darlin', I'm an old man. I might not have a week left to live."

The man next to him laughed and pointed over to the door. "Hey, Bret, isn't that your daughter coming in the door?"

With lightning speed Bret shoved the chair out and dropped to the floor under the table. Mia leaned down and asked, "What's wrong?"

Bret waved his hand. "Shoo. Get. I can't let her find me here. She'll drag me back to the house of the dead."

Mia popped her head above the table only to find his other three friends bending over and gasping for air from laughing so hard. Understanding the joke, she bent back down to Bret. "For as quick as you move, I don't think you'll be dying next week, and I think it's safe to come up."

Bret moved his head above the table and looked around like a prairie dog judging if it was safe to come out of his hole. Standing back up he glared at his friends. "You guys are a bunch of assholes."

Mia left the men to taunt each other and took a couple more orders before returning to the bar. Zoey and Derek were talking animatedly, and Mia felt a little awkward needing to interrupt them. Derek stopped immediately when he saw her and turned to the ticket printer. "Oh, sorry. I didn't see your new orders." He ripped them off and quickly began to mix the ingredients for the fruity cocktails.

He really was quite the sight to watch. His muscles rippled and flexed as he grabbed each bottle and poured with a flourish. It really wasn't fair to be that sexy and nice on top of it. She wondered what it would be like to glide her hand down his chest and...

"Mia?"

Jerking her eyes up to meet Derek's she said, "Yeah?"

"Am I missing another drink you need?"

Mia glanced at the now full glasses and shook her head. "Nope. That's it. Thanks." She nearly sprinted away so he wouldn't see the blush that she knew was now covering her face. God, how embarrassing. She was caught ogling her new boss and landlord. Yeah, that didn't reek of desperation. The last thing she needed was another man who would break her heart. And not only would he break her heart, but she would also have to move too. She definitely did not want to start over again. Nope. Not this girl. She needed to pull her shit together and not fall for the first beautiful, nice man who showed her attention. That's how she ended up where she was now.

Seeing that Derek's other server, Nicole, was back from break she told her that she was going to take her break now. Nicole just gave a nod and went on to her next table. She wasn't the friendliest person in the world, but she also wasn't outright rude either, so at least there was that. Walking into the back she saw Tiny at the grill and his assistant preparing some wings. "Hey, Tiny, can I get an apple butter burger?"

"Sure thing, sweetie. Go ahead and take a seat in Derek's office and I'll bring it over to you."

She really did appreciate the gentle giant. Tiny's size was certainly intimidating when she first met him, but it didn't take long to realize what a kind heart he had. As she waited for her food, she pulled out her phone and scrolled through her contacts list. This was usually the time she would call Jack, or her grandfather, or even Jack's sister when she was settling in and getting ready to eat dinner. This was her decompression and mental recharge time. But now what?

She leaned her temple on her hand and scrolled her contacts list up and down. She almost let some tears escape as she watched the names go by. Ten names. A whole ten people who she kept in her phone. How did that happen? Who was she kidding? She knew how it happened. She lived like a hermit at school and didn't really make any friends. Her grandfather was her life. Then Jack was her life while they cared for her grandfather.

Contact number one. Dr. Aggerman. Grandpa's doctor. She hesitated for a moment and then deleted the contact.

Contact number two. Dr. Chambers. At least that was her doctor. She could leave him in. Maybe during lunch, she could call and chat up that nice receptionist. Ugh.

Contact number three. Jack. Good old Jack. Mr. Reliable. The nice guy who didn't mind when she stayed late with her grandfather, never got mad about anything, and never fought with her a single day in their relationship. Should she delete the number? What if he called back and said it was a big mistake and that he was going to come back with all her money and things to beg for her forgiveness? She hovered her finger over the delete button and gave a final thump to the screen to delete him from her life. She knew she still had pictures of them on her phone, but those would have to wait just in case the police that she talked to earlier that day needed them.

Contact number four. Landlord. She gave a self-deprecating little laugh. "Oh, look. I get to keep one." She updated the name to Derek and hit save.

Five and six... well those were her parents. She stole their contact information from her grandfather's cell phone. Not that she would ever use it, but it was still good information to have.

Seven was McKenna's that Derek had programmed for her earlier today. Awesome. Another keeper.

Eight was Tabitha. Ah, yes, the sister... who was apparently part of Jack's con on her. DELETE.

Nine was Tiny, who also programmed his number into her phone saying it was just in case she needed anything... ever.

She stared at her last contact. "Zee best Grandpa." A small smile picked up at the corner of her mouth. When she was younger and tried to learn some European languages, she often would go around the house pointing at an object calling them by name only to put zee in front of all of them. It made her grandfather laugh at her exuberance. One day he took her hand and pointed her finger at his chest and asked, "And what am I?"

Not knowing the correct translation, she just smiled and said, "Zee best Grand-pa."

He smiled wide and replied in a bad French accent, "And you are my best girl." After that, so many times when she would leave for the day, he would ask "Who am I?" And she always gave her response with a bright smile, "Zee best Grand-pa."

Her finger grazed over his name. She would never hear that she was his best girl anymore or remind him how he was the best grandpa. She couldn't even call his voicemail anymore. She had been paying the bill to keep it on, but she got a voicemail earlier that they were turning it off due to nonpayment for the month. Just another thing she lost because Jack said he was taking care of it for her.

She finally allowed herself to hit the delete button but paused when the confirmation button appeared. She couldn't do it. Why couldn't she do it? Leaving his name on her screen wouldn't bring him back. She wouldn't be able to just dial the number one day and magically talk to him. But even with each rational thought that ran through her brain, her heart constricted tightly in her chest. Why did this feel like extinguishing the last light in her life? Her tears were falling freely now as she stared at the screen that was starting to dim.

"Mia?"

Mia dropped the phone as if it were on fire and tried to wipe away her tears. Derek gently set down the plate that was obviously her food and squatted down to look at her with his head tilted. Oh, God, not the head tilt. That look of pity that everyone hates. Yes, that's right, try to make the sad pathetic girl feel better.

"Mia, what's wrong?"

Not knowing quite what to say she blurted, "I only have six contacts in my phone."

With an obvious look of confusion on his face she continued, "One is my doctor, one is this bar, two are my parents who don't care about me, and the other two are you and Tiny." She gasped for air trying to hold back a sob as Derek tried to digest the word vomit she threw at him. Feeling a little angry at herself she continued, "I could die tomorrow and the only person who would notice is you. My very nice landlord and boss."

"I would like to think I am a little more than just..."

"I don't understand how I got here. I mean, I know how I got here. Some asshole made me fall in love with him, waited for me to inherit money from the only person who ever really did love me, and then left me at the altar unemployed and penniless."

Derek winced. That's right, buddy, blatant honesty makes everyone awkward. Taking a deep breath, she picked up her phone and showed Derek the screen she still had up. He gently took it from her and frowned. "I couldn't do it.

I couldn't even delete a stupid phone number that doesn't even work for him anymore. I can't let go of simple numbers on a screen. I deleted Jack and his sister no problem. But this. I can't do this, and I don't understand why this feels like I'm losing him all over again."

Derek ran his hand through his hair. "It's been a big couple of days. You don't need to do this now. Hell, you don't ever need to do it at all if you don't want to. We all have our things that connect us to people we care about. You lost a lot of things that connected you to him when that asshole took off with your stuff. Leave the number for now. If the time ever comes that it feels right to delete it, then do it then. But nobody has rules for grieving. We all have our own process to make us right again."

Mia nodded and looked over at the food that Derek brought in. "Is that mine?"

Derek looked back at the food and then to her. "Yeah. Tiny asked me to bring it in for you." He paused for a moment looking a little conflicted. "You need anything else?"

"Oh, no. Go ahead. I'm fine."

Lifting an eyebrow Derek asked, "You're fine?"

Mia laughed. "I promise that isn't the girl fine with a hidden meaning. Get back to the bar before Nicole gets mad at me for keeping you back here."

"Right. Just take your time coming back. We'll be okay if you need a few."

"Go! My food's getting cold."

Mia finished her dinner and didn't really want to let her thoughts spiral back down, so she dropped off her plate to be washed and went back to the floor. Things seemed to be calming down a bit. Her octogenarians had left and gave her a sizable tip. That was nice. She hoped they would be regulars.

Nicole walked up beside her and nodded to the empty table. "The old men are the best. Be nice to them and they will leave you a ridiculous tip every time."

A little confused why Nicole would give up that table if they were big tippers she asked, "If you knew that why did you give me your table?"

For the first time Mia saw Nicole look a little uncomfortable. "Thought you could use a break. I heard what your asshole of an ex did and thought you could use the cash."

Still a bit bewildered she studied the delicate features of Nicole's face. Her usual look of indifference slipped for just a few seconds. "That was very nice of you. Thanks."

Nicole huffed and returned her face to appear as if she didn't care about anyone. "Yeah, well don't expect it every day. I'm not that nice."

Before Mia could respond Nicole turned so quickly to leave Mia had almost gotten hit in the face with her swinging ponytail. "Okay. Noted."

DEREK WATCHED CLOSELY as Nicole and Mia talked after Mia came back from break. Nicole was rough around the edges, but not mean, and he could tell that Nicole liked Mia. At least as much as Nicole liked anyone.

Derek set another Diet Coke in front of Zoey. "Could you and the girls ask Mia to the next girls' night?"

Zoey nodded. "Ariel said she was going to take care of it. I will be working on a big wedding order, so I won't be there."

Derek frowned. "Don't you have Phil and Dana to help, so you aren't working so much?"

"I do, but Tyler and I are going to take a day off together just before since he is going out of town again and I don't want to rattle around at home by myself. These damn hormone shots have my mind all over the place. It's not pretty. I'm always one animal shelter commercial away from a breakdown."

"Well, to be fair, between the song and the sad animals it can make anyone cry. Anytime that damn song comes on I always change it as fast as I can."

"Right? I bet she never thought her career would forever be associated with sad puppies."

"Seriously, though, how are you doing?"

Zoey traced her finger around the rim of her glass. "I hate it. I am almost always a bundle of on the edge emotions. Tyler is being so damn supportive and putting on a brave front, but I know this is hard on him too. We go into this trying to be positive, but we've already failed once. I just can't help but feel defective. He deserves everything, and I can't give it to him."

Derek reached his hands over the bar to hold her trembling fingers. "Hey. None of that. You know that even if it never works, he has everything. He has you." Derek watched as Zoey's silent tears fell down her face. "That man loves you without conditions. If the attempts become too much, talk to him. You have options. I know Ariel already offered surrogacy if this doesn't work, or you can adopt."

Zoey withdrew her hand to wipe away her tears. "I can't let her do that. She needs time with Kyle, they just—"

"Zoey." Derek's tone came out a little bit harsher than he wanted and he lowered his voice. "Kyle wants nothing more than to help bring in a niece or nephew in any way he can. He even told me that if Ariel carried the baby, he could talk to it every night to make sure he is the favorite uncle."

Scoffing she replied, "Oh, God. Xander would be pissed if the baby came out saying Kyle's name first."

"Hell, I would carry it for you if I could."

"Now there's a picture. The eternal bachelor with a baby bump instead of the inevitable beer belly."

Offended he lifted up his shirt and looked at his abs. "Hey, not cool, these babies are never going to succumb to the beer belly lifestyle." He continued to rub them to make sure they were flat and resisted the urge not to console them with reassuring words.

Zoey rolled her eyes. "Good God, Derek. Put your shirt down before you end up on Penny's Facebook page as Hunk of the Month."

"I'm still mad that Grayson got the title last month. I had it for two months in a row. I was going for the record of four months in a row."

"Yeah, but getting a manicure with your eight-year-old makes all the women's ovaries explode."

"Maybe I should borrow one of Josie's ten kids."

"She doesn't have ten kids."

"Ten, four... whatever. It's all the same after two. Chaos personified."

Zoey looked at her phone and downed the rest of her soda. "Love you, but I've gotta go. Tyler's meeting should be over now, and I have some plans that include frosting and lots of—"

Derek covered her mouth with his hands. "Nope. Don't want details." He could feel the smile behind his hand.

When he released his hand Zoey gave a devilish grin. "You love me."

"Of course, I do. Still don't want the details though."

As he watched Zoey leave, he caught Mia looking at him with questions in her eyes. Yeah, he knew what it looked like, and it always took people a long time to adjust to his relationship with Zoey. The rumors around town about the two of them had mostly died off, but whenever someone new came it always seemed to flare back up a little. He would need to talk to Mia and make sure she really believed they were just friends. Because really it was all about controlling the town gossip mill and nothing about wanting to throw Mia over his shoulder, take her upstairs, and sink balls deep into her all night long. Yeah, that definitely wasn't the reason. Mia gave him a timid smile, and he rubbed the back of his neck. He was so screwed.

It wasn't long before Derek was getting ready to lock up the safe when Nicole walked into his office. "You guys done with the front?"

"Yeah. Renna should be here in a couple minutes to pick me up."

"Your car still at the shop?"

Leaning against the doorframe, Nicole's face fell. "Yeah. Tank said that they ordered the part, but because Beast is so old it had to be shipped from California."

"Remind me again why you aren't getting a new car?"

"Cause we're not swimming in money like some people around here," Nicole said dryly.

"I'm not swimming in money. And if you need some help, I can give you some money to help. You do a lot around here."

She narrowed her eyes at him. Great. He offended her again. "You already gave me a raise and helped me get that adoption grant. We don't want any handouts."

Derek held his breath. He sure hoped she never found out that he created and funded that grant. He had offered to pay for their expenses to adopt a child, but she had flatly refused him. Instead, he did the only logical thing he could do. Create a grant and kindly offered to help them with the paperwork and referral letter. He had so much money that he wanted to help the people of the town, and he just had to do it a little differently for each person. When they got approved for the grant, it was the happiest he had ever seen Nicole. She smiled, with teeth and everything. Before Derek could apologize a loud female voice carried through the back followed by Tiny's laugh.

"Where's my sexy wife?"

Nicole's mouth lifted on one side. "In the office," she yelled out.

Renna walked in wearing a big smile. Her presence always filled a room. She had a solid build, shaved on one side of her head and had long purple hair falling down the other side. She had several silver piercings everywhere, from her nose, eyebrow, lips, and ears. Looking at the two of them you would never put them together, but where Nicole was reserved, sarcastic, and took no nonsense, Renna was loud, overly friendly, and had no problem saying whatever came into her head to make people laugh. She was still wearing her paramedic uniform and had obviously had a long shift from the tired look on her face.

Renna spun Nicole around and kissed the breath out of her. When she finally did release her, they were touching foreheads. "Missed you," she growled.

Nicole actually flushed a little. It always amazed Derek to see just how different Nicole was when she was with Renna. He watched as Nicole's eyes focused back in and she whispered back, "Missed you too."

Renna noticed Mia standing outside the office and she nodded to her. "New girl?"

Mia looked a little flustered. "Um, yeah. I'm Mia."

"Was she nice to you?" Renna asked nodding towards Nicole.

Going back to her gruff persona, Nicole answered, "Yes. I even gave her a compliment and everything."

Renna looked to Mia for confirmation, who just nodded. "Hmmm... that's my good girl. I'm going to have to reward you later."

Nicole's lips parted, and she almost responded, but Derek interrupted them. "Okay, how about you reward her at home and not in my office?"

Looking slightly put out at her fun being ruined Nicole said, "I thought men always dreamed about two women getting it on."

Derek shook his head and looked past the couple to Mia. "Nope. I only want to focus my attention on one woman at a time and want the same in return."

Renna pinched Nicole's ass and said, "Come on, sexy. I want to have some fun before we both crash for the night."

Nicole grabbed her purse off the file cabinet and followed Renna hand in hand out the door.

Mia came in as Nicole left. She still looked almost in awe of the couple walking out the door. "I did not see that coming at all."

Smiling Derek asked, "What? Her being a mush with her love, or that her love is a woman?"

Mia tilted her head. "Both, I guess. I mean, I saw her flirt with some of the customers and she's so..."

"Rough around the edges?"

"Yeah. I mean she melted like ice cream on a hot day as soon as her wife showed up."

"Nicole flirts for the bigger tips, but they went through a lot to be together. Being part of the LGBTQIA community in a small town has it challenges. You have mostly met the good people of town, but we have our share of closed-minded people who have made their lives difficult. For the most part they don't come here. I don't tolerate hate of any kind. If people want to be assholes, they can do it somewhere else. Tiny has helped me more than once to physically remove people who don't get the message. So, if you ever hear anyone giving Nicole a hard time, or even another customer you immediately let me or Tiny know."

"Okay."

"You all done?"

"Yeah. Do I leave out the back?"

"Yeah, just wait for me. I don't want you to walk alone."

Mia raised her eyebrow. "Derek, I think I will be okay walking a few feet and going up the stairs."

He shook his head. "Don't care. All women get walked to their cars, or in your case to the entry."

"You're being ridiculous. This is a small town. Not DC or New York."

Derek sighed. "We may be small, but we have had our fair share of trouble out here. Humor me. Please."

"Fine," she said with a big sigh of resignation.

"Thanks. I'll try not to let this hurt my feelings," he said as he grabbed his keys and shut the office.

"I think your giant ego can take the small hit."

It was only a few minutes later that Derek stood in the alley staring up at Mia's living room window to make sure she was safely inside. His body was screaming at him to take the stairs two at a time and pound on her door until she let him inside her apartment and body, but his mind still had that little voice reminding him that he wasn't good enough for her. She deserved so much more than he could offer.

Chapter 6

Mia had worked three more nights and felt every muscle in her body screaming at her for jumping back into so much physical activity. She parked her car in front of Compass Securities and gathered up her notebook filled with every piece of information she had about her missing belongings and her bastard of an ex. Could she really call him an ex? He was never really with her. He just used her to get what he wanted. He never loved her.

Mustering up all the bravery she could, she got out of the car and pushed her way through the entry of the shopfront to talk to the investigator that Derek had recommended. She stopped only a few feet from the door and saw three men staring back at her. Well, this wasn't intimidating at all. "Hi. Um, Derek said to come and talk to..." She looked down at her papers and read the name scribbled in Derek's horrible handwriting. "Dexter."

A man who looked to be in about his late forties pulled away from the counter he was leaning on and smiled at her. "That's me, sweetheart. You must be Mia."

She fidgeted with her papers in her arms before nodding. "Yes. Derek said that you might be able to help me."

Dexter led her back to the counter where the other two men were waiting with matching grins. She recognized Grayson, one of Derek's friends, but the other man who had a pale complexion and red hair was new. Once he knew that he had her attention he extended his hand. "I'm Ollie. I'm co-owner of Compass, with this knucklehead," he said nodding over to Grayson.

Mia graciously took his hand and introduced herself. She thought that the meeting was only going to be with Dexter but was realizing that she would be treated to all three men.

Dexter opened her file and started pulling out the pages and pictures and put them into several piles on the counter. "I have a general story from what Grayson was able to tell me, but how about you tell me how you got into this pickle?"

"I don't know where to start."

Grayson pulled over a stool and started picking up some of the pictures of Jack and his sister. "How about you start with telling us about your grandfather?"

A small pang shot through her heart as she pulled out memories of him. "My grandpa was a great man. My parents are not the best people in the world. They don't really care about me or ever really wanted to take care of me. My grandpa took me in when I was young, and I lived with him in Virginia shortly after Grandma died. Grandpa's family comes from old money. Throughout the years there were some bad investments, but the family name held prestige on its own. He had enough to care for us and maintain the large house that we lived in since I was a child. When his health started to decline, I left school and came home to take care of him. He started to invest again and seemed to have some good luck now that he didn't care and was just playing around with the market. It just didn't translate into better luck with his health. I took some of the money and decided to hire a home health aide, because it was getting to the point where I couldn't do it all on my own. That's how I met Jack."

Dexter was scanning the notes that were attached to Jack's picture. "So, this asshole?"

Mia's mouth lifted up in the corner. "Yup. That's him. Anyway, I wanted the best for Grandpa and Jack was referred to us by one of the families from church. He had started working for them, but the person he was caring for died just the week before I started my search and needed a job. I interviewed him the next day, and he had all the certifications, background check, and experience that I was looking for. I know I overpaid him, but I thought providing a good salary would provide a better chance of consistency of care."

Dexter pulled out his legal pad and began taking notes. "When did things start between the two of you romantically?"

Mia felt her face flush. It was embarrassing to look back and see what a fool she had been. "It was a couple months. He started with the compliments and personal attention right away. But it was the devotion of care he showed Grandpa that drew me to him the most. He was so gentle and treated Grandpa with respect and not like an invalid. They watched basketball together; he took Grandpa for walks in his wheelchair around the subdivision when the weather was nice and was diligent about keeping up with the therapies that the doctors prescribed. I had never been around a man who seemed to care about people as much as he did. It was what attracted me to him the most in the beginning."

Grayson scanned over another of the pages and said, "He gained your trust and then started to pursue you."

Mia nodded. "It was a couple months before Grandpa died when he first asked me out. I turned him down, but he was persistent, and I thought that he must really like me if he was willing to keep asking me out. He would bring me flowers and books that I liked. It was all the little things that he paid attention to that finally won me over."

She continued to provide all the details to the men clarifying dates and email and text conversations up until the wedding day. The day he just disappeared. Grayson was already doing research on the computer while Dexter and Ollie wrote down notes and occasionally passed them onto Grayson. It was fascinating to watch the three of them work as a unit. They already seemed to have set roles while working. She knew that Dexter didn't work for Grayson, but he did help out with investigations as needed.

Just as everything grew silent there was a loud shout coming from the back room. "Fuck, yeah! I got it!"

While the loud voice startled Mia, none of the men seemed to react with any interest, and Grayson only lifted his head with a stern, "Language!"

A moment later a teenage boy appeared from the back with a huge look of disappointment. The boy moved closer to Grayson and shook what looked like a candy bar in his face. "You're an asshole."

Moving back in his chair Grayson looked up at him and lifted an eyebrow.

Looking appropriately scolded the boy backed down just a bit. "You said there was a hundred thousand dollars in that safe, and if I could open it, I could have it."

Looking proud of himself Grayson asked, "Is that exactly what I said though?"

The boy paused and thought for a moment. "You said there were two safes I could try to open. The hard safe had five hundred dollars and the easy one had a hundred grand."

Looking at the candy bar in the boy's hand Grayson asked, "And what are you holding right now?"

"Candy!"

Mia watched in amusement as she saw the name of the candy was 100 Grand. Oh, that was sneaky. She had to appreciate the creativity.

Grayson sighed. "I said the easy safe had a 100 Grand, but I did not say dollars. That is a 100 Grand candy bar. I did say the harder safe had five hundred dollars in it. You had the opportunity to ask clarifying questions or take the harder safe to open and have the reward of completing a harder challenge and still be five hundred dollars richer."

"Nobody would have chosen the harder safe given those options."

Grayson laughed. "And you should have known I wouldn't give a teenager a hundred thousand dollars. I want you to learn critical thinking skills, and this would have been a great time to think before acting and ask more questions."

"Your lessons suck."

"Maybe, but you did crack open the safe. You're getting better."

The boy opened the candy bar and took a big bite. "Yeah, well, you still suck." He took another big bite. "And I earned this dumb candy bar. I don't care what Coach says, I'm eating it."

The boy finally turned and noticed Mia for the first time. Looking a bit sheepish, he smiled apologetically. "Sorry about the cussing, ma'am."

Mia waved it off. "Don't worry about it. It's okay. I think I might have cussed a little if I thought I was going to get rich and found that instead." Mia extended her hand. "I'm Mia."

The boy wiped his hand on his jeans and took her hand in his. "Cam."

Mia smiled. "Hi, Cam. Is he your dad?" she asked nodding towards Grayson.

Cam's smile fell a little. "No. He married my Aunt Josie. My parents died and we live with them."

She could feel her heart fall just a bit. "I'm sorry. I didn't..."

Saving her from her loss of words Cam interjected, "It's okay. I mean it's not, but the whole town knows our story. I thought you would have heard about it anyway."

He wasn't wrong. She already knew so much gossip from the town she could write a book.

Saving her from the awkward silence, Grayson said, "You met my wife on your first night. She helped with your makeup in Derek's office."

Mia blinked. "Oh..." Then with clarity she repeated, "Oh! Yes, she was very nice."

Cam scoffed. "Nice? Wow, you got lucky. She isn't known for being nice."

Confused she looked at Grayson. "She's a bit combative with people she doesn't like, and extremely loyal to those she does. Believe me, she's very nice to me and the kids."

"Kids?"

Rolling his eyes Cam said, "There's four of us."

Four? She could barely understand how to instantly take care of one child, let alone four.

"It's not as bad as it sounds. Cam has a twin, and they are pretty self-reliant. Well, except that he'll eat everything in the kitchen in an hour if you let him."

Cam flexed his arm to show his burgeoning muscles. "I need fuel to beef up these babies."

Ollie threw a stress ball at Cam. "Put those puny things away."

Pouting, Cam replied softly, "They're not puny."

Grayson sighed. "I swear to God if you end up like a mini-Derek, your aunt is going to kill me."

Feeling defensive about her boss and landlord... and friend Mia asked, "What's wrong with Derek?"

Quirking a smile Grayson said, "Nothing, really, except that he can be a little bit cocky. I've seen him show off his muscles for women several times. He's like the pretty frat boy everyone wants, and he knows it too. Don't get me wrong, he's one of the nicest men I have ever met, but he has zero filter on his ego sometimes. The charm he can use on a woman is quite a thing to watch. They go from intelligent confident women to swoony puddles on the floor in less than three seconds."

Well, there it was. The confirmation she needed to not fall for her boss. He was nice, but she did not need to be another conquest, or worse yet a fool for falling for a man who could have anyone he wanted. Suddenly she felt an urgent need to go home. She didn't want to hear any more stories about Derek and other women. She had no right to feel the slight pangs of jealousy, but it was happening anyway. "Do you guys need anything else from me?"

Ollie shook his head. "Nah. This should get us started in the right direction."

"Okay. Let me know when you need more beyond the retainer."

Mia already gave two hundred and fifty dollars for the retainer, and she knew that wouldn't last long. She was just grateful that the tips were good at the bar, and she was able to get this started. At this point she didn't really want Jack back; she just wanted some things back that he took from her. And maybe, yes, she wanted a tiny bit of justice seeing him behind bars. The time for sadness was fading into anger, and God that felt good.

DEREK UNLOCKED THE door to his mom's house and walked in following the warm scent of fresh bread. "Did I ever tell you that you're the best mom ever," he asked as he reached for a warm dinner roll.

"Hands off, Derek McKenna," Amanda exclaimed. "I brought you into this world and I can take you out. Those are for dinner with Hannah and Mark tonight."

"The death penalty is a bit harsh for eating some bread."

"You have your own perfectly good cook at work who makes you anything you want."

"Yeah, but this is your bread, and I brought you the cornhole set."

"You said you would bring it over after you drank all my coffee a few days ago. No double dipping for rewards."

"How about if it's just because you love me?" Derek tilted his head and batted his eyelashes.

"Lord help the poor woman that marries you. You can have one."

Derek beamed and plucked one from the basket. He started to sneak a second one when he thought she wasn't looking but she quickly put a stop to it. "I said one, child of mine. Do not make me have bloodshed in the kitchen today."

"So violent."

"Your fault. So, where's the cornhole set?"

Taking a bite of the roll, he replied, "Already in your car."

"Derek, chew and swallow first, please."

Making a large gulping noise he continued. "Do you really think a bunch of old people are going to be able to toss the bags twenty-seven feet away from each other?"

Amanda pulled out a bottle of water and handed it to Derek. "It is a senior center, not a hospice. They can toss bags just fine, and if we have some who need help, I will just move them up."

"I could just buy you a new set to keep there you know."

"No, you can't. We have fundraisers and our own budget. You already donate a lot of money to the center."

"Not really. I could do more."

"If you think I didn't notice the Ten-k from you and Ten-k from Kobe Jordan, you are sorely mistaken. Did you really think you could put together two of your favorite basketball players names and I wouldn't notice?"

He shrugged. "No, not really. I didn't think you paid attention to any of the sports stuff."

"Basketball was your life for years. You loved it, so I learned to love it with you."

This shouldn't have been a surprise. Derek loved his mom so much and her heart always invested one hundred percent into anything her children cared about. For so many years her life seemed to start and stop with whatever Derek or Ariel needed or wanted.

"Just Hannah and Mark tonight?"

She fidgeted with the bottom of her shirt seeming to smooth a non-existent wrinkle. "No. They are bringing one of Mark's friends to dinner as well."

"A man?"

Amanda sighed. "Yes, a man." Then she gave a devilish grin. "Single too."

Ugh. When was the last time she'd had a date? With his dad? Derek certainly couldn't remember her ever mentioning going out with someone else since her divorce. He really wanted her to find her own happiness too. Everyone else was finding it. Hell, even Josie managed to not scare off Grayson. He knew that his mom deserved the love of a good man, but the thought of another man in her life and the possibility of that man hurting her nearly pushed him over the edge of reason.

Amanda motioned for Derek to join her at the barstools. "I can see the subject of my dating life is making you uncomfortable. How about we talk about yours then?"

"Mom..."

"What? I just thought we would change the subject since you didn't like the idea of your old mother being set up on a blind date."

"Having dinner at your house is not a date," Derek grumbled.

"Maybe not in the traditional sense, but it was what I was comfortable with. If we like each other, we can set up another date."

Derek grabbed an apple from the bowl and started rolling it around on the counter.

Glaring at the abused apple Amanda said, "You better eat that now."

Derek took a big bite and began to chew. After swallowing the bite of apple and other words he knew he shouldn't say he said, "I hope you have a good time and hit it off with..."

"Randall," she finished for him.

"Randall? Nobody has a good time with a Randall. Randall is the guy who wears a pocket protector and does your taxes. What does Randall do?"

Amanda frowned. "He's a budget analyst."

Derek laughed. "I can't tell if that is an upgrade or downgrade from a tax accountant."

"Hush. What about you? When are you going to settle down and give me another daughter to love?"

"I did give you another daughter. I brought you Zoey."

"Yes, and I love that girl as if she was my own, but you know what I am talking about. I want you to fall in love and have your own family."

For a brief moment an image of Mia flashed in his head, and he shook to clear it like an Etch-a-Sketch. "I'm not built for relationships. You know that."

"Sweetie, I am going to be brutally honest with you, because at this point someone needs to be. You are absolutely built to find love and build a good life with a woman who will be careful with your heart."

"It's not the women I am worried about, Mom. I would break their heart. What if I'm just like Dad, and I destroy someone I care about? He cheated on you time and time again, and I know I'm just like him."

Amanda placed her hand over his. "You are not. How many close friends did your dad have while you were growing up?"

Derek shrugged.

"None."

Shaking his head Derek said, "No, he had Mark."

"No. They hung out a lot because Hannah and I were good friends. Mark was never your dad's friend. They were only friends due to circumstances, and once your dad and I divorced they never hung out together again. I couldn't tell you how many times Hannah had to remind Mark not to punch your dad in the face."

"I don't see what that has to do with me."

"The point is, you have built these amazing close friendships and show loyalty with every breath you take. You wouldn't have maintained a long-distance friendship with someone if you didn't have the strength of character needed to provide a loving relationship. You're not your dad. Not even close. And even look at him now. After therapy, he has found a positive relationship with his new wife."

She wasn't wrong. Miranda was a strong woman and was a good influence on his dad. And they were taking steps to mend their relationship. It was difficult, but he was learning to set aside his anger and take steps to allow his dad back into his life. He thought again about Mia, her soft smile, and genuine personality that was slowly breaking down his defenses and making him want things he never thought he could have.

"He should have sorted out his issues while he was still with you."

Amanda sighed. "I know, but he didn't. I have to believe that things worked out the way that they were supposed to. Being with your dad gave me the two greatest things in my life. I have you and Ariel. Perhaps him and Miranda were always meant to be, and it took how things happened to bring them together."

"You really believe in all that destiny and fate crap?"

Amanda sighed as she leaned back. "I have to believe in something. I don't know if it is destiny or fate or even God. But I know that we all have a purpose and everything we do contributes to life all around us."

Derek kissed his mom on the top of her head. "How about this? I promise that if something pushes me towards a woman that I could see a possible future with, I won't fight it anymore."

"I'm going to hold you to that."

"I know."

DEREK PULLED UP TO the back of the bar and saw Mia trying to carry what looked like twenty bags into the apartment entry door. Shaking his head he jumped out of the car and strode over to help. "Mia! Wait, let me help you."

Mia shook her head. "Nope, I got it."

When Derek went to grab one of the bags, he was surprised to see it was bags and bags of yarn. Confused he looked down at the bags and back to Mia. "It's yarn."

Mia straightened her spine. "Yeah. So what?"

"It's so much yarn. You could start your own store." He looked at another bag and laughed. "Is that glow-in-the-dark yarn?"

Mia's lips thinned. "Yes, it is." She pulled the bags away from Derek and continued to climb the stairs.

No way was he going to let her just run away when he had so many questions. He followed her up the stairs and watched as she unlocked the door, her cheeks flushing a light shade of pink.

"You're not going to let this go, are you?"

Derek laughed. "Not a chance."

He followed her in as she set the bags down on the dining table. His hand itched to see exactly how many colors she had in there.

Mia shook her head. "Go ahead. Take a look, I know you're dying to."

He smirked as he nearly bounced his way over to the table. Pulling out the green glow-in-the-dark yarn he cupped his hands and put his face in the hole. "It's not very glow in the darky."

"Glow in the darky?"

"You know what I mean."

"You have to charge the yarn and hold it up to the light first."

Derek spun around and walked over with it to the lamp. After holding it for a few seconds, he tried again. Sure enough, it glowed brighter. "That's pretty cool. So, you knit sweaters and stuff?"

"No."

"Hats?"

"No."

"Scarves?"

Mia sighed. "No and stop guessing."

"But I have to know. Blankets?"

"No." Mia fidgeted with her shirt. "I make sad little monsters."

"What?"

"Sad little monsters." She pulled out her phone and pulled up a photo and handed it to him.

Looking at the photo it was so sad, it was funny. It was a purple monster with a glow in the dark chest, three eyes popping from the top and a crooked frown. Smiling he asked, "Are there more?"

She nodded. "Just swipe through. That is an album of nothing but my little creatures."

Sure enough, one by one he saw so many little monsters all with sad faces and each one just slightly different from the last. "These are great. Do you sell these?"

"No. I made those while sitting by Grandpa's bedside to pass the time. I teased him that they were all replicas of all the monsters hiding under my bed that he never scared away and now they were sad that he was leaving me."

"Were these in your storage unit that was cleared out?"

Mia's lip quivered. "Yeah. I was going to donate them to a charity here once I got settled and found a good place for them. Grandpa said that my monsters would make other people smile. I had them all around his room keeping him company when I wasn't home."

"You could probably sell these. You could set up one of those sites and I am sure orders would come flowing in. Or even set up at one of those craft markets."

"Maybe. Right now, I just like making them for me. My brain kind of shuts off while I knit."

"So, if I asked could you knit me a sweater?"

She shook her head vigorously. "Nobody needs a sweater from me. You could end up with three sleeves or it might be three sizes too big."

Derek shrugged. "If it was too big, I could always just give it to Tiny."

"Oh, no. It would just be a hot mess. I will stick to my tiny monsters. Some of them ended up with extra arms because I messed up too bad. You have no idea how many critters I unraveled because I couldn't fix something."

"What a way to die. Having your skin ripped away from your body one little seam at a time."

"You're terrible."

"So I've been told."

"Can you just imagine what is going through their head as you pull out the string?" He held up the yarn to his face and gave his best kid monster voice. "Nooooo... Don't pull me apart. I want to live... Nooooo!!!!"

Mia snatched the yarn away and glared at him. "Just for that you will never get Marvin."

"Marvin?"

"Yup. Marvin the Monster. He was totally going to be cute and now I don't think he wants to live with you. He was even going to hold a tiny little basketball."

Derek frowned. "You can't promise me something as awesome as that and then take it away from me."

"Too late. Now Marvin will have to find a new home. Maybe I can make a tiny little fireman's hat and give it to that cute guy with the Texas twang."

Austin? Oh, hell no. She was not going to make him a cute monster and let him think he could take her out and put his lips to hers. Hell no. Derek stepped closer to her. "You are not making anything for Austin."

Mia got a glint in her eyes. "Austin. That's right. I think he would love Marvin."

Derek wrapped his hand around her wrist and used his other hand to take back the yarn. He stared into her eyes and lowered his voice. "Marvin is mine."

Derek watched as Mia's mouth slightly parted, and her eyes glazed over. "Yours?"

"Mine. And Austin can keep his grubby little paws off what's mine."

Mia looked into his eyes waiting for more, but he had already said too much. Was he really doing this? Was he about to claim Mia as his? He certainly didn't follow her up the stairs with this in mind but here they were. He couldn't stop drowning in her soulful eyes and at this point he didn't care if he ever came back up for air.

"Derek," she asked with so much meaning behind it. He knew it, she knew it, but would he jump? Could he?

His phone rang breaking the moment, and he sighed as he pulled it out. He answered it not looking away from Mia. "Yeah?"

Tiny's voice came through in a rush. "We need you at the bar. Your new bartender quit, and my line prep has been puking in the bathroom for the past thirty minutes."

Derek ran his hands through his hair and looked regretfully at Mia. "Alright I'll be there in five minutes."

"Thanks. Sorry about this."

"It's alright. I'll be right down."

"I have to go."

Mia nodded. "I could hear Tiny. Do you need me to come down and help?"

"I don't think so, but I'll message if I do."

The urge to kiss her was so strong, but he resisted. If he crossed this line with her, he needed to be sure that he was all in. Did he want her? Yes, he did, but the urge to protect her, even from himself, was too much to ignore.

He nodded to the bags of yarn and said as a goodbye, "I look forward to meeting Marvin."

When Derek finally made it downstairs, he found the kitchen in chaos and his sister grabbing plates off the window.

"I don't remember hiring you? Are you new?"

Ariel turned and shifted her hip. "You didn't, but it was a nightmare out there, and I couldn't watch Tiny stress out anymore."

Tiny slammed down two orders of wings and shook his head. "I wasn't stressed. I was annoyed."

Ariel shrugged. "Either way, I don't like seeing you upset."

Derek watched as the big man's face melted into a smile. "Thanks, little one."

Ariel walked out opening the door with her butt and said, "I'm not little, you're just a giant."

Derek waited until his sister cleared the door and started to laugh. "She is little." He turned to Tiny who was back to flipping some burgers. "Do you need some help?"

He shook his head. "Nah, but you probably should get back to the bar. Josie is mixing drinks for you."

"Shit. I'm going."

Sure enough, when he got out there, she was heavy handedly pouring a mixed drink while simultaneously giving a glare at a man at the end of the bar. Derek pulled a couple of the bar tickets and reached for a bottle. "Thanks for the help, Josie."

"No problem," she replied in her silky calm voice.

He glanced at the end of the bar again at the man whose face was deepening a shade of red. "Is there a reason he looks like he wants to strangle you?"

"I told him he could be crawling through a hot desert on the verge of death, and I still wouldn't serve him a drink."

Knowing that her mean streak only rose from the depths when people usually deserved it, he asked, "Why, what did he do?"

"That girl over there ordered a Diet Coke, and I heard him tell his friend, 'Not like that's going to help.'"

"And yet he still lives."

"I know. I think Grayson is a bad influence. I'm losing my touch. He's still here."

"Nah... you are just becoming a mature adult."

"Yeah, well, I hate it. Scaring the shit out of people is what I do best."

The two of them continued to fulfill the bar orders and ignore the jerk at the end of the bar until he finally cleared his throat with a loud "A-hem."

Derek shook his head at Josie. "Go ahead and sit back down with Ariel. I've got this."

He casually walked over to the angry man and flung a towel over his shoulder. "Can I help you?"

"I've been waiting for a drink for twenty minutes."

"Yeah, I know, but we don't serve your kind here."

"My kind?"

"Yeah. Your kind." Derek pointed over his shoulder to a black and white sign that said, "We refuse to serve assholes."

"Fuck you. Give me a beer."

Derek shook his head. "No."

"I will get you fired for refusing me service."

Derek heard a snort coming from one of the locals sitting near them as he leaned in with his eyes narrowed. "I own this place. I can refuse anyone I want. And since you can't help but to be an asshole, I can refuse you service."

The man stood up and glared back. "I'll blast you on social media. No one will ever come here again."

Derek laughed as he looked around the room and saw mostly locals today. He put his fingers to his lips and gave a loud whistle. "Hey, this man says he's going to blast me on social media. What do you think, should I be worried?"

Laughter came from nearly every table as they all turned back to their food. Turning back to the man he continued, "See, you're in a small town. Maybe in that big city where you're from, people might let your little rant go viral and affect a person's business, but out here, this is our world, and nobody gives a shit about an asshole with an attitude and his tiny following. They all know me. They don't know you. Get the fuck out of my bar."

He felt the presence next to him before he saw him. Tiny was standing with his arms crossed and nodded his head towards the door. "Out."

With eyes widening the man took a few steps back and turned to leave.

Tiny grabbed a glass and filled it with some soda before he finally said, "That's disappointing. I was hoping to have a little fun with him before he left."

Thankfully, the rest of the night was busy but uneventful, but with each passing minute he found himself looking up at the ceiling where he knew Mia's apartment was and couldn't stop thinking about banging on her door and showing her what it would feel like to be devoured by him.

Chapter 7

It had been a few days since Mia saw Derek. She hadn't worked with him the past couple of nights and heard that he had poker night at his place last night. Mia was always fascinated by the game, but never quite got a handle on when she should bet or fold. Sometimes she would cling on to a hand thinking it was the best thing out there, only to get smacked back to reality and lose all her money. Her love life wasn't much different. She thought Jack was a good man who loved her until she got the hardest slap back to reality ever.

All night she kept looking over at the bar, expecting to see Derek twirling bottles or laughing with some of the regulars. Each time she looked over and saw the new guy her heart dropped in disappointment. As she reached for a takeout box Nicole said, "Enough with the pouting. You're making me look like the cheerful one."

Mia's mouth parted. "I'm not pouting."

"God, you are. You keep looking over at the bar with those sad puppy eyes all night."

Mia pulled her lower lip in and bit down in thought. "It's not sad puppy eyes."

"Yes, it is. Do us all a favor and next time just jump the man."

"What? I can't do that. I mean..."

"Yes you can. It's really simple. You just wrap your arms around his neck, pull him down and climb him like a tree."

Mia was going to say something, but words seemed to evade her.

"Don't worry, he makes the same puppy eyes at you all the damn time too. It's disgusting."

Before Mia could respond, Nicole left to take care of her new table. Mia fiddled with the box for another few seconds while she gathered her thoughts. She was not pouting all night. Sure, maybe she wanted to see Derek, but that was because he was one of her few friends right now. It was not because she wanted to see his muscles flex as he poured drinks, or because she wanted to see his magnificent chest in that sexy fitted t-shirt. Damn. Maybe she was pouting a little bit.

She felt eyes on her as she stood there and quickly made her way to her table. "Here ya go. Is there anything else I can get for you today?"

The somewhat attractive man smiled at her and took the box. "How about your phone number?"

"My what?" Surely, she didn't hear him correctly.

"Your phone number. You know so I can call you and maybe take you out to dinner sometime."

She blinked a couple times trying to process and come up with a response that wouldn't kill her tip. Maybe she should try for the sympathy route. "I appreciate the offer, but

I just got out of a relationship, and I'm just not quite ready for anything yet."

"I could be your rebound guy. You know what they say."

Ugh. Was he really going to give that line about the best way to get over a guy is to get under a new one? Gross. She put up a hand. "Yeah, I do, but I am still in the ice cream and sappy movie phase."

"How about I give you my number and you can call me when you get to the next phase?"

She really didn't want it, but it was probably the easiest way to get out of this situation. Taking the number he wrote on a napkin, she said, "Thanks."

As she turned to go back to the kitchen, she saw Derek staring at her with an unreadable look on his face. Did he see her take that guy's phone number? The closer she got to him the more certain she was that he did see it. Her heart plummeted as he shook his head and walked back to his office. She wanted to run to him and tell him it was not what he thought, but instead she watched helplessly as he slammed the door shut.

Nicole's head popped over her shoulder. "Well, you fucked that all up."

Mia shook her head. "You're no help."

"Never said I would be."

Derek never came back out from his office for the rest of the night. A few times, she saw Tiny go in only to come back out laughing his ass off. She wished she knew what that was all about. Others also went in and out but with much less humor than Tiny. She knew that she had to go in there to drop off receipts and cash, but she really didn't want to see that disappointed look on his face again. She had delayed with her side jobs long enough. Now the bar was closed and everyone else had left. Time to face the grumpy bear.

Gently knocking on the door, she prayed that Derek was in a better mood. His gruff response to come in did not sound promising though.

"Hey," she gently said as she entered his office. "Everything okay?"

Derek was entering numbers into the computer and nodded his head. "Yeah, it's fine."

"Fine?" That wasn't good. Everyone knows that fine is never fine. That's the one word in the English language that never means what the definition says. Fine means I'm pissed, and you need to figure out why.

"Yeah, fine."

He certainly wasn't open to conversation today, so maybe she should just drop off her stuff and go home. "Did I do something wrong?" Great. Her brain was deciding to make stupid decisions today. Sure, let's poke the bear and see what happens.

Derek closed his eyes and took in a deep breath. "No, Mia."

"It feels like I did."

Derek seemed to make a decision about something because he stood up and walked towards her as she backed up and hit her back to the door. He reached down to her apron and into the pocket, pulled out the napkin, and read the name scrawled on the top. "If you want to go out with... Jason, that's your choice. I can't be mad at you for that." He sounded frustrated now and his breathing was picking up speed.

Mia shook her head. "I don't want to go out with him."

Derek reached out his hands, grasped her hips tightly, and pulled her in. "What do you want Mia?"

God, she wanted a lot of things. She wanted to take advantage of that steel-hard erection she could feel against her. She wanted to run her hands along his chest. She wanted to feel his mouth caressing every part of her body. It all came down to one basic truth. "You. I want you."

He leaned into her ear and growled, "No more Jasons. You're mine."

God, yes, please. His face returned to hers with his hands holding the back of her neck, and he repeated. "Mine."

She only gave a small movement to nod her head and replied, "Yours."

Before her heart could take another beat his lips were on hers, aggressive and demanding. It felt as if he needed her to breathe. His body pressed her further into the door and he wedged himself into her until she couldn't stop herself from wrapping her legs around him. His hands explored down until they were cupping her ass and lifting her into the air. He deposited her onto his desk, and she reached for his shirt so she could finally feel his toned chest and abs under her palms.

She felt his hands trace down her shoulders, her arms, to finally reach the edge of her shirt at her waist. Gently he pulled up the edge to expose her stomach to the cold air. She gasped at the first touch of his hands on her bare skin. It was as if her skin was on fire. His touch burned her to the core. But, God, it was such a glorious burn.

She struggled to breathe as he released her lips and looked into her eyes with bright intensity and need. His hands were fisting the bottom of her shirt waiting. It took a moment to realize he was waiting for her permission. Deciding on action instead of words she pulled her shirt over her head and tossed it to the side of his desk. She was immediately thankful that she was wearing the good lace bra that pushed her breasts up and together, because he was slowly dragging his finger to trace her cleavage and used his other hand to pull her head to his and crashed his lips to hers.

His fingers delved under the lace and played with her nipple giving a slight pinch to tighten them to stiff peaks. She moaned into his mouth as the surprising feeling of pleasure mixed with the pain. He pulled down the cup to expose her breast and kissed his way down to wrap his lips around her nipple and suck. Oh, God. The way his tongue circled while he sucked was intoxicating, so much so that her hips began to move to the rhythm of his suction. "Derek. I..."

He released her nipple and gave a swirling lick around her hard tip. His hands pulled at her pants, and he gently pulled as she lifted her hips. He didn't bother to leave her panties on. Oh, no, he was going straight for what he wanted. This was crazy. She was naked on his desk, and he was fully dressed, but she wasn't feeling any shame or shyness. How could she when he was looking at her with such appreciation, such desire?

Derek gently pushed her legs further apart. "Wider, Mia. I want to taste that sweet pussy and hear you scream my name."

Helplessly, she obeyed, because fuck yes, she wanted that. His finger traced down her seam and she moaned. He smiled up at her when his finger lingered over her entrance. "You're so wet for me. You want this as much as I do, don't you?"

Want this? Was he kidding? She might die if he didn't fulfill his promise to make her scream. "Yes. I want it."

He placed a soft kiss at her thigh as his finger finally sank into her. "What do you want? Tell me."

Mia blushed and stuttered. She wasn't used to talking during sex or foreplay. All her old partners were pretty quick and quiet about it, but she was realizing that Derek was different, and it was hot as hell. She gasped as he sank a second finger into her channel.

"Mia. What do you want?"

"You," she replied breathlessly.

"Me, to do what?"

"Ah. I ... oh shit... I want you to eat my pussy."

Smiling, Derek said, "As you wish."

Derek's mouth replaced where his fingers were just pumping in and out and he was absolutely going to deliver on his promise. His tongue glided in a maddening pattern and moved in and out while his hands spread her wide apart. Mia's body rocked into him as he continued to devour her. Her moan only seemed to fuel his efforts. "Derek, I can't—"

He moved his mouth away and smiled up at her. "You can. Just let go."

His fingers once again thrusted into her and his mouth latched onto her clit. Before she knew it, she felt as if she was starting to float off the table. She leaned back on her elbows and finally just relaxed into his expert hands and tongue as he turned his fingers inside her and made a quick curling motion hitting that spot she thought was a myth. She screamed out his name so loud it surprised her. She started to slump back on the desk, but she felt Derek's arms wrap around her and picked her up onto his lap. A momentary thought of protesting crossed her mind, but really who would have the energy for that after that magnificent orgasm he just gave her?

"Are you okay?" he asked.

Okay? She'd never felt better in her life, but as she sat naked in his lap... in his office, she began to panic. What had she done? She couldn't look at him. Nope. She needed to find her clothes and hide out in her apartment. No, not her apartment. Maybe she could just move to some other small town and maybe not throw herself at her boss and landlord. Just as she was about to calculate the best way to make an exit with some dignity, she felt his hand on her chin moving her to look at him.

"Mia? Are you okay? Please tell me you're okay."

She could see his worry lines setting in. She didn't know what to say. "I'm... okay."

He must have seen her unease and handed her shirt to her so she could cover up a little. After she pulled the shirt down, he gently grazed his thumb across her cheek and gave a light kiss to her lips. "Please don't freak out on me. I can see your cute little brain starting to formulate an escape plan."

Mia's eyes widened. "I wasn't."

Derek put a finger to her lips. "I'm going to stop you right there before you try lying to me. You're going to overthink things, so let me help you right now. I like you. In fact, I can barely make it through the day without thinking about you at least a thousand times. I meant it when I said you were mine. Let me show you that I deserve it, that I deserve you. Go to dinner with me tomorrow."

Mia's brain was not functioning at full speed. "I can't."

Derek frowned. "Why?"

"I have to work."

A blinding smile fell across his face. "I think I can convince your boss to give you the night off. How about I pick you up at seven?"

Finally feeling a little more comfortable she smiled and said, "Sounds good."

He kissed her again and gently let her slide off of his lap. "Get dressed. I am going to check up front and then I'll walk you home."

Mia rolled her eyes. "Yes, that incredibly far distance to my apartment."

"Hey, you never know. You could walk into the great magical fight of your pickle fairy and my troll that lives under the stairs."

"You have a troll?"

"Of course, I do. He moved in just after the fairy did. They spend all night fighting and casting spells against each other."

"All night, huh?"

"Yes. They can't fight during the day, or he will turn into stone in the daylight. He likes me. If you're with me, you'll be safe."

"Well, then, how could a girl refuse an escort under those circumstances?"

Derek winked. "Exactly."

It was only a few minutes later when Derek was following behind her up the stairs to her apartment. She stopped halfway and leaned over the railing to see the bottom landing. Derek raised an eyebrow at her. "What are you doing?"

"Looking for your troll."

"Hodag."

"What?"

"Hodag. His name is Hodag."

Mia shook her head and continued up the stairs. "Do you think Hodag is a sexy name for a troll? Like everyone cringes if you say you are going to date a guy named Gilbert, but if you are going out with a guy named Ford, or Roman everyone thinks he is a sexy guy from a romance book."

"I think Hodag is definitely the sexy name of the troll world. It's a strong name. Ho-Dag. You can hear the strength in his name."

Mia laughed. She loved his sense of humor. He always seemed to have a lightness about him. She could see why people were always drawn to him.

After reaching the door Mia turned around only to find Derek a whispers breath away. He leaned down and gave her a gentle kiss and said, "I'll see you tomorrow."

Mia slowly opened her eyes and replied, "Uh-huh."

Derek slowly took the keys from her hand, then unlocked and opened her door. "Go inside, Mia, before I pick your sweet ass up and take us both inside."

Nearly breathless at the idea she asked, "Would that be so bad?"

"I'm trying to be good, Mia."

"Oh," she said with a note of disappointment.

"But tomorrow..." He wrapped his arm around her waist and drew her close. "I make no guarantees about my behavior."

After kissing him, she said, "Tomorrow then."

Chapter 8

Derek found himself awake at 4 a.m. just staring at the ceiling. He was anxious to see Mia and for all the things that the night could bring, but this was actual dating. She would expect things from him that he had never done before like having more dates and doing boyfriend type things for her. He did not know how to do that. What do boyfriends do exactly? He needed some advice. Ugh. That meant he would have to ask Kyle and maybe even Tyler.

Looking at the time on his phone again he thought about texting Kyle. Was it too early to text? Yes. Did he really give a shit? Not really.

Derek: Hey.
Derek: Hello, Asshat.
Derek: You awake?
Kyle: WTF? Now I am.
Derek: Good. I need to talk to you.
Kyle: Now?
Derek: Yeah.
Kyle: Can't still sleeping. Zzzzzzz
A separate text from Ariel appeared on his phone.
Ariel: Are you dying?
Derek: No.

Ariel: Do you want to?
Derek: Not really.
Ariel: Then stop texting Kyle in the middle of the night and waking our asses up.
Derek: Sorry, I thought you would sleep through it.
Ariel: Grrr (angry face emoji)

Pulling up Kyle's text chain he continued.
Derek: Fine, sleep, but meet me at the trails at seven.
Kyle: As long as it will shut you up now.

Hours later Derek was leaning against his car watching Kyle pull into the parking lot with an annoyed look on his face driving Ariel's little clown car. Good. He could use a little annoyance in his life now.

Kyle unfolded himself out of the little Karmann Ghia and just barely missed hitting his head on the doorframe.

"What are you doing with Ariel's car?"

Kyle turned back and glared at the little sports car. "Mine wouldn't start. I think I need a new battery. Ariel said she would call Tank's and have them take a look."

"And you're mad at her car?"

"I hate that car. I feel like I'm driving one of those toddler cars when I get in it. Then my back and legs hurt from crunching up while I try to drive it. At least when we have kids, I can convince her that we will need a bigger car for her to drive around all the baby crap."

"You do realize that she will still want to keep that one and just get a separate one for the family car, right?"

"Probably, but at least I can tell her that is her special car for her alone time, and I won't have to go to the chiropractor every time she decides she wants to drive us somewhere."

Kyle nodded to the opening of the trail and asked, "You ready?"

Derek grabbed his water bottle and said, "Yeah, let's go."

They walked for a couple minutes in silence until Kyle finally broke it. "What did you want to talk about so bad that you had to wake my ass up for?"

Without turning back to look at him Derek replied, "I'm taking Mia out on a date tonight."

"Mia, your new waitress?"

"Yes."

"Mia, the girl who was supposed to get married not too long ago?"

"Yes."

"Mia, the girl who lives in your apartment?"

"Jesus, yes."

With a small laugh Kyle said, "I just wanted to make sure I knew all the little ways this could go wrong before we talked about this."

"What makes you think this will go wrong?"

Kyle hesitated. "Well, because it's you. You don't date. The whole damn town knows that you don't date. Hell, you don't even sleep with locals."

"I know, this is why I wanted to talk to you. I don't know what the fuck I'm doing."

Derek heard Kyle's feet stop moving and he turned around to see his friend's face appear dumbstruck. "What?"

Kyle pulled out his phone.

"What are you doing?"

Grinning, Kyle said, "I'm calling Ariel. If the world is going to end, I just want to call and let her know how much I love her."

Derek turned around and kept walking. "Asshole."

He heard Kyle laughing as he started walking again. "I'm sorry. I couldn't help it. You're going on a date with the new girl; that's great. What's the problem?"

"I really like her."

"I don't think that's a problem when dating a girl."

Derek sighed in frustration. "No, asshole. I want to be around her all the damn time. I can't stop thinking about her, and I don't want to fuck it all up. I don't know how to be in a real relationship. I'm in my fucking thirties and I have the mental relationship capacity of a twelve-year-old."

"I blame your dad for that."

"Yeah, me too. So, help me, what do I do?"

"I can't really tell you what to do."

"What? Why not? I let you live after sleeping with my sister."

"Yeah, I'm also marrying her."

"Eh. As her brother I can still legally put you in the grave for touching her."

"Pretty sure that's illegal in all fifty states. Look, being in a relationship is different for everyone. No relationship is the same. I mean you've got the basics. Make her feel wanted. Make her feel loved. Don't be a dick, but you have to customize all that crap for each person. Some girls like flowers, some don't. Some like to go out and party it up, while others would rather stay home and read a book cuddled up on the couch with you."

"Women should come with handbooks."

"Shit. That would be fantastic. Like when they say they're fine, which fine are they talking about? Like, is it really fine, or is it fine, do what you want, but you're gonna pay for it later?"

"How many times have you gotten the fine wrong?"

"Enough to err on the side of caution. How much do you know about Mia?"

"A little. Her parents are the special kind of selfish assholes. They basically dumped her on her grandpa when she was little and only care about money. Her ex is a liar and thief. She doesn't really have many friends. She likes to read and knit these little stuffed animal monsters."

"She's an introvert then."

"How do you figure that?"

"How do you have a female best friend and *not* know that?"

"Do you really think a girl who likes to party it up at bars on her days off is into reading and knitting? This is a girl who will enjoy the quiet nights at home with you. She will probably need reassurance at the beginning because of how people have constantly left her behind and have used her to get what they want. Spend time building trust and show her that you aren't going anywhere. And show her the real you. The guy we all love and not that fake prick who picks up women on the daily."

"Hey. It wasn't on the daily."

"Weekly. Whatever. She's going to hear all the gossip about your sexual history, and it will be best to be upfront about it. Where are you taking her?"

"I was going to cook her dinner."

Kyle let a disbelieving laugh out. "On a first date? How is bringing her to your place to cook a dinner going to show her you're not just trying to get her into bed?"

Derek thought about it for a couple minutes. "Okay. Maybe you're right. Casperelli's then?"

"Good place, but maybe you should avoid the gossip mongers for a little bit."

Derek threw his hands up in the air. "That's why I was going to cook at home."

"Get out of town, dumbass. Hop over to Willow Springs. They have that new farm-to-table place that is really good. I took Ariel with me when I interviewed the owners last month. The food is amazing and the whole layout is great for intimacy. It's perfect for a first date and getting to know someone. They also have a walking garden that leads to the lake after dinner."

"What are the chances that you're not going to run and tell my sister everything?"

Kyle laughed. "Absolutely none."

"Figured."

IT WAS JUST BEFORE seven when Derek stood outside of Mia's door looking down at his makeshift bouquet, wondering if it was too cheesy and if he should toss it in the can before knocking. He shook his head and decided to take the chance that it wouldn't make him look desperate.

Mia opened the door looking amazing in a soft blue and pink dress with a white sweater hugging her shoulders. She smiled first looking at him and then down at six small balls of yarn setting on top of knitting needles make to look like a bouquet of flowers. "Is that for me?" she asked.

"Yeah. I wasn't sure if you liked flowers so I thought I would get you this instead."

With a smile that could light up the world she took the makeshift stems and said, "It's absolutely perfect. I love it." She gently laid it on the couch next to a small pile of yarn and what looked like a partially completed monster.

"Is that my Marvin?"

Mia looked back and her face blushed when she looked at Derek again. "Oh, no. That's for Tiny. I'm making him a monster chef. Marvin is almost done; I just need to do a couple more things to him."

"I can't wait."

"And I can't wait for you to meet him."

"Are you ready for dinner?"

"Yes. I'm starving."

It was a short drive to Manfield's. The large, converted barn was brightly lit in the front and held much of the farm's produce set up on one side like a farmer's market and the other side with several tables and an opening to the backyard where additional outdoor seating was provided with several strands of lights above with vintage Edison light bulbs. Kyle was right. This was the perfect place for their first date.

Derek gave his name to the hostess who immediately sat them outside towards the back next to the lighted waterfall.

Mia looked around taking in all the elegant touches. "This place is perfect. I've heard about these farm-to-table places, but I've never been to one."

"Me either. Kyle suggested it to me."

"That's your sister's fiancé, right?"

"Yeah. He was also my best friend growing up, but the two of them have been into each other since we were kids."

"Oh. They've been together that long?"

"Nah. Kyle didn't make his move until recently. Actually, the whole story is kind of messed up. At first, he didn't want to mess up our friendship, then he wanted to let her have a chance to spread her wings at college, and he also went to college out of state and took a job in Philadelphia for a major paper. Long story short, he pissed off some major gang leader and moved back home. This guy basically threatened that he would kill Ariel if Kyle tried to be happy and get what he wanted out of life... my sister. So, he stayed, took over the paper, and lived his life just staying friends with her. That is until the gang was basically wiped out in a war with an MC."

Mia's mouth was open in shock. "Well, that's more drama than I anticipated."

Derek's mouth quirked up. "Actually, our entire little group has quite the little dramatic backstories. Your photographer almost died twice in car accidents. When she was in high school, she was in a car with her best friend and her best friend's mom when another car hit them. Dixie was the only survivor of the crash and she and her best friend's older brother became very close. It was years later before they got together, and just when they did, another car crashed into a field where she was waiting for a tow truck. Chase asked her to marry him at the hospital. They were only together for about a week. And a couple days after she was released from the hospital they got married."

"What about Zoey? I'm sure her story has to be less traumatic."

"Not really. We went to college together. Her then fiancé died of a brain aneurysm."

"Oh, my God."

"Yeah. I moved back home after graduation, and she stayed in Lexington and eventually ended up with a narcissistic abusive asshole. She left him and moved out here to open the bakery. She met Tyler, who is Kyle's brother, and they almost immediately fell in love. Her ex didn't like that she was moving on with her life and decided to destroy the bakery just before the opening. And when that didn't stop her from being happy, he came back and tried to kill her and Tyler. She jumped in front of a bullet for Tyler and the asshole ended up getting shot and arrested by Chase. This also led to a hospital proposal. But to be fair, Tyler was planning to propose the night all this went down."

"I'm almost afraid to ask about Josie."

"Honestly, she has probably the saddest story out of all of us. Her dad died while serving in the military in the Middle East. Her mom was addicted to drugs and left her with her grandmother. The grandmother died, and she went into foster care. After several abusive homes, her and another girl ran away and were living on the streets until they were kidnapped and held in a psychopath's home with another boy. They were locked up in reinforced dog kennels until they finally were able to escape and were adopted together by the cop who rescued them."

"Wait, I've heard about this on the news. I remember Grandpa saying that they should suffer and be locked in dog kennels as their punishment for the rest of their lives. God, that was so long ago, but a story like that really stands out in your mind."

"Yes, it does. And the other girl and boy that Josie was trapped with fell in love and got married. They had four kids but then died in an accident and Josie got custody of all of them. She went from perfect and organized, to a house of chaos. Grayson lived next door to the new house she got when she took guardianship of the kids. He's the perfect calm to her storm."

"Would I sound like a horrible person if I said that I don't feel so bad about my past now?"

"No. We all have stuff in our past that messes with our head, but thankfully all the people I care about haven't let it define who they are."

"What about you? Do you have a hidden hot-mess past?"

Derek played with his wine glass and shrugged. "Nothing like the others. My dad cheated on my mom. She forgave him once, but he did it again, and when she found out she kicked him out. It kind of soured me to love and relationships for a while."

"What changed your mind?"

Without thinking how it would sound he replied, "Zoey."

Mia shifted her head down and quietly said, "Oh."

Realizing his mistake, he took her hand in his. "No. Not like you think."

"Then how?"

"Zoey's fiancé in college. His name was Trevor. The two of them were completely in love. And I mean the kind of healthy love that you don't see very often. They laughed together. Supported each other and had a trust that I'd never seen before. For a long time, all I saw were my mom's tears and the hurt in her eyes when she would remember how it used to be. Watching Zoey's relationship in college was eye opening, and I became close friends with Trevor. I never really connected with anyone like that, so I didn't see the point in having a relationship with someone if I couldn't have that. And then he died." Derek's voice grew softer.

"His death did to Zoey something I had never seen up close before. It decimated her. I mean, down to bare bones soul ripping despair. In books you hear about someone almost fading away, but let me tell you seeing it happen is something I never wanted to experience. Watching a person fading from existence is the most helpless feeling in the world. All I could think while I was trying to help breathe life back into her was that I never wanted to feel the devastation of loving someone so much that it could shatter you into a million little pieces."

"Has that changed now?"

"Yes. I watched Tyler and Chase as they thought they were going to lose the women they loved, but also all the happiness that they got to have as well. It's hard to be around my friends and not think maybe it is all worth it." After saying those words, he found that he really did believe them. He was tired of the life he had been living and seeing just how happy everyone else was, especially since Ariel moved in with Kyle. When she lived in the apartment above his house, he felt like they were in this together. Now when he went home, it was just too big and quiet.

The waiter brought out their bread and took their order. The friendly teenager was funny and energetic, and he loved the way he made Mia laugh. As he walked away, she smiled. "I bet he gets great tips."

"Yeah, I bet he does. Ariel used to be a waitress at Daisy's diner when we were in high school, and she said she made more money there than she did working at Dad's office as an assistant. She really hammed it up for the customers. The tourists just threw money at her."

"I bet a lot of it had to do with her looks, too."

"Oh, yeah. The men who came into town definitely gave her plenty of attention and tried to overtip to get a date."

"Did that work?"

Derek shrugged. "Sometimes. I mean she was in love with Kyle, but he was away at college, and he never allowed them to be together. I heard whispers about some guys she went out with, but thankfully not too much since I was at college, too."

"I've seen the articles at the bar from your college days. You seemed like a pretty big deal."

Not wanting to seem like he had a big ego Derek underplayed it. "I was alright. Good enough for a scholarship."

Mia rolled her eyes. "To the University of Kentucky. For basketball."

"What?"

"Come on! I don't watch sports much, but even I know playing basketball for UK is a big deal. You were all right."

Derek bit his lip trying not to smile. "All I cared about was a free education. My parents didn't make a lot, but enough to where we couldn't get grants, and I didn't want to drown in student loans. I worked hard, or I guess I should say I played hard. I went to all the basketball camps, read books about playing strategies, stayed late at practice, and sometimes played a little too late in our driveway where Dad put up a hoop on the garage."

"Did your sister play with you?"

Derek scoffed. "No. She has always been the little princess who loved dressing up. She didn't even hang out with me while I played outside until I met Kyle. Then I couldn't get rid of her."

"That's cute."

"It was annoying."

"I used to wish I had a brother or sister. I was so lonely before I started living with my grandpa. Do you have any idea how boring it is to play checkers by yourself? After a while I started playing chance games that didn't take any strategy like Candy Land. It was all luck of the draw. I was a little weird though. Even though I was both players, I always ended up rooting for one over the other."

"Ariel always tried to make me play dress up or barbies with her. One year, Mom gave me some money to get her a birthday present, and I made the mistake of getting her this princess dress-up kit. It had a plastic tiara, this crazy pink dress with lace and flowers, and those ridiculous plastic high heels."

"I remember those. The shoes always broke in a day."

Derek scoffed. "I wish. She wore those damn things for a month. Every day she would run around the house wearing the whole outfit clopping those heels on the floor like her life depended on making as much noise as possible. I remember Dad offered to dog-sit for the neighbors just hoping it would eat her shoes."

The remainder of the dinner continued with stories of their childhoods, and it was remarkable just how different their experiences were. Mia was denied so much love by her parents, but she didn't seem resentful. She loved the life she had with her grandpa and was grateful for the time she had with him. Derek started to feel a little guilty at how much anger he had towards his dad after his parents' divorce. Sure, his mom deserved better, but his dad still tried his best with both him and Ariel. It was only just recently that the two had begun to repair their relationship, and that was still only because Ariel finally put her foot down and forced Derek to deal with their issues.

Once dinner was over Derek extended his hand out to Mia to help her out of the chair. "Do you still want to walk the garden path?"

Beaming, Mia nodded her head. "Yes, please."

The walking path really was magical. The path was paved with old red bricks that according to the dedication sign at the start was reclaimed from the old mill that burned down nearly thirty years ago. At the first bend towards the lake was a series of arches covered in greenery and small white fairy lights. Derek stopped them in the middle and looked around. "Do you think your fairy used to live here before she moved to your apartment?"

She looked around seeming to consider the possibility. "Maybe. I bet she wanted to spread her wings and find out what the world was really like outside of the perfect magical place."

Derek cupped her face and looked into her bright eyes. "I think you're magical."

Before she could say something that would try to refute his statement, he brought his lips to hers and softly kissed her until she relaxed in his arms. He wanted to let his hand journey down to her ass, but he heard soft laughter not far from where they were hidden in the canopy of greenery. He let a soft groan escape as he released her. "I think we are going to get some company."

"Well, I guess we better keep moving then."

They made their way to the back of the path as it opened up to a large moonlit lake. The water had small ripples from a couple of canoes that passed with couples gliding by. He watched her as she watched the couples slowly moving further away from them. "Are we taking one of those?" she asked.

"I didn't know they had this as an option. Do you want me to get one?"

She gave a soft little sigh and finally said, "No. I think this is perfect just how it is."

Derek entwined his fingers with hers. "Me, too."

The drive back home was almost agony. Derek couldn't stop himself from constantly touching her, but the more he grazed his hand up and down her thigh the more he thought about pulling the car over and taking her right there. While that might be incredible, she might not appreciate their first time being contorted in the front seat of his car.

She was looking out the window at the woods as they drove by and said, "I love all the trees. This was one of the reasons why I chose to move out here. Jack had wanted a big city at first. I thought that I had convinced him that small-town life would be better. I guess he knew the whole time that he wasn't really coming, so it didn't really matter to him." She gave a little scoff before continuing. "And here I thought it was my sexy charm that convinced him. I'm so stupid."

Derek frowned. "You're not stupid. Yes, you fell for his act, but he had this all planned out. He took advantage of you when you were most vulnerable. You were losing your grandfather, and he started filling in another piece of your heart. He knew you wanted to grasp onto something that provided you hope, and he used it."

Mia played with the bottom of her dress. "Yeah, I know. It still doesn't make me feel any better about it."

"What if I told you that your sexy charm could convince me to do just about damn near anything, would that help?"

Mia lifted one corner of her mouth. "Yes, it would."

By the time they made it back to Mia's apartment Derek was done taking it slow or holding back. She seemed hell-bent on torturing him though. She swayed her hips and took each step on the staircase with slow precision. Yup, he was done with slow. Derek put his hands on her hips and turned her around. "Derek? What are you... ooomph."

Derek threw her over his shoulder in a fireman's carry and quickly took the stairs to her front door. He stopped only long enough to take her keys. Once they were inside, he nearly sprinted into the bedroom. He stopped dead in his tracks at the sight of her bed. Staring back at him were nearly fifty knitted monsters in every color imaginable.

Still upside down and facing the hallway Mia asked, "Derek? Is something wrong?" Derek gently slid her down his body and watched as she realized what he was looking at. "Oh. We can just toss them on the floor."

Derek swept his gaze from one end of the bed to the other. It would take forever to move them. Too long. "You sure?"

"Yeah, why?"

With childlike enthusiasm he grabbed one side of the comforter and swiftly lifted it from the bed causing all the creatures to fly in the air and scatter across the floor.

Mia laughed. "Well, that's one way to do it."

He looked from the bed over to Mia. "The bed's too empty now." He scooped her up in his arms and tossed her onto the bed. Her face flushed as he prowled over the top of her. "I've been dying to get my hands all over your body all night."

"What are you waiting for?"

"Not a damn thing anymore."

Derek lowered his lips to hers and felt the hunger only grow inside of him to claim her as his. With each stroke of their tongues together Mia's hips began to move up and down. The heat coming off of her body could be felt through his clothes. He wanted that heat on his bare skin. He stopped kissing her only long enough to help her get down to her underwear. It was a sexy white lace matching set.

Derek's hands traced the edge of the lace bra and slowly down her stomach to the top of her underwear. His hand dove under the delicate fabric and found her clit. He gently took two fingers and started a slow circling motion.

Mia's head bowed back as she raised her hips. "Oh, God. Yes."

Slightly moving up, he brought his lips to her ear. "Do you want me as much as I want you?"

She only moaned in response.

Derek stopped the movements on her clit and slid his finger inside of her. "Words, Mia. Do you want me as much as I want you?"

Before she could respond he added his thumb to her clit as his finger grazed that magical spot just enough to keep her on the edge.

Mia growled and replied, "Yes. I want you more than anything."

The words were sweeter to him than the finest wine. He devoured her lips and continued to move his hand in and out. He wanted to feel her grip around his finger in sweet release. He crooked his finger and stroked relentlessly until she screamed out his name with her orgasm.

With her face still a beautiful shade of red he pulled her underwear down her legs and helped her up to have them both on their knees. He cradled her face and kissed her slowly.

With frantic movements and kisses Mia helped Derek shed his clothes. The awe and desire he saw in her eyes would have brought him to his knees if he wasn't already there. His cock was bobbing and nearly reaching out for her. He guided her down underneath him and took her mouth devouring her.

Mia wiggled under him so that his length rubbed up and down her folds. It took all his strength not to plunge right in. "Condom," he groaned.

Mia started to reach for the nightstand, but Derek took over and yanked the drawer open. Thankfully, there was a new box just waiting for him. But that wasn't all. There was also a pink vibrator with a clit stimulator. Mia's head turned and saw what he was looking at. "Oh, God, ignore that."

Derek opened the box and gave his best devilish smile while he protected himself. "Not only am I not ignoring that, but we will also play with that later."

Mia gasped. "I…"

"Later. I promise, you'll love it."

Derek finally settled back over her and gave her a soft kiss while stroking her cheek with his thumb. "Ready?"

Mia could only nod.

Unable to hold back any longer Derek slowly worked his way in. He moved back and forth gaining small ground until he was finally full seated within her. This. This was heaven. Her warmth surrounded him and tugged at his heart.

"Derek, I need you to move," Mia whispered while she tried to force him to give her the friction she desired.

"So eager," he growled as he gave her what she wanted. His mouth covered hers as he continued to rock his hips in and out. Each time his hips met hers in his deepest thrusts she gave out a tiny moan of pleasure. It didn't take long to lose himself in a faster pace and he could feel her walls quivering around him.

Mia called out his name in a strangled voice and that was it. He couldn't hold it any longer. His spine tingled, and he finally let his release go.

Derek returned the soft smile that Mia gave him. That was incredible, and he knew there was no way he would ever let this amazing woman go. "I'll be right back," he said as he gave her another soft kiss.

After retreating from her body, he went to dispose of the condom. He expected to have a small freak out in the bathroom, but it never came. The only thing that occupied his mind was getting back to the soft, intriguing woman waiting for him to return. Once he returned, he joined her in the bed as she lifted the covers in invitation and settled in for a night of a little bit of rest and a whole lot of fun.

Chapter 9

It had been two days since Mia's date with Derek. Today was Derek's day off and he was spending it with Kyle getting ready for the wedding. The boys were doing a tux fitting and helping to make arrangements for a special surprise for Ariel. Mia was grateful for the small bit of alone time. While she loved the things that Derek was doing to her body every waking chance they got, her body was also sore in places she never knew could hurt so much.

This morning, she also felt like she might be fighting off a cold. Her head was a bit woozy, and her appetite was nearly non-existent. At least her shift wasn't for a couple hours. She could get some knitting done and finish the chef's hat for Tiny's monster. The big man had certainly taken up a place in her heart. She knew his past and that he served time for nearly killing the man who had beaten and almost killed his sister. The town mostly overlooked his criminal past especially since many would have done the same or worse if someone did that to their family.

She had just finished when her cell rang. She expected Derek but was surprised to see Compass Securities light up her screen. "Hello?"

"Mia?" the man asked on the other line.

"Yes?"

"This is Ollie, with Compass Securities."

"Oh. Hi, Ollie. How are you?"

"I'm good. Thanks. Look I have good news for you."

"Really? You found Jack?"

"No, but we did find a storage unit that we think he used to take your stuff to."

"Oh, my God. That's great. Can we get into it?"

"That's what I wanted to talk to you about. We have a couple options. We can give the police the information right now, or if you want, we can get you in to see if there is anything you want to rescue before we do."

"Is that legal?"

"Do you want me to answer that?"

Mia sighed. "No. Not really. Where is it?"

"It's in Alexandria."

Mia thought for a few minutes. It would be about a five-hour drive one way. She couldn't exactly go right now. She was scheduled to work the next few days in a row. Sighing she finally replied, "Go ahead and call the police and let them do their thing. Just let me know when I can go if any of my things are there."

"Are you sure? It could be a while before it gets released."

"Yeah. I don't want to risk anything to prevent him from getting what's coming to him."

"Okay. Whatever you want. I'll let Dex know. He is up there now with the storage facility manager."

"Thanks, Ollie. Let me know if you hear anything else."

After getting assurances from Ollie that he would keep her updated, Mia went to the kitchen for some juice. Her hands shook as she poured the contents from the jug. Was she doing the right thing? Should she call Ollie back? The whole thing was making her stomach turn. Deciding that the juice was not a good idea for now, she poured the glass back into the jug and resigned herself to getting ready for work.

Thankfully, McKenna's was busy today with a healthy lunch rush. The dining room was filled with tourists coming in for the next rounds of weddings for the weekend. Originally Mia was going to have Tiny fix her a burger before her shift, but she saw Nicole getting swamped and decided to punch in early to help.

A while later, her stomach and head were still doing a number on her. She was having trouble focusing and a couple times had to lean on the counter in the back to catch her breath.

"You look like shit," she heard Nicole say as she hefted her tray to unload her dirty dishes.

"Thanks."

"Hey, I just call it like I see it. I've seen you look better, and that is even after I saw you on your wedding day."

"Great, thanks. I'll be fine. Just give me a few minutes and it'll be all good."

Nicole shrugged. "I know you are working a double today, but if you need me to cover, I got you. Renna is working today anyway. No biggie."

Mia smiled. "Are we bonding?"

Nicole scoffed. "God, no."

Taking in a deep breath Mia pulled away from the counter and grabbed the tray to take the next order. Nicole may have offered to cover the shift, but if Dexter traveled to Virginia to track down her stuff, she needed to keep working. She knew the investigation bill would only keep growing.

Another hour went by, and Mia thought she had gotten past the worst part of her dizziness, but as she took another order from a friendly middle-aged couple, the room started to blur and suddenly the sounds of the bar muffled, and blackness surrounded and created a small tunnel of light. She heard someone say, "Shit, she's going down." And then there was nothing.

The next thing she knew, she was lying down with someone cradling her head. She raised her hands to her pounding head. "What..."

"Shhh... take it easy."

Mia looked over to where the voice was coming from. "Tiny?"

"Yeah, sweetie. You gave us a scare."

Us. He said us. Oh, no. Where was she? She looked around and sure enough she was in the middle of the dining room with a lot of onlookers. Just great. She started to get up, but Tiny's hands prevented her from moving. "Tiny. Let me up."

"No can do little girl. We've got the paramedics coming to check you out. You fainted and hit your head on the table before that guy over there could catch ya."

Mia looked over and found the man whose order she was taking before she passed out. He gave a small wave. "Sorry. I tried to catch you, but the table got you first. I was able to stop you from hitting the floor though."

That would explain the headache. Mortified at the scene, she just wanted to get up and go home. "Tiny, I can..."

"Uh-uh."

Nicole's face peered over her. "Stay the fuck down. Thanks to you I get to see my wife. Give me something to brighten my day."

Mia narrowed her eyes at Nicole. "You're so weird."

Nicole shrugged. "You're just now figuring that out?"

Mia heard someone say that they needed a beer. She watched as Nicole straightened and bellowed back, "Hold your damn horses, can't you see we're dealing with an emergency over here?"

Mia mouthed the words, *Hold your damn horses*. Nicole must have seen her because she said, "I blame my mom for that one. She says it all the time to Dad." She looked over at Mia again and shook her head. "You seem like you're gonna live. I'm gonna go deal with the gawkers."

It was only a couple minutes later when she heard the doors loudly open and the distinct sound of a wheeling gurney come in. Before she knew it, Renna was placing a neck brace on her while her partner was taking vitals and asking questions. This all seemed a bit like overkill. Really, she just fainted. Okay, fainted and hit her head but this was excessive.

Renna shook her head. "I know you want to argue with us, but save your breath. We're going to take a little trip down to the hospital and let them check you over. No way I am letting Derek give my woman a hard time for not making us take proper care of you."

She didn't want Nicole mad at her. They seemed to almost be friends and Renna was right. Derek seemed to have a bit of an overprotective streak for the people he cared about. "Fine, but really it isn't nece—" Before she could finish that sentence Mia's head throbbed and she felt the world spin.

Renna gave her a small smile and said, "Let's get going." Less than a couple minutes later Mia was loaded up into the back of the ambulance and headed out to the hospital.

Nearly an hour later, Mia sat with her hands folded in her lap. At least they had released her from that awful neck brace, but this waiting around was getting out of hand. She had been hooked up to an IV and had a couple vials of blood drawn after chatting to the doctor for a few minutes. He didn't think there was anything to get worried about from the fall, but he wanted to run a couple other tests before releasing her.

"Mia?"

She jerked her head up to see Derek's worried face in the door.

"Hi," she meekly replied. "Sorry."

He shook his head as he walked to her and pulled up the chair beside her. He took her palm and kissed it. "You don't have anything to be sorry about."

"I should have called in. I wasn't feeling good, but I needed the money and..."

"Hey, it's okay. I am just glad to see you're okay. When Tiny called I kind of panicked. I may have broken a lot of laws getting back here to you."

"You did?"

Derek laughed. "Oh, yeah. Kyle almost threw up in the car."

Finally feeling a little more relaxed Mia sighed and smiled. "Well, thanks for coming. You saved me a long walk back home. I mean I could have pulled out some cleavage and possibly found a ride."

"Oh, she has jokes now."

"A few."

"What did the doctor say?"

"Not much. They are running some tests before setting me free."

A knock came from the door and the doctor walked in carrying a tablet. She was very pretty with chestnut hair pulled back in a ponytail and an air of confidence that Mia could only dream of. "Hi, Mia. I was able to look at some of the results and wanted to go over them with you." She turned to Derek and gave a small smile. "Derek, can I have a few minutes with Mia?"

Derek started to nod and stand but Mia tightened her grip on his hand to hold him in place. "He can stay. He's my... my, uh."

"Boyfriend," he interjected.

The doctor looked a little confused but quickly recovered and smiled. "Okay. Everything came back with your blood work, and I don't have any major concerns outside of the pregnancy."

Mia's mouth fell open, and she squeaked, "Pregnancy?"

The doctor looked at Mia and then Derek. "I'm sorry. You didn't know?"

"Pregnant?" Mia looked at Derek and back to the doctor. "Pregnant?"

Derek tightened his hand into Mia's. She assumed he was doing it to stop her freak out. "As you can see, we did not know about this."

The doctor looked back down at her tablet and said, "Your last cycle was eight weeks ago, correct?"

Mia felt her face flush. Oh, my God, how could she be so stupid? Apparently stupid and pregnant. "Yes." Feeling ashamed she felt her tears begin to fall.

"Okay. Let's get an ultrasound done and make sure everything is okay and get you started with some prenatal vitamins and next steps."

The doctor left the room just as quickly as she came in leaving Mia alone with Derek. Derek who was her boyfriend. Derek who was *not* the father. Derek, the nicest man she had ever met who would certainly dump her now that she was pregnant with her ex's baby. She couldn't stop the tears from coming. They were falling fast, and she was starting to gasp for air. Breathing was becoming a challenge. She felt the bed dip as Derek sat and pulled her on his lap. Saying goodbye to him was going to kill her. She was a horrible person. Pregnant with one man's kid and sleeping with a new man. "I'm a slut," she cried in between sobs.

"You're not a slut," Derek said soothingly while he kissed the top of her head.

"Yes, I am. I'm having sex with you while I'm pregnant with Jack's baby."

"Yeah, but you're only a slut if you were still with Jack while pregnant and sleeping with me."

Mia pulled away from his chest and wiped her tears. "Don't you try to be all rational with me right now. I am allowed to have this. I deserve to have this breakdown."

"Okay, but only for like ten minutes."

"Ten minutes?"

"Yeah. I figure that's about how long we have before that machine comes in here to show us the baby. Do you want your memory to be of you freaking out or being calm and hearing the heartbeat of the miniature bean?"

How could he be so calm right now? Why wasn't he storming out in anger, or yelling at her? He was just accepting it like they told him we were having spaghetti for dinner. She needed to think for a few minutes. Time to get her thoughts together. "Can you do something for me?"

"Of course. Anything."

"Can you get me a drink and some candy?"

"Sure. Anything special?"

"No. Just chocolate something."

"Okay." Derek stood up and gave her a light kiss. "Don't think I can't see through this as you getting rid of me for a few minutes."

Mia widened her eyes. "No, I—"

Derek smiled. "It's okay. Take a few minutes and I will come back with goodies."

ONCE DEREK GOT OUT of the room, he bent over, put his hands on his knees and took out a long breath. Holy shit. She's pregnant. With Jack's baby. For a brief second, he thought the baby was his. Yeah, he knew it would have been way too soon for that, but his heart leapt at the idea of him and Mia having their own child. It was completely irrational, but for that split second, he wanted it.

He stood back up and ran his hands through his hair hoping it would clear his head. Just as he turned the corner, he saw Kyle sipping out of a cheap hospital coffee cup and handed another one to Derek. "Thought you could use this."

He needed something a bit stronger than this, but beggars couldn't be choosy. Derek took his first sip and winced. "God, that's terrible."

"They do that on purpose, I think. You okay?"

"Yeah. I mean..." Derek started to say Mia was pregnant but stopped himself.

Kyle sighed. "I have a confession."

"Not now. If you tell me something about my sister and your sex life, I may have to kill you."

"Ha. No. I heard that Mia's pregnant."

Derek hung his head. "Shit, you heard that?"

"At least this side of the floor did. She was a bit loud repeating that she was pregnant a few times."

"Fuck. Yeah, she had no idea."

"That was obvious too. I assume not yours."

"Nope." Derek let that settle in the air for a minute before he continued. "But you know what? I wanted it to be. Is that fucking crazy?"

"Nah, man... well, maybe a little. But when you know you know. What are you going to do?"

"Whatever she wants. It's her decision, but I will fight to stay in her life if she tries to push me away."

"And you are good with being a father to another man's child?"

"Would I have preferred for us to have one? Yes, but I can love this one too. It's a part of her, and I love her."

Kyle placed his hand on Derek's shoulder. "Alright. Good enough. She ready to get sprung yet?"

"She needs an ultrasound, and after that we should be able to go."

"Do you want me to find a ride home or are you good with me as the awkward third wheel?"

"I have been the third wheel for you and Ariel several times. Your turn."

IT HAD BEEN SEVERAL minutes since Derek left and Mia had calmed down to only a small panic. She was going to be a mom. For a brief minute she considered adoption, but the thought quickly faded as she absently rubbed her belly. There was going to be a small person that was all hers. Jack certainly wasn't going to just show back up and demand visitation. Of course, she wouldn't get child support either, but that was okay. She could figure it all out. After all, her rent was paid for a while, and she ate for free a lot at the bar. She was going to need to take it easy on the fried foods though.

"I have tons of chocolatey goodness," Derek said as he came back with a plastic tub of candy.

"How many did you buy?"

"I dunno. I just kept hitting buttons. Did you know that vending machines have credit card readers now?"

Mia laughed. "Yes. Where have you been?"

Derek shrugged. "Blossom Hills. Where they only upgrade when needed. The vending machine at the senior center still works on the pull knob things. Mom makes Tiny fix them every now and then when they get stuck."

"They're friends?"

"Yeah. Tiny recently bought the house next to Mom's. She helped him with the landscaping in exchange for him cooking for her."

"That man needs to get out of the kitchen sometimes."

"He says it is his happy place. You going to argue with him?"

"Nope," she replied with a giggle. Mia grabbed the Milky Way bar and took her first bite. "Mmmm... that is so good."

Derek groaned. "Do you have to make little sex noises right now?"

"Sorry."

"No you're not."

Mia grinned. "Nope. Not even a little bit."

They both looked over as they heard the cart being wheeled into the room. The tech smiled at them both. "Hello, Mia. You ready to see the baby?'

"Yes, please."

Within minutes they were both looking at the screen and listening to the steady thump of the heartbeat. Mia gasped. "Look. There're her little legs."

"Hers?" Derek asked.

Mia nodded. "Yeah. Hers."

Derek looked over at the tech. "Can you tell that now?"

She shook her head. "No. It's too early, but I can't tell you how many times I have seen the mommas be right. Their intuition is crazy sometimes."

The tech continued to take measurements while Mia looked on in wonder. That was her baby. A little life inside her. Derek stayed close to her stroking the top of her hand with his thumb. They both seemed to be enjoying the constant sound of the heartbeat and were completely mesmerized.

All too soon the tech pulled the probe away from her stomach and began clearing the gel off of her. She left and advised that the doctor would be back soon.

Mia bit her lip and turned to Derek. "I'm keeping her."

Derek nodded. "Of course you are."

"I'm keeping her, and if that is too much I understand. I mean we just started dating and I can't expect you to—"

"Mia," Derek groaned.

Mia put her finger over Derek's mouth. "Let me say this then you can talk. Understand?"

Derek smiled behind her finger and nodded.

"This is Jack's baby biologically, but he won't be around. It is going to be just me and the little bean. You didn't sign up for this. I mean, you met this weird girl who lives in your building and felt sorry for her. I don't want you to stay out of some weird sense of duty or obligation and then regret it. Regret us. So, if you need to cut and run now, I get it. I'll hate it, but I get it."

Derek didn't respond at first, and Mia looked down. Quickly Derek had his fingers lifting her face to his. "Are you done?"

"Yes."

"Great. My turn. Is this a surprise? Not gonna lie. I nearly fell over when the doctor told us, but you being pregnant doesn't magically change how I feel about you. Life throws curveballs at us all the time. You were a curveball I wasn't expecting, but you are the best curveball. I believe that little bean was part of the plan for us. You're going to be an amazing mom, and I hope that you will let me be by your side with this next best curveball. I know this is going to be a challenge and I am almost certain there will be days I drive you crazy and you'll want to kick me out, but like today I will just keep coming back for more. You can't get rid of me that easy."

Mia looked into Derek's eyes, searching for some untruth, some kind of deception, but it wasn't there. "It's gonna be a lot."

"That's okay. I'm kind of a lot."

"People are going to talk."

Derek shrugged. "They'll get over it. Someone else will have a crisis drama and the focus will move over to them."

Mia wanted to talk about it some more, but they heard a knock on the doorframe again. It was the doctor. She looked down at her tablet and gave a big smile. "Everything looks good, Mia. You were a little dehydrated, so make sure you are drinking plenty of water. Do you have an OBGYN here?"

Mia shook her head.

"Okay. I will have the nurse give you some names of good doctors. I'm afraid locally it isn't a big list, but I can personally vouch for each one. I will get you set up with some prenatal vitamins and just ask that you monitor for any increase in symptoms from your fall. There will be more information in your discharge papers. Do you have any questions?"

"No. Thank you."

Within a few minutes Mia found herself in the car with Derek and Kyle on the way back to town. Kyle insisted on driving and Mia was leaning her head on Derek's shoulder in the back seat.

Kyle was nervously tapping on the steering wheel when he finally said, "I hate to break the peace, but I have something to tell you guys."

Mia felt Derek's chest tighten. "What?"

"News about the pregnancy has already broke out."

Mia sat up quickly and winced in pain when her head reminded her it was still injured. "What?!"

She saw Derek narrow his eyes. "Are you fucking kidding me, Kyle? Seriously, you published that?"

Kyle's eyes widened. "What?! No, not me. It's on Penny's Facebook page. Between the ambulance being called at the bar and what I can assume was Mia's loud voice repeating she was pregnant in the room, one of Penny's spies already leaked it out."

"I want to see it," Mia said.

"You don't need to read that shit," Derek said calmly.

"Yes, I do. I want to know what everyone already knows or what they think they already know."

Sighing Derek took out his phone and pulled up Penny's Page.

Things got rather exciting today at McKenna's bar. The beautiful, jilted bride, and our new favorite bar server had quite a nasty spill while working today. Patrons said she didn't look like she was feeling well since the start of her shift and while she was taking an order, she swayed a bit and fainted. Not only did she faint, but she also hit her head on the table as she went down. Blossom Hills finest responded to the scene where she had regained consciousness but was taken out by the ambulance to the hospital. While she was there, she also found out that the reason she fainted may have been due to her pregnancy. As we all know she has captured the heart of our very own Derek McKenna, but this reporter knows that it is very unlikely to be his child. It seems like an empty bank account and a broken heart was not all her ex-fiancé left her with. Will our commitment-phobe favorite son run for the hills? Will he stand by his new girl? Or will he be the second man to break her heart?

Derek locked his phone screen and growled. "I'm going to kill that old bat."

"You can't kill her," Kyle replied dryly.

"Why not?"

"You have a kid to raise now. It would set a bad example."

Mia smiled. "He's got a point."

Derek exhaled and squeezed Mia's hand. "I'm just pissed."

Kyle shook his head. "You're pissed? She called herself a reporter. I'm offended."

Chapter 10

It was the next day, and Derek was working in the bar while Mia rested in the apartment upstairs. He went up several times to check on her, but he thought it was starting to get on her nerves. At least the text messages were dying down. His friends and family were blowing up his phone asking if Penny's post was true and what he was going to do about it. He did verify that it was true but continually asked for some time before having to talk about it to all of them. Some eased off quicker than others, but he was grateful for the silent phone today.

There were some people who stopped by the bar hoping to catch a bit of gossip and give long stares at him, but he just ignored them. Taking a small break, he went into the back kitchen to find Tiny talking to his mom. "Mom, what are you doing here?"

"I came to give you back the cornhole set."

Derek rolled his eyes. "Right. And it had nothing to do with what you read on Penny's page?"

His mom gave an over-exaggerated gasp. "No. Penny's page? I haven't heard anything about what she wrote this time."

"Uh-huh. Come on. Let's go into my office and talk."

"We need to talk about something?" she asked too sweetly.

Derek heard Tiny snort trying to hold in his laughter. Derek pointed back at him. "It's not funny."

Tiny didn't even try to hold it in this time. "It's fucking hilarious."

They made it into his office where he offered his mom the chair while he leaned on the desk. "God is going to strike you down for lying."

"Please. If he didn't strike you down when you used to lie to me about sneaking out and hooking up with some girl in high school, I think he'll spare me."

"You knew?"

"Of course, I knew. I'm your mom."

"But you didn't stop me."

"You knew what a condom was, and I knew your secret spot. If I needed you, I knew where to find you."

"Wow, you just let me run amuck all around town."

"No laws were being broken, you weren't doing drugs, you weren't sneaking out to get drunk. I was choosing my battles."

"How did you not freak out with worry all the time?"

Amanda laughed. "Oh, I was a mess when you guys were little. Every fever, your wobbly steps, seeing hazards in every little thing around the house. It got easier though." She paused and he could tell she was trying to read his face. "Are you asking for a particular reason?"

"You know Mia's pregnant." It wasn't really a question, but she nodded her confirmation anyway. "It's not mine."

"I figured that out, too."

"Yeah, but I want it to be mine. God, I wish it was mine."

"It doesn't take blood to be your child. If you and Mia decide to stay together and get married," she said the married part with a bit of hesitation and hope, "that child will be yours in every way that matters."

"I'm worried though. What if he comes back and tries to take her?"

Amanda grinned. "Her? It's a girl?"

"We don't know for sure. Mia seems positive it's a girl, though."

"Well, then. A girl it is until we find out otherwise. Now when can I meet her?"

"Mom, you've already met her."

"Me showing her the apartment and having her sign the lease does not count, and you very well know that, Derek McKenna."

Crap. She used his full name. At least it didn't include his middle name. "Okay. How about dinner next week? You can come to the house, and I will make dinner?"

Amanda stood up and patted his cheek. "Absolutely not. My house and I will cook."

"Mom. You are not showing her my naked baby pictures."

"I have very few things in life that give me joy, and embarrassing the hell out of my children is one of them. And since I squeezed your giant head out of my body, it is my God-given right to do whatever I want."

"Ugh. Too much, Mom."

Amanda gave him a kiss on his cheek. "Never too much, sweetie. Let me know what day is good for you and what she likes to eat, or at least what doesn't make her queasy."

MIA HAD A SURPRISE visitor. Derek's sister stood before her with a bright smile and a pink bakery box. "Hi! I heard you might be able to use some baked goodies."

Mia was a little nervous. Was Ariel really bringing her something to be kind, nosy, or a bit of both? Thinking it was a bit of both she tried her best to give a welcoming smile and opened the door to allow her in. "Yes, that's very sweet of you. Come on in."

"Thanks," she replied as she went straight for the kitchen. She must have been here before because she had no issues finding the plates and forks. "I brought the chocolate swirl cheesecake from Zoey's shop."

That sounded like heaven. Everything she had tried from Zoey had been amazing and she was feeling like having a treat. That grilled cheese and soup she had for lunch was hours ago and her stomach was now celebrating with a rumble for the new treat.

"Should I be expecting a visit from Zoey, too?"

Ariel's face fell a bit as she plated the first slice. "No."

Mia suddenly felt her stomach drop. Did Zoey not like her and Ariel was trying to find a kind way to tell her? What chance would they have if Derek's best friend hated her? "Oh. Okay."

Ariel plated the second piece and sat on the other counter stool next to Mia. "It may take a couple days."

"Oh, I understand that. She must be busy with the shop all the time."

Ariel played with her slice for a second before she set her fork down. "I'm going to be honest. She is going to need just a couple days to adjust."

"Adjust?" Was she in love with Derek too? Mia thought Zoey was happy with her husband.

"I feel kind of bad telling you about all this, but it is out there on Penny's page and the whole town knows anyway. Zoey and Tyler have been trying to have a baby. She has been taking fertility treatments, and it hasn't worked yet. I don't know the details of your plan with Derek and the baby, but I know he told me that he still wants to be with you and be a part of both your lives. You make him happy and that makes me happy. That makes Zoey happy too, but hearing about him raising a baby with you just hit... differently than she expected."

"Oh." Mia didn't know what to say. She couldn't do anything to change the situation and honestly there wasn't anything she wanted to do to change it either.

Ariel reached her hand out to Mia. "Please don't feel bad. She would never want you to feel awkward or that you can't be happy around her. When Dixie found out she was pregnant Zoey handled it great, but by the time the baby shower happened she was knee deep in hormone injections and it was rough on her. There is a lot more that I probably don't know, but she never wants people to feel like they can't share their happiness around her either. It was her concern for you that brought this amazing cheesecake to you. She was going to bring it with me, but at the last minute she asked me to take it alone."

"Is there anything I can do?"

Ariel shook her head. "No. Just understand if she gets lost in thought sometimes it isn't about you. At least not in the jealous 'you're taking away my best friend' way."

"Thanks. That's actually helpful."

"Enough about that. How are things going with my big dumb brother?"

Mia felt the room lighten and was grateful for the topic change. "He's amazing. A bit on the overprotective side, but good."

"Overprotective?"

"God, yes. He has been up here several times today to check on me. He keeps asking me about my head and has been falling down the rabbit hole of online pregnancy articles."

"Oh, no."

"Oh, yes. Want an example?"

Ariel bounced in her seat. "More than anything."

Mia pulled out her phone and read off a text from earlier that morning. "You are not allowed to slice the lemons at work anymore. Pregnancy increased your blood volume by up to fifty percent. If you slice your finger at work, we could end up with a fountain of blood like old faithful. No more knives."

Ariel gasped. "No, he did not!"

Mia nodded. "But wait, there's more." She scrolled down and read another. "You can crave nonfood items. If your yarn starts looking like a tasty treat, we need to take you to the doctor, because you are not getting enough nutrients."

"I have no words. I swear he was a normal kid."

"It's kind of sweet, but if he is like this the whole time I may have to kill him."

"Damn. I'm going to miss having a brother. I guess Tyler will have to step up his game."

"Tyler?"

"My fiancé's brother, and Zoey's husband."

"Oh, that's right. Sorry, you guys are all interconnected around here."

"Small-town life. Kind of hard not to be. Everyone knows everyone."

"Yeah. Even the doctor at the ER already knew who Derek was."

"Which one? Old man, the young hot guy, or the pretty woman?"

Mia blinked. They only had three? Really? "The pretty woman."

Ariel nodded. "She was the one who took care of Zoey when she was shot, and she was around when Dixie got hit by that car."

"What?" Mia was confused for a moment but remembered what Derek told her on their date. God, she had completely forgotten about all that.

"Yeah. We had kind of a rough patch for a while where we were all in danger or getting hurt. Things have been pretty calm for a while though."

"That's not very reassuring."

A couple hours passed while the girls talked. Mia really liked Ariel. She was very sweet and also enthusiastic. She seemed to have an endless supply of energy. Mia could feel her social battery draining while it seemed like Ariel could talk for hours more.

Ariel started to fill her in on some of Derek's past antics until the man himself came in with two takeout containers. He looked at his sister and said, "Hey. Wasn't expecting to see you here."

"Just getting to know Mia better and I brought her cheesecake from Zoey."

Derek looked over to the pink box and smiled. "That was nice of her. Was she here too?"

Ariel shook her head slowly. "No. Maybe next time."

Derek's face dropped only slightly before he stopped it and smiled. "I'll go visit her later. Maybe pick up some muffins for breakfast," he said with a questioning look to Mia.

"Yes, please!"

Within a few minutes Ariel left them alone to enjoy dinner and Mia found herself devouring the burger and fries that she knew had to come courtesy of Tiny.

"Good to see your appetite is back."

Mia looked down at her plate and then back to his still half full one. "Yeah, and it shouldn't be. I ate two pieces of that cheesecake."

"Soooo.... Mom invited us to dinner."

"Oh?"

Derek rubbed the back of his neck showing a bit of nervousness. "Well, invited might not be the right word. She is insisting that we come for dinner."

Mia's mind raced. Was she going to be upset that she was pregnant with another man's child? She probably didn't want her son with a knocked-up woman who can't get her life together. She seemed nice when she'd met her before though. Her stomach churned as her doomsday scenarios were kicking in. Maybe his mom would ask her to leave Derek or even leave town. Just as she headed down a secondary path of outcomes, Derek placed his fingers under her chin and made her look at him.

"Hey. Breathe, Mia."

She gave a slow blink and then took in a deep breath.

"That's better. Now, whatever horrible idea you were creating in that mind of yours, get it out of that pretty head. Mom loved you before and that isn't going to change now. She already knows about the baby and is excited about it. Honestly, I think you could show up without me and she would be perfectly happy."

Mia shook her head. "No, she wouldn't."

"Sure, she would. I was a bit of a challenge sometimes and the idea of having another girl to give attention and love to has put her in her happy place. Besides, if you don't go, I will get in trouble and you don't want me to get in trouble, do you?"

How could she resist the puppy eyes she was getting? "Okay, when?"

With a brightened face Derek said, "Whenever you want. Mom doesn't have anything going on."

Mia frowned. "That is awfully presumptuous of you. Maybe she has a date." Derek's mom was beautiful, and she wouldn't have any trouble finding a man to go out with.

Derek's eyebrows drew down. "Trust me, Mom doesn't date. She'll be free whenever we can come."

Oh, that man was going to be in for a rude awakening one day. She couldn't wait for the day that Derek just invited himself over and would get more than he expected.

Chapter 11

After a couple reschedules, it was almost a week and a half before Derek and Mia were able to have that dinner with Amanda. Mia took Derek's hand as he helped her out of the car. The house was amazing, not in the grandiose manner she saw back home, but instead it overflowed with charm and coziness. The house was a soft blue with white trim and was adorned with a beautiful landscape that was well taken care of.

When they reached the top step, the front door opened wide to show Amanda at the door. She was dressed in jeans with a brown V-neck sweater and looked stunning. Mia nervously tugged at the side of her floral dress and tried to give a confident smile in return. Amanda opened the door wider to allow them in. "It's so good to see the two of you." She gave Derek a brief hug and then tightly wrapped her arms around Mia. It was so warm and comforting she found herself longing for her grandparents.

She soon discovered that she was embracing Amanda just as much in return. "Thank you." She wanted to say more, but she was at a loss for words.

Derek cleared his throat. "Geez, Mom. You didn't greet me like that."

Amanda released Mia and smacked Derek's arm. "Hush, you. Lord knows you are not suffering for affection."

"I am. I'm totally neglected. I need therapy and everything."

Amanda ignored her son. "Come on into the kitchen. Dinner is ready."

As they entered, Mia marveled at how Derek jumped right in and pulled out the items needed to set the table. He didn't hesitate or ask what he should do. He looked around and took the initiative to take care of what was needed. But isn't that what he always did? He just knew how to take care of everyone.

"What can I do?" Mia asked.

Derek passed her by with glasses in his hands and kissed her on the head. "Nothing, babe. Just sit your cute ass down."

"Derek," his mom warned.

He rolled his eyes. "Your cute butt. Better?"

Amanda sighed. "Not perfect, but yes better."

They made it through the first bites before Amanda brought up the topic Mia was desperately trying to avoid. "How are you feeling? Is the pregnancy going okay?"

"It's not too bad yet. I get a little sick in the morning, but it's not as bad as it could be."

Derek shoveled some food in and mumbled, "Yeah, I only had to hold her hair twice this morning."

Amanda smiled. "Your dad was a sympathetic vomiter. I was sick all the time with Ariel. Every time he got too close to me while I was getting sick, he had to run to the other bathroom. I remember one night all three of us were sick all day. We ended up on the couch eating crackers and watching movies. By the end of my pregnancy, I was so swollen from all the salt I ate from those crackers, my ankles looked like they had tennis balls on the side."

Mia gave a small laugh. "I have been pretty lucky so far. I swear once someone told me I was pregnant it was like giving a hall pass to my stomach to get a little puffy. I am going to need to buy some maternity clothes soon."

Derek swung his head. "I'll take you shopping tomorrow."

"You don't need to do that. Josie already offered to take me this weekend."

"Take my credit card. You'll need it with her."

Mia shook her head. She was not going to take advantage of Derek. No way. She would pay for her own clothes. "Nope. I've got this."

"Mia."

"No. I have been taking extra shifts and if you remember correctly, I paid my landlord up front for a nice discount, so I don't have many bills right now."

"I want to do this."

"Derek, let me have this. If you want to buy a couple things for the baby, then fine, you can do that. But if it is something for me, like my clothes, I've got this."

Derek tilted his head. "So, I can buy for the baby, but not for you?"

Mia, happy with her victory, replied, "Yes."

Derek's mouth tilted up at the corner. "Okay. Then maybe I will get something for little bean this weekend too."

Just before Amanda took a sip of her wine Mia heard her whisper, "Oh, boy."

After dinner a small knock sounded from the front door. Derek answered it to a tall boy who looked to be about twelve years old. "Hey, Derek. Saw your car. Do you have some time to shoot?"

Derek looked at the basketball tucked under the kids arm and then back to Mia. "Go, have some fun. I can talk to your mom for a bit."

"Are you sure?"

Amanda walked over and started pushing Derek out the door. "Get out. Girl time."

Almost immediately they could hear the bouncing of the ball and the young boy's laughter.

Amanda glanced out the window before saying, "That's Sean. He's an only child living with his mom and stepdad. They both work a lot of hours, and that poor kid gets lonely. Derek has always made time for him over the years. I let Sean use our hoop that I never had the heart to take down after Derek moved out. If Derek sees him playing on his way home, he will usually stop and try to teach him some things."

"Wow. That's awesome. Most people wouldn't bother."

"Derek has always wanted to make a difference. I sometimes worry that he will try to do too much and wear himself out, but he still seems to have boundless energy."

Mia started to fidget with her hands. Was she just a charity case to him? Another person he was trying to make a difference with? She didn't want him to be with her out of pity. First, she was stood up at the altar, then she was penniless, and now a soon to be single mom.

Amanda must have immediately noticed because she sat down with a concerned look. "Did I say something wrong?"

Shaking her head Mia replied, "No. I just..."

"You just?"

Taking in a deep breath she blurted, "Maybe he just feels sorry for me."

Amanda blinked and finally gave a small laugh. "Oh, no, sweetie. He truly cares for you. I have watched my son his whole life and how he interacts with others. If he felt sorry for you, there would be a distant concern. He would try to help but still keep a solid wall between you. I've seen how he looks at you and how he tries to predict your needs. He has never looked at his other, uh... women, like he looks at you."

"I don't want him to feel trapped with me and the baby. I mean he started dating me and then, bam! There's a baby."

"I hate to tell you this, but you are not the one doing the trapping. Derek is quite known for his scheming to trap people into doing his bidding."

"Really?"

"Ask him one day how his best friend from college moved here."

"I thought she moved here to start over after her bad ex and start a bakery."

"Oh, she did. But Derek may have overly helped the stars to align to get her here. He missed his friend and thought starting over here would be what was best for her."

"What did he do?"

"You will have to ask him to tell you that story one day. We only have a few minutes before Sean will go home and I have years' worth of embarrassing stories to tell."

DEREK SPRINTED UP THE stairs of the porch only to hear the laughter of his mom and his girl. He had a smile as he opened the door, but it quickly fell as he saw the two laughing over a picture album. "Ah, shit. Mom."

"Derek. Language."

"Sorry. But seriously?"

Mia pointed her finger at a picture and looked up at him. "This... is amazing."

Sighing he walked over to the couch to see which horribly mortifying picture they were looking at.

"You look so pissed off."

Derek rolled his eyes. "Of course, I was. I was a stupid freaking white rabbit."

"You guys were so cute, though. Ariel's Alice dress is adorable. And you were the good big brother to dress up with her."

Amanda nodded. "I always dressed them up to match since they were little."

"I still say Ariel cheated."

"Cheated?" Mia asked.

"Cheated. She was a cheaty McCheaterson."

Between her laughs Amanda said, "She did not cheat. It was Candy Land. Not poker. She got the better cards. Get over it."

"What would you have gotten if you won?" Mia asked.

"Choice of costume. I wanted to be a cop, and she could have been my criminal. I was going to have Dad build a prison cell out of the wagon. It was going to be awesome."

Amanda shook her head. "Oh, yeah. Locking your sister up all night."

"Hey, I was going to pull her around all night. It would have been quicker, we would have gotten more candy, but nooooo. She cried because a criminal wasn't pretty. Then Mom over here had the bright idea to let the Candy Land winner take all for the costume idea."

"He did get to pick the next year at least."

"Yeah, but it was still lame. I dressed up as the scarecrow from the *Wizard of Oz*, because this girl I had a crush on was going to go with us as Dorothy. I made Ariel be Toto, because she screamed bloody murder when I suggested being the wicked witch. She really doesn't do ugly well. Anyway, on Halloween we got stood up."

"We?"

"Yes, WE. Stay focused. WE got stood up. We had no Dorothy, because at the last minute she got invited to a high school party and ditched us. So here we were just the scarecrow and the dog. All night people kept asking where Dorothy was, and Ariel had no problem telling everyone she dumped me. So much for man's best friend."

"Oh, you poor thing."

Derek tilted his head on Mia's shoulder. "Yes, and I'm still broken-hearted about it all. Will you take me home and make me feel better?"

"I'm still here," Amanda said in a dry tone.

Derek popped his head back up. "Sorry." Then he looked at Mia who had the most amazing soft look in her eyes. "Well, not really."

Once they finally made it to Mia's place, Derek began slowly kissing her neck.

Mia giggled and breathily said, "You know, Halloween is coming up soon. You will definitely have to dress up with me."

Standing behind her Derek slid his hand down past the scoop neck and under her bra. "Oh, yeah? Maybe I can be a pirate. You can be my wench, and I can plunder your body."

Mia gasped as she leaned back into his chest seeming to love when he pinched her nipple. "Maybe I could be fat Thor, and you could be Captain America."

Derek continued to pinch and caress her breast as he replied, "I do have a great ass."

His lips trailed kisses up to her ears where he gave a playful bite. Mia gave a small squeak. "America's ass."

Releasing her breast Derek lifted the bottom of her dress and dove his hand under her white lace panties. He groaned as he found her already wet and waiting for him. "It's such a turn on when you quote Marvel to me."

His fingers glided up and down driving him nearly as crazy as it was driving her. He could tell she wanted more. He wanted to tease her. Let her go a little wild. She was moving her hips trying to maneuver his fingers inside of her. It wouldn't take much. "God, you're so ready for me."

"That's my secret, Cap; I'm always ready around you."

Fuck that was hot. Derek turned her around and backed her up against the wall. "I need you now."

"Oh, thank God, cause I'm dying over here."

Derek pulled his shirt over his head with that one arm behind his back way and he heard Mia take in a sharp breath. "God, that is so sexy."

He smiled as he unbuttoned his jeans. "Oh, yeah, better than this?" he asked as his pants fell to the floor and his cock sprung free pointing straight towards his target.

Mia started to reach out and then pulled her hand back. "Almost."

"Mia, I need your hands on me. Now."

She didn't waste any time. She wrapped her hand around his cock and gave a slow stroke from his base to the tip. He crashed his lips onto hers and quickly found the zipper on the back of her dress. Before she could stroke him a third time, the dress was sliding off of her body.

Captivated by her curves he watched as she let go and allowed the garment to fall to the ground. He gazed appreciatively and demanded, "Panties."

Without looking away she pulled them down and kicked them next to her dress. He decided that he wanted to be the one to free her perfect breasts and quickly unclasped her bra. They were slightly fuller now. The pregnancy was giving him just a little more than a handful. They were perfect, and he couldn't resist latching his lips onto her tightening nipple. Just as her moaning grew louder, he released and lifted her so she could wrap those long legs around him.

They kissed and devoured each other as he walked them to the kitchen. She gave a little shriek when he placed her on the counter.

He pulled away to look at her. "You okay?"

She delved her fingers into his hair and nodded. "It was just cold."

With a low growl he said, "I will fucking warm you up."

"I'm counting on it."

Derek was kissing the slope of her neck as his fingers found her clit and began to rub in small circles. The small moan that Mia let out only fueled his desire. His two fingers glided in and began thrusting in and out. She leaned back a little further on the counter laying out for him as an irresistible feast.

Removing his fingers he lowered his face and gave a slow languid lick all the way up her center and to her clit. She tasted like the sweetest honey, and he couldn't get enough. His tongue continued to alternate between her clit and then fucking and diving deep inside of her. He knew she was close to coming. Her hips were thrusting into his moves, and her reactions were the hottest thing he had ever seen. To know that he could make her feel like this, was a powerful thing.

Once her whole body shook with her release, he couldn't hold back anymore. Derek pulled her ass down to the edge even further and wasted no time thrusting into her.

Derek's cock slid into her welcoming body, and he moaned once he was fully seated. "Mia. God, you feel so fucking good."

"Right back at you. But I really need you to fuck me now."

Derek smiled and began to move back and forth. Mia leaned back, but Derek pulled her up and placed both of his hands on the back of her head and neck so she was looking at him. He slowed his pace and kissed her. When he slowly backed his lips from hers, he tilted his head, so their foreheads were touching. Being able to see her eyes as he continued to slide in and out created a powerful pull on his heart. She was his. He would make sure that Mia always knew she would be his priority; she was his forever.

"Come with me baby," he whispered against her lips.

She nodded in reply, and he quickened his thrusts until she threw her head back and her walls shook around him. He gave a groan as he gave one final push and allowed his release to spill inside of her. He brought her face back to his and gave slow kisses as they caught their breath.

Mia finally smiled and asked, "Round two?"

Derek picked her up off the counter and walked them to the bedroom with a satisfied smile. "I am going to love your pregnancy hormones."

Chapter 12

Today was shopping day and Mia was not really looking forward to it. She needed some maternity clothes... desperately. She was wearing leggings and even those were getting too tight. She took one look in the mirror and frowned. "I'm getting too big too quick."

Derek came up behind her and kissed her neck. "No, you're not. You are perfect."

"You're only saying that so you can get laid."

"Well, the sex would be great, but I'm not lying. Your body is just making some room for little bean. You can't keep her all cramped up in a tight firm belly. She needs room to move and groove."

Mia sighed. "And thus, the reason for shopping today."

Derek wrapped his arms around her and placed his hands on her stomach. "Make sure to find something sexy for dinner tonight."

Mia rolled her eyes. "Sexy and maternity clothes are not something that goes together."

"You're going shopping with Josie, right?"

"Yeah."

"Trust me, she'll find it."

Just then a loud knock came from the front door and Josie's voice loudly followed. "Derek, get your horny ass off the girl and open the door."

Derek slumped his head to Mia's shoulder. "Speak of the devil."

Mia giggled. "Don't let her hear you. She might bring down some wrath on you."

As he walked to the door he said, "Thank God, Grayson mellowed her out."

"She was worse?"

Derek put his finger to his lips in a shushing motion and nodded his head just as he opened the door.

Josie pointed a finger at him and narrowed her eyes. "I heard that."

Looking skyward he replied, "Of course you did."

Ignoring him Josie went to Mia and gave her a hug. "How are you doing?"

"Pretty good today. No sickness and I actually ate more than toast this morning."

"Good. Ariel is downstairs waiting for us. We have a busy day. Let's get a move on it."

Knowing better than to throw off Josie's schedule Mia got into her sweater with Derek's help and gave him a kiss goodbye.

"Stay out of trouble."

"I'm always well behaved," he said. Even as he said that she saw a spark of mischief in his eyes. Good lord what did he have planned?

It wasn't long before Josie had them at their first stop. It was a darling boutique in Willow Springs dedicated to pregnancy and new moms. A pleasant woman greeted them as they walked in. "Welcome to Bump it Up. Is there anything I can help you with today?"

Josie had no problem speaking up. "My friend has zero maternity clothes and has quite a bump developing."

Mia sighed. "She's not wrong."

The woman smiled. "Well, we can certainly help with that. Do you have a certain style you prefer?"

Mia blinked. "Uh, comfort and doesn't make me look like a cow."

Ariel placed her arm around Mia's waist in a comforting gesture. "You could never look like a cow. Just an amazing woman carrying a baby." Ariel's focus turned to the sales clerk. "She needs a couple of really nice dresses for date nights and a wedding, some black pants for work at the bar, and lazy day clothes."

In a blinding speed the clerk picked out several choices that Ariel and Josie were more than happy to either veto or approve. As she was trying on the first dress, even more clothes came flying over the fitting room door at her. "Hey, can I at least get the first dress on?"

Ariel giggled. "Sorry. We're done now."

"Really? I think there might be some clothes still left out there." This was really going to kill her budget. She would absolutely have to weed out some even if she liked them. Nobody needed this many clothes.

As she straightened the first dress she beamed. It was so pretty. This was something she would have chosen even in a regular size. It had a V-neck and long lace bell sleeves. It was a soft black material with a beige floral lace overlay and the flowy skirt hit just above her knees.

"Get your butt out here," Josie said.

Mia opened the door to her friends and was relieved to see their smiles.

"Oh, you look so pretty," Ariel exclaimed.

Josie nodded. "That dress is a good choice for your date night."

Mia took a second look in the big mirror and twirled. She loved the swing of the dress. "I think so too."

Ariel said, "Okay, next. Try the one I just threw over at you."

She thought she caught a bit of an evil smirk from Josie before she returned to the dressing room.

As she took the next dress off the hanger she dropped it, but once she picked it up, she turned it a few times and couldn't figure it out. It seemed to have way too many holes. "Um, guys, I think there is something wrong with this dress. Maybe it is missing something?"

Ariel laughed. "Nope. Here, this will help."

Mia moved back as a phone slid under the door with a picture on the screen. Mia picked it up and tilted her head. "Are you guys freaking kidding me? Nope. No way. Uh-uh."

Mia's eyes studied the picture and then the dress that was on the fitting room chair. The woman in the picture was wearing a long black dress, but really that was being generous. It was floor length with long sleeves, scoop neck, but it was backless with a slit that went to the top of the thigh. But that wasn't the worst part of it. Oh no, the belly was completely cut out too. Have they lost their minds?

There was no way she was going to throw out her belly with all the stretch marks to come for all the world to see. Pregnant and proud, sure, but this was about a thousand times too much.

"Come on. Try it. You never know. It could be good for date night at home if you don't want to wear it out."

Mia took another look at it. It was sexy. There was no doubt about it. Derek would lose his mind. "Okay, but I am not showing it to either of you."

"Spoil sport," Josie shouted through the door.

After a couple of minutes Mia looked at herself in the mirror and gasped with surprise at the boost of confidence she felt. While it was risqué, it didn't really reveal anything. Her cleavage was completely covered, and the slit was only noticeable when she drew her leg forward.

They must have noticed her silence because Ariel finally said, "You love it, don't you?"

"Yes," she replied as she turned side to side.

"Knew it," she said in a sing-song triumph.

DEREK PULLED UP TO Chase's house in Tiny's large SUV just as Chase was pulling the front door closed. While Chase fit his large body in the seat Derek handed him a small white box. "Bear claws."

"Thank God. I'm starving."

"Didn't you eat breakfast with Dixie?"

Chase nodded. "Yeah, but that was like two and a half hours ago."

"I would hate to see your grocery bill."

Chase laughed. "That's nothing compared to the diaper bill these days."

"This is why I brought you. I need an expert. What are we going to need for the baby, and where are the best stores?"

"We need to go to the big stores in Raleigh. The big box stores will have most of the stuff you need, but there are a couple small independent stores that have some cool things too."

"Okay. We're on a tight schedule, and I am taking Mia out for dinner tonight too."

Chase nodded. "I am the world's best speed shopper. I can spend all your money in ten minutes or less."

It wasn't long before they reached the first store. They were in the baby aisle and Derek's eyes began to glaze over. They started at an independent store just outside downtown. They had several nooks that were decorated like a real nursery.

Chase rubbed his palms together and grinned. "Alright. What color crib are we looking for? Natural wood, cherry, white, black?"

Derek rubbed his hand at the back of his head. "Uh, natural?"

"Did you do any research before we came out today?"

"Yeah. I read about different things we might need, but I figured that you could help me figure it all out."

"Dude. Girls dream about the nurseries that they want just like they do weddings. They know down to the theme and music box that should be in there." Without letting Derek respond any further Chase pulled out his phone. He must have called Dixie because he greeted with a smile and said, "Hey, babe. Are you friends with Mia on that Pinny site?" There was a pause before he continued, "Yeah, Pinterest. Great. Can you send me her page for the baby? Thanks. Love you, babe."

Within seconds a ping sounded, and he opened the link that Dixie sent.

Derek raised an eyebrow. "You already have Pinterest downloaded on your phone."

"Of course, I do. Dixie pins all kinds of things on her boards. It makes buying gifts easy as fuck. She pins it, I buy it."

"Huh. Nice."

As Mia's page loaded, it was easy to see her preference from the nearly hundred pins of baby room ideas. She definitely wanted white wood with either soft pink accents for a girl or blue celestial accents for a boy.

This narrowed down their choices of cribs easily. There were three sets that were in white, and one nearly matched for several of her pins that also had a matching dresser and rocking chair.

Derek looked at the price tags and blew out a breath. "Why is this stuff so expensive?"

Chase shrugged. "People will pay for it. If there is one thing you shouldn't cheap out on it's stuff for a baby. There are so many things that can go wrong if proper safety protocols aren't followed. Do you know how many calls we have because of kids getting body parts stuck in cribs or getting into something they shouldn't? Hell, I got my head stuck between the posts of the stairway when I was like four."

"Seriously?"

"Yeah. I was trying to make Summer laugh because she wouldn't stop crying so I played peek-a-boo in the stairs and somehow got stuck in one."

"How did you get out?"

"Dad ended up having to cut and remove one of the rails. Mom made him redo the railing with super wide posts. At least I did get her to stop crying. She laughed the whole time I was stuck."

"Such a good big brother."

Chase's lips thinned, and he nodded his head as he whispered, "Yeah."

Damn it. He saw that look of self-blame cross over Chase's face. While he had dealt with his sister and mother's death over the years, there were still moments that he struggled with it. Tyler was better at this with Chase than he was. No one blamed Chase for the accident, including his wife who was also involved and had lasting injuries that she still struggled with at times. Derek knew Chase played out the what if in his head. What if he hadn't stayed longer at school and picked up Summer and Dixie himself instead of his mom, but Derek knew all too well that you couldn't linger in those what if clouds. He clasped his hand on Chases shoulder. "Hey, help me pick out some toys."

The two large men proceeded to squeak, squish, and rattle nearly a hundred toys. So many choices it was hard to pick out favorites. Derek's first choice was, of course, a soft white basketball that made a rattle noise.

"What if it is a girl?" Chase asked.

"Duh, that's why I got the white one. I'm good either way."

They were able to take the crib today but had to order the dresser and rocking chair to be delivered in a few days. As they got in the SUV Derek noticed Chase eating one of the suckers he bought.

"What do you think you are doing?"

Chase removed the sucker with a loud pop of his mouth. "What? Eating candy."

"That wasn't for you."

Chase shrugged. "I'm starving and you haven't fed me."

Derek started to smile. "Does it taste good?"

Chase pulled it out and stared at it for a second. "Eh. It's a little sour but not bad. I will buy you some more at the big store."

Holding in his laugh, he said, "We can't get those there."

"Why not?"

"Those are preggo pops. You know, for pregnant women."

Chase slowly pulled it back out and stared at his chest in mortification. "Like hormone stuff? Am I gonna grow boobs or something?"

"No, jackass. It's for nausea."

Chase gave the sucker a side eye and shrugged. "All good then."

Derek gave him a slight shove. "Get your ass back in there and buy some replacements."

A few hours later Derek was sitting on the floor with parts of the crib scattered across the floor, a stack of diaper boxes in the corner, and bags of baby clothes and trinkets on the couch. He may have gone a bit overboard, but actually it was kind of fun. At one point he and Chase were just tossing baby items in the cart like they were playing basketball. An older woman smiled at them and commented how they reminded her of her grandson and his husband when they adopted their first baby.

Chase looked a bit shocked, and Derek seized the moment to wrap his arm around Chase and smiled. "Thanks, we're so excited."

Chase still couldn't talk while the woman gave them her congratulations. It was nice to find something that could render the big man speechless besides food. It really was a good day.

Just as Derek finally got about half of the crib done, the door to the apartment opened and Mia and his sister came walking in with several bags themselves.

Mia stopped in her tracks and looked around the room. "Oh.. my... God. Derek. You said you wanted to buy a few things."

Derek looked around the room in slight confusion. "I did buy a few things."

Mia still wasn't moving. "No. No, this is an entire store."

"Not an *entire* store. We just got the necessities."

Ariel quietly took the bags from Mia and said, "I'm just going to take these to the bedroom."

Mia shook her head. "Derek, I can't let you buy all this stuff. It's too much."

"No it isn't. Too much would have been hiring that custom builder to do all the furniture."

Mia's eyes widened. "You didn't!"

Derek laughed. "No, I didn't."

He saw his sister come out of the bedroom with wide eyes. "Uh, Mia. There's more."

Mia's head swung over to the bedroom with accusing eyes and then back to Derek. He jumped up and followed her into the bedroom.

He noticed her eyes land on the giant life-sized polar bear in one corner and the two car seats still in boxes in the other.

Hearing a squeak come out of Mia, Derek said, "I know Snuggles is a bit big, but the baby will love it, and he also makes a good barrier when the baby starts to sit and falls over. Bean will just land on a soft comfy leg or like a pillow."

"Is that what the sales lady told you?"

"No," Derek replied defensively. "It was Chase."

A little softer Mia asked, "You named him Snuggles?"

"Yeah. Chase had to snuggle with him the whole drive home because we ran out of room. It seemed to fit."

Mia sighed. "And the *two* car seats?"

"Well, yeah. It would be a pain to keep moving one car seat from each other's car all the time."

"He's got a point," Ariel said.

"Is your brother always this over the top?" Mia asked.

Ariel tilted her head. "Yes, but he is usually a little sneakier about it."

"Sneakier?"

Derek pointed his finger at his sister to stop her from continuing. "Zip it."

Ariel rolled her eyes. "Funny. What are you going to do if I spill all your secrets? Tell Mom?"

"Don't you have a fiancé to get back to?"

Ariel giggled. "I do. Maybe I will wear that sexy lingerie I bought for him tonight."

Derek pinched the bridge of his nose. "Ariel, I swear to God..."

Suddenly he felt arms wrap around his waist in a tight hug. "Love you, big brother."

Derek sighed. "Love you, too."

Chapter 13

"Derek, you better get your cute ass moving or I am going to leave without you," Mia shouted towards the bathroom.

Derek was pulling a shirt over his head and smiled. "I'm coming. We wouldn't be running late if you hadn't interrupted my shower and then kicked me out."

Thinking back to the orgasm she needed and received, she wasn't sorry about it one bit. "You loved it."

Derek leaned over to kiss her. "Yes, I did."

"Don't start something we can't finish. Let's go."

Shaking his head he grabbed Mia's sweater from the couch. "Here. It is getting a bit colder."

Mia shook her head. "I already have a built-in heater. This baby is like a little furnace."

"Just humor me."

"Fine, but if I spontaneously combust, it will be all your fault."

"I'll take my chances."

Mia looked over her shoulder at Derek as he locked the apartment door. "Where are we going?"

"Casperelli's."

"Just us?"

Derek swung the keys around his fingers and smiled. "Well, that is the intention, but I make no guarantees we won't run into anyone."

"Yes, I am learning small-town life always has that hazard."

As predicted once they were sat at the booth Derek sighed and said, "Dad is here."

Mia spun her head around trying to find the man she had not met yet. "Where?"

Derek nodded his head behind Mia. "He's with his wife."

"Is that bad?"

"No. She's a very nice woman and genuinely seems good for him. Remember how I said we are working on building a better relationship?"

"Yeah," Mia replied cautiously.

"Well, he is working on it more than I am. I know I need to do a little more, I just still have that bit of pissed off teenager in the back of my head saying he is an asshole."

Mia laced her fingers through his. "But he cares about you, yes?"

"Yes."

"So, you are in much better shape than I am. My dad doesn't care about me at all. And if you really are going to be with me and little bean, I would love to have a grandpa around. My most cherished memories are with my grandpa. Bean should have that too, and it isn't going to happen with my dad."

Derek hung his head down and sighed. "Well, shit. Come on. Let's go say hello."

Mia allowed Derek to help her out of the booth and could feel his hesitation with each step. Just as she was going to say they didn't need to do this, he kissed her palm and said, "Love you."

It only took a few steps before Derek's dad obviously noticed them approaching the table. The smile that the man had was a mix of surprise and happiness. He stood up before they could reach the table. "Derek."

"Hey, Dad. I wanted to introduce you to Mia. Mia, this is Jeremy, my dad."

Mia was so proud of him. There was almost no grimace to his voice when he said Dad. From what Ariel said it wasn't long ago he refused to call him Dad at all instead of any other insulting names.

Jeremy stepped towards Mia and shook her hand. "It's so nice to meet you. I've heard a lot about you."

Mia's mouth opened, but she wasn't quite sure what to say.

Miranda stepped out and broke the burgeoning awkward moment. "Hi. I'm Miranda, this lug's wife."

Mia greeted her politely and then looked at Derek who asked, "You already know about Mia?"

Jeremy nodded and put his hands in his pants pocket. "Yeah. I read about it online first and then talked to your mom."

Mia got bumped by a person walking past and Miranda invited them to join them at the table. After settling in Jeremy continued, "It was a bit of a surprise, and I never know if that old bat is posting the truth or just stirring up some trouble."

Miranda shook her head. "Oh, she wants to cause a little bit of trouble, but she didn't lie."

The corner of Jeremy's mouth lifted slightly. "Have to admit I miss the old days when gossip was whispered in dark corners instead of being written on the internet for all to see."

Mia felt Derek tense up a bit, before he said, "Yeah, you got lucky."

Mia turned to him and tilted her head and softly admonished him. "Derek."

Jeremy's eyes drifted back down to the table. Mia could see the confidence pour back out of his body and was replaced with waves of guilt and shame that consumed him.

Derek sighed. "Sorry... Dad, I didn't mean..."

Jeremy put his hand up to stop him from continuing. "I know. We're still a work in progress. Thanks for the apology, though."

Miranda was the first to break the obvious tension. "Any special occasion for dinner tonight?"

Derek laced his fingers into Mia's under the table. "Mia went and bought a bunch of new clothes, and I had to take her out to show off this new amazing dress."

Mia shrugged. "I had to get some maternity clothes. I didn't have much to begin with and now this little one is taking up all the extra room I had in them."

"Oh, a friend of mine just had her last baby and bought all these ridiculous designer clothes for her pregnancy. She got her tubes tied and was thinking about donating the clothes. I'm sure she would love to give them to someone who needs them," Miranda said.

"Oh, I couldn't..."

"Nonsense. I can call her this week."

Mia could see that this was important to her for some reason and just nodded in acceptance. "Okay. Thanks."

It wasn't long before the server made accommodations for the two extra people at the table and the order for dinner was in. Mia relaxed as the tension between Jeremy and Derek left and they managed to have a normal conversation. The two talked about sports and some of their businesses. Jeremy was the local insurance agent and talked to Derek about the fundraiser for stuffed animals, clothes, and blankets to help families who lost their homes.

Mia brightened. "I want to help."

"Oh, yeah?" Jeremy asked.

"Yeah, I make these knitted stuffed animal monsters. It is a time filler, and I make so many I would love to give back to the community. Especially since everyone has been so kind to me."

"That would be great. You can drop them by my office anytime or Derek can bring them to me."

Derek's smile grew, and he said, "I can bring them. I have some other donations I can swing by later this week." He only paused for a few minutes before he continued, "Okay, be honest. Did Melvin really wreck his car trying to avoid a deer or is what Tank said true that the inside of the car could light the whole garage under black light?"

Mia nearly spit out her drink. "Do you mean he... that he?"

Jeremy laughed. "Redecorated his car in bodily fluid?"

Miranda shook her head. "You guys are gross."

Lifting the wine glass to his lips Jeremy responded, "I can neither deny or CONFIRM that it is true."

"Poor Tank." Miranda sighed.

Derek laughed. "Poor Tank, my ass. He made the newbie take care of it. That dumbass made some rude comment about Tank's sister, and it was the perfect punishment. At least he had someone to do it for him unlike Ariel."

Everyone stared blankly at Derek in obvious confusion. "Oh, shit, you guys don't know?"

"Does this look like the faces of people who know this story?" Miranda asked.

"Well, I should clarify. It wasn't that type of bodily fluid, but it was vomit. Just before Kyle and Ariel got together some guy was in the store with his buddies all hungover and acting like an idiot. Then he threw up exorcism style all over the cards and Ariel. Kyle showed up and they made this guy and his friends pay for all the damaged stuff and compensate for Ariel's dress. And in one of the many signs that Kyle was a goner for Ariel, he helped clean it all up."

"Oh, my God, I forgot all about that. She came to my office shortly after that happened. My poor girl. She always tries so hard to stay pretty and clean, but it never seems to work out that way for her."

"She says that she is God's personal court jester and that he just enjoys seeing how much she can take before she cracks."

The remainder of dinner was pleasant, and Mia enjoyed getting to know Derek's dad and his wife. As they were leaving, she weaved her arm through his and smiled. "Ariel would be very proud of you for being so nice to your dad."

Derek's sigh was accompanied by a low grumble. "Yeah yeah. It hurt a little."

"Want me to kiss it and make it all better?"

Mia gasped as he pinched her ass. "God, yes. Move your butt a little faster."

Chapter 14

Mia burst into Derek's office with excitement. "Dex called. He has found some of my things and the police are releasing what they found at the storage unit."

Spinning in his chair to face her, he grunted as she landed in his lap. Kissing him more forceful than normal she started to wiggle. "Keep moving like that and I will have to bend you over this desk."

Mia lightly moved her finger over his lips and grinned. "Was that supposed to be punishment?"

"It could be if you play your cards right."

Mia shook her head. "Nope. Can't. We're super busy. It's trivia night and half the town showed up today."

"That is because we chose retro pop culture tonight. Everyone thinks they are an expert on eighties and nineties trivia and they want that gift card."

"Yeah, not many showed up for local history last time."

"Tiny's fault. I let him pick the topics and questions every now and then. He is kind of a secret nerd. His time off is filled with documentaries and cooking shows."

"I think he could host one of those cooking shows. He's so talented."

"And a little rough around the edges. Not sure the audience would appreciate him like we do."

"Oh, I don't know. Look at those shows where the chefs always scream at the staff."

As if the man could hear them, he walked by the open door. Mia yelled out to him. "Hey, Tiny."

The large man stopped in his tracks and leaned into the doorway. "What's up?"

"Ever think about trying out for one of those cooking shows?"

"Not a chance in hell."

Mia pouted. "Why not?"

"I had years of assholes telling me where to stand, when to eat, when I could piss, and what I could cook. Bossman treats me like a man and not something to order around. I don't need some guy in a suit telling me what I can and can't do."

Mia sat staring at him for a second before she responded. "Oh, sorry. I didn't think about all that."

Tiny shrugged. "All good. I wouldn't expect you to. I don't wish what I know on anyone. Anyway, gotta go. Chase just got here and ordered like four appetizers."

Mia watched as Tiny disappeared around the corner. "It still bothers him, doesn't it?"

"The prison time?"

"Yeah."

"Believe it or not, he is better than he used to be. He was quiet at first and didn't talk to anyone. Then he started opening up to Mom and Ariel when they would come visit me."

"And he is close with Grayson too?"

Derek nodded. "They were cellmates for a bit."

"That's right, I heard about that. He broke into a church to take a selfie with some rare artifact."

"Yeah. Don't break into a church... It's classified as a felony."

"Wow, but didn't he get caught because he was saving the life of the priest or something like that?"

"Yup. Just goes to show... no good deed and all that. Okay, we got sidetracked. When do you want to go get your stuff?"

"I was thinking Monday. I have Monday and Tuesday off so I can go up and see what I can bring back and visit my grandparents' graves."

"Want some company?"

"Yes, please."

DEREK LIFTED MIA'S suitcase in the back of Tiny's SUV. "Ready?" He really needed to think seriously about buying his own SUV soon.

"Yes. Do you really think we needed the SUV?"

"We are not sure how much we will be bringing back. I thought about Kyle's truck, but that would expose everything to the elements, and it might rain on the way home."

"Good thinking."

"So, we are meeting Dex first at the storage unit. And he also has a few new leads on some of the jewelry at the pawn shops."

"Oh, I hope we find some."

"Me, too. Now I have road snacks, a knock-your-socks-off playlist, and plenty of time to dig into your deep dark secrets."

Mia sat down and smirked. "I have no secrets, but you, kind sir, I believe have plenty."

"Never. Small-town life, remember? No secret too small to be blasted to the town."

"What about the college years with Zoey?"

"Everyone knows what happens in college stays at college."

"Does it really?"

"Well, it should," Derek said as he started the car and found the first song on his so-called kick-ass playlist.

As the music started Mia laughed. "Five hundred miles? Really?"

"Seemed appropriate."

THANKFULLY, AFTER HOURS of driving, they reached the storage unit's front office. They found Dex waiting for them already on the phone arguing with someone.

"I don't pay you for a bunch of I don't knows. I pay you for answers. You're the hacker... go hack something."

After he disconnected the call Mia asked, "Problem with my case?"

"Nah. Different case. I am a man of many juggling talents. I have your case and a couple others. One should be super easy. Dad took off with the kid and thinks that he can get a new credit card while on the run and we won't figure it out. People are dumb."

"I wish Jack was dumb."

Dex huffed. "He was at least a little dumb. It wasn't too hard to find the dump-and-run site. Normally, he sold off the goods to a buyer when he did this before, but this time he just took what he thought he could make quick cash off and left the rest. But I have to warn you what's here doesn't amount to a lot."

"Better than nothing. I'll take it."

They followed Dex to the unit where he unlocked it for them. As the loud metal door rolled up Mia gasped. There were a several boxes that were opened and papers and pictures scattered around the floor. Mia ran over to the first picture she could find and picked it up with trembling fingers.

She felt Derek's hand on her shoulder before she whispered, "This is Grandpa and me when he took me to the beach. I think it was the first summer I stayed with them while Grandma was still alive. He was so excited to take me on a boat hoping to see some dolphins. He said they were so smart, just like me."

Looking around Mia took in a deep breath. She was not going to cry. Not now. Her next focus needed to be gathering up what was left and making some decisions on what to keep.

After about an hour they had loaded up a few boxes and had picked up whatever was loose on the ground. There was one box left, and she heard Derek curse before she could get to it. "What?"

"Fucking assholes."

Annoyed at the situation she asked a little louder. "What?"

"I found your knitted monsters."

Mia raced over and bit hard on her lips to avoid screaming. There were her creations that her grandpa loved so much, but each one was destroyed. Gutted and unraveled with stuffing mixed in all around the carnage. "Arrrggg. Seriously? Just why... I mean, I get it. Take my stuff and sell it, get your money and run, but to kill my little monsters. You weren't taking them. You could have left them the fuck alone, but no. Let's hurt me even more."

Derek tried to wrap his arms around her, but she was too pissed off. "No! Don't! I just want to smash something, but I don't even have anything here to smash. I would settle for anything that was his. His goddamn stupid ass coffee mug, the plate he made on our paint your pottery date, or how about that picture frame with him and his sister. Oh wait, that's right. That's not his sister. That's his fucking lover. His criminal partner who made me think she was my friend." Not seeing anything else to take her frustrations out on, she picked up the box full of stuffed animal carcasses and threw it against the wall.

As it went flying across the unit pieces of yarn and stuffing released into the air creating a blizzard of white fluff and colorful yarn falling around them.

Dex looked around and shook his head. "Well. That was a choice."

Mia turned around and glared at the man. Before she could respond he said, "I'm gonna go get a broom."

Derek started picking up the mess and Mia whispered, "You don't have to do that."

He shrugged. "I know, but I want to."

"I shouldn't have done that."

"You were entitled to your angry breakdown. Honestly, I expected it way before now."

"Really?"

He gave a half laugh. "Yeah. I mean this whole thing has been a shit show. But once we make the rounds to the shops Dex wants us to look at, we can close the door on all of this. We have everything we need, right? You, me, and bean. At least we found some pictures and things here. It was more than I thought we would get."

"Yeah, me too. I still don't understand. Why spend the extra time to kill my critters?"

"I don't know. Someone had some rage that they needed to get out."

THEY WERE ENTERING the third pawn shop; they had luck at the first one, but not at the second one. She was able to get a pair of her grandmother's earrings and two necklaces at the first shop.

Dex held the door open and said, "I saved the best for last." He nodded at the clerk as they entered, and the man smiled and walked into the back. When he returned, he held a metal lock box and placed it on the counter.

Mia was silent as she was hopeful to find a few more pieces.

The middle-aged man stopped and started to speak before opening the box. "Dex explained what happened. I am so sorry for everything you are going though. I couldn't imagine how hard this must be for you. Dex had showed me a picture of your ex and I remembered him clearly. The woman who was with him was a real piece of work and made several rude comments to my daughter while she was writing up the tickets."

Not sure what to say to the kind man, Mia apologized.

"No apologies needed. I just hope this is everything you are looking for."

He opened the box and piece after piece was laid out before her. Grandpa's watch, his wedding band and cufflinks, several of her grandmother's necklaces, earrings, bracelets, and the ring.

Her hands shook as she picked up her grandfather's ring and read the engraving.

Leaning over her shoulder Derek asked, "What does it say?"

"Written in the stars. Grandpa used to take Grandma out to the lawn, and they would lay on the blanket and stare at the stars holding hands for hours. For their anniversary one year she took the ring to get it engraved. She didn't think he would notice it gone since he was tinkering in the garage. He got done early and freaked out." Mia laughed a little. "He kept muttering that Grandma was going to kill him if he didn't find it. She got back, and he looked so guilty, like a kid who got caught eating dessert before dinner. She only let him squirm for a couple minutes before she gave him the box. This ring was his most prized possession."

Gazing down at the collection of items, she asked, "How much for all of it?" She would have to max out her new credit card, but it would be worth it.

She noticed a quick look to Derek from the man and then back to her. "Don't worry, miss. Take them, they're yours."

"I couldn't possibly. At least let me pay you for what you paid for them." He didn't respond but instead looked uncomfortably between Dex and Derek. Oh, he didn't. He couldn't have. She turned to look at the man she had fallen for and saw him fidget before he could say anything. "Derek."

"Yeah?"

"Did you already pay the man?"

Derek raised his hands in surrender. "No. I did not pay this kind man."

She looked again at the shopkeeper who was now taking special interest in the lighting in the ceiling. "Sir, did this adorable idiot already pay you?"

With a big smile the man replied, "Nope. That man did not pay me."

Whirling around to Dex, she said, "You paying by proxy is the same thing!"

Dex pulled out his phone. "Oops, important call. I'll be outside." And with a speed like she had never seen from him he was out the door holding what she was sure was a phone without a call to his ear.

Deciding against making the poor shopkeeper witness the disagreement they were going to have she sighed. "Thank you, sir. I will take these home."

He pulled out a few jewelry boxes and began placing each item into them carefully. Derek, the big chicken, joined Dex on the sidewalk. As the man handed the bag to her, he said, "Miss, may I say something?"

"Of course."

"Seems like you found a fine man out there. That last one was a real piece of work. Hang on to this one. He meant well."

She looked out the window and smiled. "I know he did. I'll only make him suffer a little."

"Good idea," he replied with a wink.

DEREK WALKED UP BEHIND Dex who was still on his fake phone call. "Dude, you left me out to dry."

"Hey, I was paid to find people and property. I was not paid to stand in the line of fire of my pissed off client."

"You could have played it off better."

"Ha! None of us were going to win any Oscars with that performance. Grayson's toddler could have figured out we were lying."

"True. How mad do you think she is?"

"What like on a scale of one to ten?"

"Yeah."

Dex looked back to Mia, who was smiling at the shopkeeper and then back to Derek. "Six, maybe five if you are lucky. You'll get to keep your balls."

Just as Derek started to relax Mia came through the door and walked straight to the car. She pulled on the handle and realized it was still locked. She looked over and arched an eyebrow waiting for it to be unlocked. Once the doors unlocked with the telltale click, she opened and shouted over the car, "Are you two idgits getting into the car or what?"

Dex walked by Derek and muttered, "Six. Definitely six."

Chapter 15

It had been about a month since their trip to retrieve Mia's things and Derek was thankful that he only had to grovel for one night and was easily forgiven with a few orgasms. Not that he minded his consequences. Nope. Not at all.

Things had been pretty quiet. Mia's pregnancy was in its seventeenth week. Her appetite had been increasing exponentially. Tiny started making a basket of fries that he said was for the servers to munch on, but in reality, Mia's crankiness could rise with each hunger pang and the fries help a lot. But what was also rising was her libido. Those glorious pregnancy hormones were absolutely something Derek was taking advantage of.

He also loved caressing her small swollen stomach during the night. He was looking forward to feeling the baby and just how much more beautiful she was going to be with each passing day.

For the most part, Mia had moved on from what happened with Jack and Tabitha. She said that as long as he didn't come back and try to make things difficult, she was happy. He could live his life wherever he was now. There had been a few nights, however, when Mia had woken from a nightmare where he would return and take the baby away from them. At first, it was rare but as the pregnancy progressed the nightmares became more frequent. She asked Grayson to stop searching, but Derek often wondered if that was the best course of action. He would feel better at least knowing where he was. There were times he also felt like he was waiting for the other shoe to drop.

While Derek was pouring a beer for the new guy at the counter, he heard a small giggle coming from his latest customer. "Hi, Derek!"

Turning around he saw one of Grayson and Josie's kids sitting at the stool twisting it back and forth. "Hey, Jessica. Let me just drop this off and I will make your favorite drink."

Bouncing in her seat she gasped. "The big one?"

"Of course, the big one. I mean, it isn't special if it isn't the big one."

Derek dropped off the beer and grabbed the non-breakable glass from under the sink he reserved for the kids that visited. "Where's your Aunt Josie?"

"She's outside talking to my teacher."

"And you aren't eavesdropping? That's very mature of you."

"I know, right?!?"

Derek placed the fruity soda mix in front of her and topped it off with a sliced strawberry. "You're not afraid of what the teacher is going to say?"

While sipping her drink she shook her head. "Nope. I have all As except that dumb project I got partnered with Nicholas on. He made us get a B. All he had to do was color in the map with the right colors, but nooooo. He mixed them all up. If it wasn't for my report, we would have gotten a C."

"Well, we can't have that."

"No way. I'm gonna get all good grades so I can go to college and run the company like my mom and dad did."

Derek's smiled dropped just a bit as he thought about the young couple who died too soon. "I have no doubt you will rule the world someday."

"That would be amazing. And I would make it against the rules to do group projects. They're stupid."

"Aw, kid, hate to break it to you but when you get a job with that amazing big company, it is nothing but group projects all the time. It takes a lot of people to make things run well in a company. Take this place, for example, do you think I could do this on my own?"

Jessica looked around tapping her finger to her lips thinking, just as Josie sat down next to her and set down a bag on the counter. Finally, Jessica responded, "It would be hard, cause you would have to serve people at the tables, make the drinks, and cook the food."

Derek nodded. "Seems like a lot for just me, doesn't it."

"Yeah, but you are the boss. You can just order people around."

Josie smirked. "Do you like it when your brother and sister just boss you around when you all are splitting the chores?"

"No. They don't listen to anything I say, and it makes me mad."

Leaning in Derek whispered, "Could you imagine me just bossing Tiny around all the time? Do you think he would react well?"

Jessica's eyes nearly bulged out of her skull. "No. He might pummel you." Then as if she realized something important, she placed her hand palm up towards Josie. Josie quietly opened her wallet and handed over a dollar.

Confused, Derek looked between the two and asked, "What did I just miss?"

Folding up her dollar Jessica replied, "I used my vocabulary."

"We made a deal with the munchkin. She gets a list of new words each month and if she can find an appropriate time to use that word naturally in a conversation she gets a dollar. She has all month to complete all twenty-five words. If she uses them all in the month, she gets an extra ten dollars."

"Wow. How many do you have left for the month?"

"Twelve. She keeps making it harder though. How am I supposed to just say valiant like normal? Who says that? She won't let me just say, 'Valient is my vocabulary word for the month.'"

Josie shook her head. "That's cheating."

Jessica rolled her eyes and mocked, "*That's cheating.*" She looked over at Josie who had her eyebrow cocked and then added, "Sorry."

"You're forgiven. You still want those cheese sticks?"

"Yup."

Derek nodded. "You got it. Anything else?"

Josie shook her head. "Just an iced tea for me."

Derek put the order in and caught up on a few more drinks. Derek resisted the urge to text Mia to check up on her. She'd grumbled the other day about him being too overprotective by calling and texting several times a day when she wasn't with him. At least she added the Life 360 app. She only agreed after finding out the whole group had it installed. Call him paranoid, but his best friend was shot by a psycho ex, and his sister was kidnapped by a desperate man because of Kyle. Now the woman he had grown to love had a criminal ex with a bitchy crazy girlfriend/pretend sister.

Setting down the cheese sticks that Jessica ordered, Josie shoved a bag towards him that came from his sister's shop. "Trade. I told Ariel I would bring this over to you."

"Thanks. I was going to pick it up later today."

"Yeah, we were there picking up a gift for Mia's birthday too and the munchkin over here wouldn't stop telling the whole store how hungry she was."

Derek placed the bag under the sink. "Have to admit I am kind of nervous about tomorrow. She has said that she doesn't like surprises, but she also hasn't had a real birthday party in years."

"I think once she gets over the shock, she'll be happy. She went from little to no friends to a somewhat large group in a very short amount of time. It can be an adjustment."

Jessica started to kneel in her stool and tried to peer over the counter. "What is it?"

Derek pulled out the silver trinket box with an engraving on it and placed it in front of Jessica. She squinted as she read. "Written in the stars. It's pretty, but you just got her a box?"

Derek laughed. "No. There is a necklace too."

"Oooo... can I see?"

Without responding Derek opened the lid and turned it towards her. "Wow. It's so pretty and different."

"Thanks. It is in the shape of Andromeda. It was the first constellation she pointed out to me when we went star gazing."

"You *are* a softie," Josie said with humor.

Defensively, Derek took the necklace and box and placed it back in the bag to put under the counter. "Like you're not?"

The huff of aggrievance that came out of Josie was loud and quick. "Certainly not. I am still the bad as—" Josie stopped and cleared her throat. "I am still the strong independent woman that I have always been. People still fear me."

Chewing on her cheese stick, Jessica said, "Uncle Grayson doesn't. He said he loves your squishy heart."

Trying not to smile Josie replied, "He does, does he?"

Nodding she replied, "Yup."

"I love him too, but I may have to remind him who he should fear."

"Can you remind him after we go to bed? Last time you guys made out in the kitchen. It was gross."

Josie rubbed her temple. "Just finish your food." Turning back to Derek she asked, "What are your plans for tonight?"

"Just a quiet romantic dinner at home. I have a small cake from Zoey, and I will be making pork chops with red potatoes and green beans. I was going to take her out, but she just wanted a quiet night with just the two of us. I figured if I get her the small cake and celebrate tonight, she won't expect another party later."

With impeccable timing Derek's part-time bartender came in to relieve him. "And that is my cue to leave. Let Joe know if you guys need anything else."

"Enjoy your romantic dinner," Josie said with a wink.

As he turned to leave, he heard Jessica shout, "Don't forget to wrap it up!"

Derek stopped dead in his tracks as did most of the conversations in the bar. "What?" Did that sweet angel just tell him to wrap it up?

"You know. Wrap it up."

Josie for once looked speechless with her mouth agape.

Jessica seemed unbothered by it all. "Wrap up the present before you give it to Mia. Geez what is wrong with you guys?"

Derek let out a deep breath. If this is what it was going to be like to have a kid, it wouldn't ever be dull, or it might even kill him.

MIA WAS STARVING AND if Derek didn't hurry up with the last of the cooking, she might dig into that delicious cake on the counter without him.

Without even turning around he said, "Stop eyeballing that cake. Dinner is almost done."

"You said that half an hour ago."

"No that was ten minutes ago. You have moved into the pregnancy timing phase. Everything seems to take longer."

"Let's not forget the non-stop hunger."

"What have you had today?"

"I had oatmeal for breakfast."

"That's good."

"With a muffin, a banana, and a bowl of cereal."

Derek stopped stirring. "That's not too bad for the day."

Mia slumped and put her head on the table. "That was just breakfast. I had a sandwich, chips, soup, and two croissants for lunch." She did feel that it was reasonable until she added the croissants an hour after lunch.

"It will all even out soon. I promise."

"Oh, yeah. It will even out in extra pounds all over my body. And I won't be one of those cute pregnant girls who wear it all in their stomach. Oh, no, I will have fat everywhere like someone put an air hose in my body and blew me up."

Derek set down the spatula and walked over to her. Cupping her face he said, "No matter where the food goes you will still be the most beautiful woman to me. You are making a perfect little baby and your body has to make changes to accommodate that. Try not to worry too much. Okay?"

"Okay." Mia looked over at the stove where dinner was still cooking. "But can we eat now?"

Derek kissed her on her forehead. "Yes. Take our drinks and sit down. I'll bring our plates."

After digging into the first few bites, Mia moaned. "This is sooo good. Did you get this recipe from Tiny?"

"No, actually Mom. I called her this morning to get the recipe."

"Aw, How is your mom?"

"Good. She was going over to Hannah and Mark's tonight for dinner."

"That's Tyler and Kyle's parents, right?"

"Yeah, they were like second parents for me and Ariel. We were almost always at one house or the other growing up. When Mom and Dad got divorced, I spent a lot of time over there. Mom was so sad, and I didn't want to bother her for anything. If I was upset about anything Hannah always was there to listen. If it was too serious, she would encourage me to talk to Mom about it, but mostly I just wanted someone to talk to that wasn't directly involved."

"You are so lucky to have that second set of parents. I just had my grandparents. As amazing as they were, there were times I wished I had a younger adult I could talk to."

"I'm sorry. I wish your parents could have been what you needed."

"Me, too." Mia absently rubbed her stomach. "I won't ever let this little one go through what I did. They will always have me."

Derek placed his hand over hers. "They will always have us."

Mia leaned over and kissed him and silently prayed that would always be true. As the kiss grew deeper, she could feel the warmth of desire warming her body up, but also a grumble from her stomach.

Derek smiled against her lips. "Maybe we should finish feeding you before we get too far."

"Good idea."

"How did your meeting with Tyler go this morning?" Derek asked.

"Really well. We went over some basic concepts for the website. I showed him some example sites of other crafters that sell their work, and what I thought would work well. He said what I am looking for would be fairly simple and I just have to come up with some branding colors and logos to give him. He said he could create everything now while I get the proper licensing for the business. I will also have to take pictures of the monsters too."

"Josie's oldest daughter might be able to help you with that. She is learning photography with Dixie and would probably love to get some more experience on her own."

"Oh, you think so? I would pay her, of course."

Derek laughed. "You pay her too and that would make her the happiest girl on the planet."

"It won't be much."

"Believe me, getting paid as a kid to do something you love is a gift. Oh. Speaking of gifts, I have something for you."

"Derek, you didn't have to," she said as he was already getting up.

"Too late."

He returned with a small box sloppily wrapped in pink wrapping paper with a haphazard ribbon and box. "Wrapped this yourself, did ya?"

Derek frowned looking down at the gift and back to her. "Maybe."

"Thank God."

Derek's eyebrows drew down. "Why thank God?"

"Finally, there is something you're not good at. I mean you are nearly perfect." Holding the hot-mess, gift-wrapped box up in one hand Mia beamed. "This is quite possibly the worst gift wrapping I have ever seen. And to think, your sister owns a gift shop."

"Hey," he said in mock offence. "My sister owns it not me. I don't expect Zoey to code a computer just because her brother and husband can."

"True."

"But my present selection skills are not to be doubted."

"I'll be the judge of that," she said as she tried to remove the ribbon. Mia pulled and yanked, but it was not budging. "What is this crap made out of?"

Laughing, Derek said, "Here, hand it over."

Mia placed it in his hands and sat back as he pulled and stopped just short of using his teeth. She pulled the box down and shook her head. "Get the scissors."

Derek moved his body away from her and shook his head. "Never. I will not be defeated by the clearance bin ribbon."

"Clearance bin?"

"Don't judge."

"Oh, I'm judging."

He placed the box on his lap and rolled his shoulders, then shook his whole body.

"What are you doing?"

"Loosening up for the battle."

Mia picked up her fork and said, "You just let me know when you're done."

She managed to get at least three bites in while Derek grunted and got a little red-faced as he finally broke the ribbon. Shaking out his hand he gave it back to her.

Happily taking the box, she asked, "Have we learned a lesson?

"Yeah. Next time just do the bow on top."

"Or we can always use scissors."

"Nope."

"Why?"

"Real men don't need scissors."

"Can I open this now?"

Derek sighed. "Yes, please, while I still have some dignity left."

"Do I need to go to the store tomorrow?" she asked as she removed the paper.

"No, why?"

"Well, I think you might have used all the tape in the house."

Derek tickled her side. "Smart ass."

Mia laughed. "I'm sorry. That was the last jab. Promise."

Once the wrapping paper was finally removed Mia gasped. "Derek, it's beautiful." She moved her fingers over the engraving and weakly smiled.

"Open it."

"There's more?"

Derek kissed her neck as she sat frozen and opened the lid to reveal the necklace. "It's Andromeda," she whispered.

He nodded. "I did a little research after you showed me her in the sky. You both have a lot in common."

"You think so?"

"Yes. First, her mom bragged a little too much about her beauty, and then when things kind of went to hell in a handbasket her parents sacrificed her to keep their own happy little world."

"I wasn't chained to a rock to serve as a sacrifice to a monster though. I lived with my grandpa, who loved me very much."

"True, but work with me. Your grandpa guarded over you until I was able to rescue you, and we could build our family."

"I think she had like nine kids. I am not doing this whole pregnancy nine times."

"We could have nine kids. That would be fun. We could have our own baseball team."

"No."

"What if we could squeeze them all into like four pregnancies?"

"Derek."

He pulled her onto his lap and kissed her again. "I could have super-sperm, and we could get it all done kind of quick like."

Mia gripped his shirt tightly and smiled. "Three. Your limit is three. One for this little bean, and then two more. Whether that happens in one pregnancy or two, your limit is three."

"Five."

"Three."

"Four if I can get twins out of one round."

"You really want to see me pregnant that much?"

"Yeah. I mean sure the grocery bill will be astronomical—" Derek blew out a breath as she smacked his stomach. "Ow. As I was saying I may have to buy more groceries, but you are sexy as fuck when you're pregnant."

"You have technically never seen me not pregnant."

"All the more reason to see you that way more often. Besides, these horny pregnancy hormones are a great side effect."

Mia felt his cock growing harder under her ass and she decided to give a little encouragement by wiggling her ass. "It is kind of fun."

"That's it," he said as he picked her up to carry her into the bedroom.

"Wait!"

Derek stopped immediately. "What? What's wrong?"

"Grab the roll first."

"Are you kidding me?"

"No. The hungry pregnant girl is not kidding. Grab the roll. I'll be done before you get your pants off."

"Wanna bet?" he asked as he dutifully grabbed the roll and took her into the bedroom. He did, in fact, lose the bet.

IT WAS THE NEXT DAY when they were pulling into Ariel and Kyle's driveway. Mia was excited to have dinner with Derek's sister. Derek seemed to look up and down the driveway before providing his hand to help her out of the car. "Such a gentleman."

Derek shrugged. "You know me."

"I'm getting there. Every now and then you still surprise me."

"Oh, I am just full of surprises today."

"What?"

"Nothing. Come on."

As they walked up to the door Ariel greeted them both before Derek could knock. "It's so good to see you!"

"Thanks—"

"Surprise," the crowd cheered as they entered the room.

Mia gasped as she looked around. There were so many people. Just off hand she saw Tiny, Amanda, Zoey, Dixie and Josie, and all of their men. "Oh, my God." She wanted to say more, but she was overwhelmed.

One wall was decorated with a balloon arch and waterfall streamers of blue, green, and white. There was a letter banner that said "Happy Birthday" and a two-tier cake decorated in replicas of her tiny little monsters holding balloons. Before Amanda could be the first to greet her with a hug, tears began forming. She tried to hold them back, but as Amanda whispered, "Happy birthday, sweet girl," the fat drops fell down her face.

"Thank you." Before long she greeted everyone with a hug and was even given a giant bear hug by Tiny who slightly lifted her off the ground.

"Put her down. She can't breathe," Derek said.

Tiny put her down and frowned. "She's fine. She needed that."

Mia nodded. "I really did."

As the night went on Mia began to realize that she actually liked surprises. At least when they came from people who cared about her. Everyone was laughing and having fun. The food was great, and she found that she was so busy talking that she wasn't even overindulging in the yummy treats.

Zoey was cutting up the cake and serving everyone while Mia was talking to Amanda and Ariel.

"I heard you were able to recover some of the jewelry your grandparents owned," Amanda said.

Mia nodded. "I did. We found quite a few pieces at the pawn shops."

"Did you have to buy them back?" Ariel asked.

"I did at the first place, but the majority was at the last place and Derek bought them before I could with his little co-conspirator."

"Who?"

"Dex. Grayson's investigator. They arranged it ahead of time that he would pay for them and the shopkeeper tried to play it off like he was giving them back to me."

Ariel smiled. "He couldn't pull it off, could he?"

"No. It was like watching of bunch of teenagers trying to lie to their parents. It truly was quite pathetic. I was going to use my credit card, but he already had it all taken care of."

Ariel shook her head. "That is just like Derek. Always trying to rescue everyone. I remember when he created and funded that grant so Zoey could open her bakery."

Mia looked just behind Ariel to see Zoey standing behind with a stricken look on her face, and Ariel just continued. "Zoey wouldn't take any money from him, so he just up and—"

"Ariel," Amanda said to try and stop her daughter from continuing, but it was incredibly too late for that.

"He did what?" Zoey asked hoarsely.

Ariel's eyes widened as she turned to face Zoey. "Nothing. He didn't do anything."

Zoey shook her head with her reddish curls bouncing back and forth. "No. Not nothing. You said he created the grant and paid for my bakery. He told me it was from the city's Chamber of Commerce."

"Zoey, I—"

Zoey shook her head again and handed the two plates to Mia. "Excuse me. I need to talk to Derek."

Before any of them could stop her, she had made a beeline straight towards Derek where she grabbed him by the shirt and said, "We need to talk. NOW!"

With a frantic look toward Mia, he was led out of the room with Zoey pulling him by his shirt. Ariel was the first to follow them trying to apologize as they went into Kyle's office and closed the double doors.

Mia couldn't help it. She followed and leaned in close to the doors, attempting to listen in. She was shortly followed by Josie and Dixie. She leaned in closer only to hear Tiny grumble. "Scoot in. I can't hear."

Well, at least she wasn't alone in her curiosity.

ZOEY WAS PISSED. DEREK couldn't remember a time when she was this pissed off. At least not at him.

"How could you?" she asked in a tone that was both angry and sad.

"How could I what?"

"You lied to me."

"Zoey, you're gonna have to help me out here. I don't know what you're talking about."

"You don't know? How many lies have you told me?"

"None. At least not that I know of."

"Really? You can't think of one teeny tiny lie you have ever told me?"

Derek tried hard to think, but he was never good in panic mode outside of sports. High pressure, have to make last-minute decisions to save a game... sure, all over that, but interpersonal connections and conversations not so much.

"You said there was a grant I could get by opening a shop in Blossom Hills."

Oh, shit. Okay, so maybe he lied to her once, twice if you counted the time he said her dress wasn't ugly that she wore that one time for a wedding. But these were good lies, right? "There was a grant. It was the first year for the grant."

Zoey stepped closer, and he instinctively took a step back. "And I seem to remember telling you that I didn't want your money, and that I wanted to figure this out on my own."

"And you did."

"No, I didn't, because you funded this grant and just handed it over to me."

"Zoey, I—"

"I swear to God, don't right now. I had a man who was controlling every move I made. I couldn't make one decision on my own without Shane's permission or interference. He guided every decision that I ever made. Nothing I did while I was with him was mine. Any small accomplishment he made sure that he had his hand in it. And here I was starting a new life, excited that I was doing this all on my own and it turns out it had your hands all over it too." Zoey's lip quivered, and she sucked in some air. "You just manipulated the situation to get your way and still use your money."

"It wasn't mine at that point. I did create the grant and gave it to the Chamber. They were the ones who decided who to award it to and have every year since. It is a good program; I still donate every year."

Zoey sighed. "I'm glad you're doing that, but answer this one thing for me... truthfully."

Derek nodded. "Okay."

"How many people applied for that grant the year I got it?"

Derek slumped. "One."

"I want to pay you back, but you know I can't, and that just pisses me off. Tyler and I have been sinking every penny we have into getting pregnant, but now I just..."

"Zoe, please don't. Don't pay me back. You would have won that no matter what. Your application would have stood out on its own. It was something that I had been thinking about doing anyway. It just solidified when we realized that you could open your bakery."

Zoey's anger seemed to subside just a bit as she leaned on the desk. "You have to stop trying to rescue everyone all the time. Sometimes the people you want to rescue want the choice of saving themselves. It is kind of crushing to think you did something all on your own only to find out that you didn't."

"But you did do it on your own."

"No, not completely, and now I will have that nagging little voice in the back of my head always saying that I needed your help to get my life back together... again."

He knew what that again meant. She was talking about when her life fell apart when Trevor died. Trevor died, and she became a shell of herself. She barely ate and did the minimum of self-care, then even after that when she was dealt another life-changing blow with losing the baby. He couldn't let her sink back into that shell when she left Shane. He wanted her close. He wanted her here in Blossom Hills where she could start over and have a supportive friend network. As much as he was sorry that she found out before he actually told her, if he ever would have, he couldn't bring himself to be sorry about what he did.

"Don't listen to that voice, Zoe. Even if I didn't get you that grant you could have figured it out with another loan or something else. Look, I'm sorry. I didn't think it would upset you."

Zoey sighed. "Yeah, you did. Otherwise, you wouldn't have hidden it from me." She pushed off the desk and stood there looking at him quietly for a moment. "I'm gonna go."

Hoping for the best he asked, "Can I have a hug before you go?"

Zoey bit her lip and shook her head. In a whisper she replied, "Not right now. You kind of broke my heart a little. I just need a couple days, okay?"

Derek nodded. "Okay. You know I love ya, kiddo, right?"

"Yeah, I know that." Zoey turned and opened the door to find most of their friends scattering around down the hall in a hurry. "Looks like we won't have to explain this to everyone later."

She found Tyler who was leaning on the hall doorway. "Did you know?"

Tyler looked at her and then Derek. "No. I didn't."

"Good. Can we go home now?"

Tyler kissed her on the top of her head and said, "Of course. I'll grab your purse and be right behind you."

She nodded and walked over to Mia, giving her a hug. "Sorry for ruining your party."

Mia shook her head. "You didn't. And it's still the best party I've ever had."

Derek watched as Tyler gathered Zoey's purse and sweater and then came over to him. "Kind of a big fuck up, you know?"

Derek ran his fingers through his hair. "Yeah, I know. But to be honest I would do it all over again."

"Don't get me wrong, I am so grateful that you did, but it has been years now. You should have been the one to tell her."

"Think she'll forgive me?"

"Yeah. She just will need a few days to cool off. I just don't think I have ever seen her mad at you before."

"She hasn't been. At least not like this."

Derek sullenly looked at the door and sighed. It was going to kill him to give her time, but he could do that. He just hoped he could find the right words when she did.

Chapter 16

Four days. It had been four days since he had his fight with Zoey. Derek was, in the words of Mia, a hot-mess express. His mind could not focus. He nearly fell down the hillside during the run with Kyle this morning. Did Kyle bother to give him a pep talk or maybe some good advice? No, of course not. He didn't even give any advice at all. He just gave a hand to help him up and told him to get his shit together. Yeah, that's helpful.

Now he was punishing his body yet again hitting the punching bag. He was trying to help, and now his best friend wasn't talking to him because of it. Most guys get to grovel with their bodies and giving orgasms, but that had never been an option with Zoey. Maybe he'd get her flowers. Poppy could make a nice arrangement. Wait, were flowers supposed to be for romance? Same for jewelry. Not that she had ever been into that too much either. Maybe he would give her a few more days.

He kept hitting the bag until the music he was listening to abruptly stopped. What the fuck? Turning around to take a look at what happened to the music he nearly jumped out of his skin seeing Ariel standing by the now silent speaker.

"Oh, look, it's my dumb ass brother."

Derek grabbed the towel off the stool and wiped his face. "Oh, look, it's an intruder. Maybe I should call the cops on you for breaking and entering."

"Wow, you *are* in a pissy-ass mood."

"What do you want?"

"I want to smack your head until you come to your senses, but you're all sweaty and gross, so I'll have to settle for some slightly mean words."

"Slightly mean?"

"I still love your dumb ass, so I don't want to crush your soul or anything."

"Thanks."

"You need to apologize to Zoey."

"Don't you think I have tried? She won't talk to me. She isn't even returning my text messages."

Ariel sat down on the stool. "God, guys are so stupid."

"Hey!"

"What? Am I wrong? You messed up. You got caught."

"I was trying to help."

"So am I. We are all worried about you. You take rejection worst out of all of us."

"If you are all worried about me, how is it you are the only one here?"

"I drew the short straw. Literally." She paused and quirked an eyebrow. "At least virtually I did."

"Virtually?"

"Yup. Tyler found this website that lets everyone draw straws. I drew the short straw."

"Thanks for taking on the burden of your brother's misery."

Ariel rolled her eyes. "I was going to talk to you anyway, but this just made it official. I can't have your morning runs turn into some sad cable movie where you fall to your death."

"It wasn't that bad."

She shrugged. "Kyle said he saved your life."

"It was a small decline, not a ravine. He's such a drama queen."

"Doesn't matter. Do you have a plan?"

"I did. I went to her shop to talk to her, and she practically ran away from me. Then I got the stink eye from her assistant."

"Phil?"

"Yeah, Phil."

Ariel tilted her head almost looking sympathetic. Almost. "And it didn't occur to you that maybe she didn't want to talk about it at her work? That maybe you both should talk about it in private and not where the whole town would find out within thirty minutes?"

Derek felt his face flush. Guess that was kind of stupid. "No."

"Okay, so step one. Go to her place. Step two, beg for forgiveness. Women love it when you take accountability."

Derek waited, but she didn't continue. "Is there a step three?"

"Each woman is different. You could bring a gift, but don't make it some weird gift that should only be given by Tyler."

"I figured that out on my own, thanks."

"Aw, you do have a couple brain cells to rub together. Look, you can't go solving everyone else's problems with your money. Life doesn't work that way."

"Mia let me buy back her jewelry for her and she didn't get mad."

Ariel let out an exasperated breath. "She did get annoyed, though. And you have to remember Mia and Zoey come from very different worlds. Mia grew up around money and understands that people who can afford it don't look at it as a big deal to help someone financially, but Zoey comes from the world you and I grew up in."

"And what world was that?"

"Middle class. We didn't struggle paycheck to paycheck, but Mom and Dad didn't overindulge us all the time. Vacations were special and something we saved up for. If we wanted something, Mom and Dad earned it and were proud of what they could do for us. You took that from Zoey. She had already told you that she didn't want your money, so you just went around her and did it anyway."

"Alright. I get your point."

Ariel popped off the stool and went to give him a hug but stopped in her tracks and must have thought better of it. "Nope. You're still gross." She began to leave and turn around again. "I'm sorry I blabbed. I had some wine, and I couldn't stop it. I didn't think about Zoey being there."

Derek nodded. "Thanks, but this is solely on me. I should have told her by now or helped her find another way that didn't come from me."

"Aw... you can learn from your mistakes."

Derek threw his towel at her. "Get the fuck out of here."

"Love ya, big brother," she bellowed as she walked down the hallway.

"Love you too, you little monster."

IT WAS A FEW HOURS later when Derek found himself fidgeting on Zoey's doorstep. *Good God, man. Ring the doorbell, say you're sorry, and get her to forgive you.*

He pushed the button and dying chimes of the doorbell rang throughout the house. He heard footsteps that were obviously not Tyler's and sighed in relief. The door swung open, and Zoey's smile dropped. "Nope." And just as quickly as it opened it shut in Derek's face.

"Zoey, please open the door."

"No."

"I just want to talk. Please."

"No. I'm mad at you."

"I have Diet Coke."

"Don't care about a stupid bottle of Diet Coke."

Oh, she is really pissed. "It's a whole twenty-four pack."

The door swung open, and Zoey held out her hand. Derek handed over the goods and before he could think about taking a step she slammed the door in his face again. "Aw, come on Zoe. Let me in."

No response this time. Just silence. He looked at the door and back to the street. He wasn't leaving until he could talk to her face to face. Sighing, he sat on the steps of the porch and rested his arms on his knees. "I'm not leaving."

An hour later he felt a light droplet of rain fall on his head. At least he hoped that was rain and not some bird giving their opinion about him too. Splat, splat, splat. Yup, rain. That seemed about right. At least he could take cover under the porch.

It appeared that it wasn't going to be a bad storm as light thunder rumbled, but then the rain started drenching him and blowing in sideways. Just as he thought he could handle a little storm, a lightning bolt nearly blinded him and lit up the entire street and the crack of thunder had him scooting closer to the wall. "Holy shit!"

Debating on running for his car the front door suddenly flew open. "Get your ass in here before you get killed."

He scrambled to his feet and sprinted inside. Zoey shut the door shaking her head. "Let me get you a towel."

Derek shook his head and water droplets scattered all around. "No need. I'm all good."

"Yeah, you're freaking wonderful," she said as she disappeared down the hall and returned with a towel.

"I don't need—"

"It's not for you. Wipe up my floor and wall you just got wet."

Derek looked down at the towel and resigned himself to cleaning up his mess. "Sorry."

Zoey stood with her arms crossed. "Uh-huh. You want a drink?"

"A beer would be nice if you have one."

Zoey left and joined Derek as he sat down on the couch. "Thanks for letting me in."

Returning with his drink Zoey's eyes drew down. "I'm mad, but I still care about you. I'd be sad if you got fried by lightning."

"Thanks, I think."

"Plus, Tyler would have to clean up all your bloody bits and he doesn't deserve that."

"And you still love me, right?"

Zoey sat back and pulled her legs under her. "Of course, but do you still not understand?"

"I do, but all I wanted to do was help you."

"Mmm."

"And maybe help myself too. I missed having you around and it seemed like everything had just fallen into place for you to move out here. I didn't want to wait too long, and have it all fall apart and we spend another several years living so far apart. You didn't have a good support system out there, and I knew you would thrive here."

"You lied."

"I did, but it wasn't meant to hurt you."

"Just because you're a bagillionaire doesn't mean you can throw money around to solve all your problems."

Derek frowned. "I'm not a bagillionaire. I'm not even a billionaire."

"How much?"

"What?"

"How much are you worth now?"

Derek played with the label on his bottle, not sure if he wanted to say it now.

"Derek."

"A little over two hundred."

"Million?"

Derek lifted one shoulder up in a shrug. "Yeah. I just kept playing around in the market and then kept buying real estate in town and out. What Josie said is true, when you have money, it just seems to make more."

"And to think you started with just a few thousand your dad gave you for college. I still can't believe you let everyone in town think you are just a simple bar owner."

"They would treat me different if they all knew. Some know I own other rental properties, but figure I am like the Glovers. Small-town rich."

"If I wanted your money, I would have asked."

"I know. I can't undo it now. What can I do to make it better?"

"I can't just pay you back. We don't have the money."

"I don't want you to. I want a niece or nephew to spoil more than money."

Zoey gave a small smile. "You think you still get to have that title?"

Derek bumped his shoulder to hers. "I hope so."

Zoey sighed. "You are teaching sports to the kid. You know I am not coordinated enough for that. And don't tell Tyler, but he is terrible too. I swear you guys let him on the softball team out of pity."

"So mean. It wasn't out of pity."

"No?"

"No. He's Kyle's brother. We didn't have a choice. Alright, lifetime coaching sessions, what else?"

"You will never pay for food at the bakery again."

"Except my wedding cake."

Zoey immediately gasped and smiled. "You're engaged?"

Derek laughed. "Not yet. But I plan on asking soon. She's it, Zoe."

Zoey leaned over and gave him a big hug. "I'm so happy for you!"

For the first time in days Derek felt a weight lift off his chest. They certainly had longer stretches of time where they didn't talk, but never before because of a disagreement. "Thanks."

"When are you going to propose?"

"I want to do it after Ariel's wedding next month. I don't want her to feel like we are taking attention away from her. She deserves the spotlight to be on her."

"That's good. They deserve their fairy tale wedding. Did you see the design for the cake yet?"

"No."

Zoey reached for her phone and thumbed through some pictures until she pulled up a sketch of a gorgeous pale-blue cake with cascading white flowers topped with an elegant castle.

"She keeps changing her mind about the castle. Sometimes she wants a carriage, sometimes the Cinderella couple dancing, then back to the castle."

"I like the castle idea. I've got the carriage taken care of."

Zoey gasped. "You didn't."

Derek lifted one shoulder. "Maybe."

"Oh my God, she is going to freak out. We have a surprise for her at the rehearsal dinner too."

"Really? What?"

"Uh-uh. Not a chance. You are still in the dog house."

"Can I at least be out of the dog house and maybe at the back door?"

"Fine. Just don't lie to me again."

"I can do that."

DEREK STAYED AT ZOEY'S until just after Tyler got home and the storm had moved on. He was looking forward to spending some quality time with Mia. She was working tonight but was on the first-cut rotation so she should be home soon.

Derek looked at the stairs leading up to Mia's apartment but decided to surprise her at the bar instead. He walked directly passed Tiny who said, "Hi, Bossman." Derek gave a wave and kept walking. Tiny laughed. "Bye, Bossman."

Once he opened the door to the dining room, he relaxed hearing her laugh coming from the drink station. She was talking animatedly to Nicole who also seemed to be in a good mood. Not caring who saw him he walked up behind Mia and kissed her neck. "Almost done?"

Mia smiled and slightly tilted her neck to give him more access. "Yeah. Just have one table left."

"Let Nicole finish and come home with me."

Laughing, Mia shook her head. "No. I can't do that to her."

Nicole grabbed a towel and shook her head. "No, please do. I really don't want to see him panting over you the rest of the night. It's gross. Besides, your side jobs are done anyway. Get out of here."

"How about you keep the tip since you will have to clean up after them."

"Nah. I'll put it in the office for you. Just keep this in mind for me one day."

Mia lifted one corner of her mouth. "I can do that."

"Great. Thanks," Derek said as he pulled Mia behind him.

She didn't say a word until they were safely inside her apartment, and he had devoured her mouth for a few minutes.

She ran her fingers through his hair, and he leaned into her touch. "Things went well with Zoey, then?"

"I feel like it could have been better, but honestly the storm helped."

"The storm? How?"

"She wouldn't let me in at first. Then I told her about the Diet Coke, and she opened the door and then slammed it on me again."

Mia covered her mouth as a laugh escaped.

Derek tilted his head at her. "Really? Hit a man when he's down why don't you."

"Sorry. Couldn't help it. Go on."

"Anywayyyy. I sat on the porch for a while hoping she would cave in, and it started to rain. Then I almost got hit by lightning and she had me come inside."

"That's good. I would hate to find another boss to fall in love with me."

Derek tickled her side. "Not funny."

"It's a little funny."

"We had a good talk. We figured out that I'm a moron, she's an amazing friend, and I won't try to interfere and always play the hero."

"Do you think you can stop yourself?"

"I will try. At least with Zoey I will be more conscious about it."

"As a girl who used to have a lot of money, it doesn't always fix everything."

"Maybe not, but you have to admit it does help."

Mia cupped his cheek and gave a devilish grin. "It does, but you know what also fixes a lot of things?"

"What?"

"Orgasms. Lots and lots of orgasms."

"Thank fuck for that."

Chapter 17

The month leading up to Ariel's wedding flew by. It was the night of the rehearsal dinner and Derek was standing next to Tyler at the altar. Ariel was talking to their mom, but the girls were notably late. Mia had been acting weird all day. She did confess that she was in on the surprise for Ariel but wouldn't give him any hints. What good was having a girlfriend if they wouldn't tell you everything?

Just as Derek looked down at his phone the church doors burst open with a commotion from the women entering the church. It took a second, but he recognized the first one through. It was Josie dressed in old lady makeup and some fancy gown. Then following behind her were Dixie and Zoey dressed in ridiculous wigs fighting over a dress. Holy shit. They were the evil step mom and the two stepsisters.

Josie approached Ariel regally barely holding in a smile. "Who said you could come to the party? We only RSVP'd that your sisters would be here."

Ariel's mouth dropped open wide, and she started to laugh. The two "sisters" continued to fight over the gown like toddlers with a toy while Josie lifted her eyebrow that commanded everyone's attention. Getting into character Ariel bowed her head and said, "I'm sorry, Stepmother, I—"

Before she could finish Mia walked in dressed in a blue robe holding a giant wand. "Wait! I am here to grant your wish. Would you like to go to the party?"

Beaming, Ariel nodded. "Yes, please."

"Follow me then for a little magic."

Practically bouncing on her toes, Ariel followed out the doors, with the girls and Mia following close behind. Derek turned around to find Kyle, only he went missing as well. With only a few people left in the church they quietly talked anxiously waiting for everyone to return.

Kyle was the first to join him at the steps of the church altar complete in a prince's uniform.

Derek elbowed him and said, "Nice outfit."

Kyle straightened. "Laugh all you want. I look fucking amazing."

"You would do anything for my sister, wouldn't you?"

Kyle turned his head and smiled. "Wouldn't you for Mia?"

Before he could respond Mia tried to sprint up to the front row as fast as her expanding belly would allow her. He watched her wink as she took her seat.

"I would change the world for her."

Kyle nodded and slapped his hand on Derek's shoulder. "Good. Bout time."

Within a few seconds they were told to take their places. Kyle remained at the altar while the men went back to the front hall to walk the women down the aisle. Hugging Ariel, who was now in a full Cinderella gown, he whispered to her, "So happy for you."

"Hey, save the sappy stuff for tomorrow."

Derek rolled his eyes. "Okay, brat."

"Better."

After what they were calling the Cinderella surprise, they all met for dinner and drinks. Everyone was having a good time and Derek even saw his parents talking like old friends and not like the cautious exes that they had been. It was good to see.

Holding a glass of sparkling cider Mia looped her arm through his. "I don't think I have ever seen your parents together. I mean in the same place at the same time."

Derek lifted one corner of his mouth. "I knew what you meant. To be honest, I can't remember the last time they were either. It's good to see them both moving on in a healthy manner."

"I think the steps you took to mending fences helped with that."

Derek tilted his head, still looking at them talking and also including Miranda in the conversation. "You think so?"

Mia leaned her head on his shoulder. "I do. It had to be hard on your mom to heal when all of your relationships were fractured. Can you imagine our little one hurting and not also hurting inside knowing you can't fix it?"

Derek stepped behind her and wrapped his arms around her resting his hands on her belly. "It would kill me."

Mia tilted her head and exposed her neck. "Ready to go home and take advantage of some raging hormones?"

"Do you still have that costume?"

Giggling, Mia asked, "Yeah, why?"

"Oh, I have some wishes that I need granted."

"Well, let's get going before the clock strikes twelve, and the magic wears off."

Chapter 18

One thing Mia quickly figured out, was that small towns did not equal small weddings. Looking around she thought half the town was at the reception. The wedding had been beautiful, and the incredible glass pumpkin carriage that delivered the bride to the ceremony looked like a fairy tale come true. The happiness between Kyle and Ariel filled the entire room. Mia had gone through several tissues during the ceremony. She blamed the pregnancy hormones for most of that.

Several times, she caught Derek looking at her during the vows and it seemed as if they were having a conversation in front of everyone. Without words he was telling her that he loved her, and this would also be their future someday. At least that is what she hoped he was saying. And hopefully, she was giving an understanding look back and not the weird crazy eyes thing. He made fun of her last week for the crazy eyes thing when she devoured that molten lava cake. But really who could blame her? Chocolate cake, vanilla ice cream, and hot fudge. Heaven on a plate.

Speaking of heaven on a plate, when were they going to serve the cake? She could really use some sugar right about now. Derek placed his hand into hers and stood them up. "Dance with me?"

Mia nodded and allowed Derek to lead them to the dance floor, all the while turning her neck looking longingly at the cake.

Stopping to begin the dance Derek looked over to the cake and back to her. "Really? The cake looks better than me?"

Mia bit her lip to stop her smile. "I never said that."

Now swaying to the music Derek shook his head. "No, but the drool at the corner of your mouth did."

Mia gasped. "I am *not* drooling!"

"Want to sneak into the back and I can give you something to drool over?"

Not wanting the man's ego to take over too much Mia responded, "Why? Do you think they have more cake in the back?"

Derek placed his hand on his heart like he had been stabbed. "You wound me, woman. Give a guy a break."

Laughing, she said, "You got two breaks last night during the wish-granting nonsense. And again this morning to thank you for that amazing breakfast."

"It was amazing, wasn't it?"

"Yes, the food was amazing."

Derek growled and lifted her off her feet. Mia giggled and squirmed. "Okay, okay. You were amazing, too."

Derek set her down and kissed her. "That's better."

"Yup. You were a very close second to the bacon."

She knew that look that was coming over his face and she was going to get carried off to teach her a very fun lesson, but they couldn't do that just yet, so she quickly stepped away and greeted his mom at the table just next to them. "Hi, Amanda. How's it going?"

Derek was slightly shaking his head at her but let it go and kissed her on her cheek. "I'm going to get us some drinks. Mom, do you want anything?"

"No, baby. Go on. We'll just have some girl talk."

Mia watched as he walked away and Amanda said, "You make him happy."

"Huh?"

"Derek, you make him very happy."

Mia smiled. "He makes me very happy, too. What about you? Anybody making you happy?"

Amanda waved her off. "No time for that nonsense. I wanted to focus on having Ariel's wedding and now we have you and the little one coming. That is enough excitement for me."

But just as she finished her statement, Amanda's eyes drifted over to the bar where Tiny was talking to Derek. She also caught Tiny's eyes meet Amanda's and hold for just a little too long. Mia couldn't help it. Maybe just a little nudge. "He looks good all dressed up, doesn't he?"

Amanda let out a barely audible sigh. "Yes, he does." Shaking her head, she smiled. "I mean Derek always looks good in formal wear."

Mia leaned in a little closer. "I wasn't talking about your son."

With the worst cover up Mia had ever heard, Amanda replied, "Oh? I thought you were talking about Derek."

Realizing she only had a minute or two before Derek made his way back with what looked like Tiny in tow, she said, "It would be a good thing to take happiness where you can find it."

Amanda's eyes widened. "I can't—"

She was cut off by Derek handing the glass to Mia. "Take a sip and come back out on the floor with me. You still owe me a dance."

Wanting to nudge a little more she replied, "Only if your mom and Tiny come with us."

Completely oblivious to the world, Derek helped Mia up. "Alright, come on you two what my lady wants she gets."

Tiny tugged at the cuff of his sleeve and extended his hand out to Amanda. "Think you can handle a big lug like me?"

Amanda's face flushed from what Mia was certain was not the wine as she said, "Oh, yeah. I definitely can."

As they danced, Mia watched as Tiny and Amanda moved in a world of their own. She saw him take deep breaths in as he closed his eyes as if he was trying to sear the memory into his brain. She wished that they would act on their obvious feelings for each other, but Amanda needed to take those steps on her own. Not to mention it would be a bit of a mess with Derek being Tiny's boss.

As the dance went on Mia started to melt into Derek's arms as they moved to the rhythm. So much had changed since she'd moved to Blossom Hills. She lost a fiancé, was financially wiped out, got a new job, a baby on the way, found a new wonderful man who loved and supported her, and so many friends it was almost overwhelming.

A couple nights ago she had that recurring nightmare where Jack returned and took the baby away from them. She had jolted upright in bed and was gasping for air. Derek had still been at work. It wasn't uncommon for him to work until one or two o'clock in the morning and her pregnant body wouldn't let her stay up to wait for him. While her brain knew that Jack didn't want the baby, and that he wouldn't come back, her heart continued to have these panic-inducing episodes where she would lose everything again.

The song stopped, and the host announced that they would be cutting the cake. They made their way over just in time to see the knife being pushed down to slice the first piece together. Thankfully, they didn't do the smash and run. She knew Ariel had vocalized her opinion about that tradition and Josie had threatened disembowelment if Kyle didn't comply. A little over the top, but it worked.

Before the cake was passed out, it was time for the garter and bouquet toss. Mia felt a little strange standing out there with only a few other women and several children. The close group of friends she made were all already married. She was pretty sure that Ariel was just going to aim for her, but maybe she could sidestep discreetly out of the way.

Nope. There was no discreet sidestep. That thing came straight at her and she was surrounded by kids who didn't let her move out of the way. Were they in on it? A tiny human conspiracy?

Derek kissed her on the forehead and said, "Well, I guess I better go catch that other thing. No way in hell some other guy is touching your leg."

"So possessive. I love it."

Derek stood amongst the bigger group of men bouncing on his feet like waiting for a fight. Once Kyle was in position, he played with it moving back and forth and Derek making adjustments as needed. With the garter stretched to its max, Kyle let it fly over his head. Everyone stopped and looked around for a second before finally seeing it hooked onto the chandelier at the center of the dance floor.

Derek stood with his hands on his hips shaking his head. Kyle joined him and stared at the elegant light fixture and said, "I think it looks good up there. Maybe we should just leave it."

"Works for me."

The rest of the night was more dancing, laughing, and cake. Maybe a few pieces of cake. But who was counting? As they made their way to the car, Mia frowned. "I left my phone on the table."

"I'll get it. Be right back."

As Derek left Mia saw Tiny loading some gifts into Amanda's car and opening the door for her. She drove off as he stood under the lamp post threading his hands together on the top of his head. Poor guy. She had never really seen this side of him. He never showed any interest in the other women who approached him at the bar, but wow, the emotion that was coming off of him was staggering.

Tiny walked back into the hall just as Derek returned with her phone. "Ready to go home and take off those torture devices you call shoes?"

"They are not torture devices. They are strappy sandals."

"Call them what you want but if you don't take them off soon those poor swollen feet of yours will rip them open."

Mia frown down at her swollen belly. "I blame you for this."

Once they were both in the car, he leaned down towards her stomach and said, "Don't listen to Mommy. You're perfect and nothing is your fault."

"Oh, you're gonna be that dad."

"What dad?"

"You know. Spoiling the kid and being the fun one, while I get to be mean mommy."

"I promise to be the mean one sometimes. Maybe we can rock-paper-scissors it."

"Or just take turns."

"Nah. Where's the fun in that?"

"Just drive."

"Am I in trouble again?"

"Maybe."

"What if I said I grabbed a few extra slices of cake?"

"I would say you are forgiven, and maybe I will share and let you lick some of the frosting off of me when we get home."

MIA FRANTICALLY RAN down the hall to the crib only to find it empty. Where was she? Where was the baby? She could hear crying, but she was nowhere to be found. Seeing the front door open, Mia ran out to the sidewalk in her bare feet where she just saw the back of Tabitha's head putting her baby into the car and Jack getting into the driver's seat.

"No!" She needed to run. She needed to stop them. He took everything away from her once, but this, she would never recover from this. "Stop!" The guttural scream from her lungs caused a pain in her chest. She couldn't breathe.

"Mia! Mia! Wake up."

Mia's eyes flew open as she started sobbing. "He took her. He took her."

Somehow, Derek had her cradled in his arms and was soothing her like a child. It was mortifying, but she couldn't stop crying. And why did it hurt her chest so bad?

"We can't lose her. I can't—"

"We're not going to lose her. It's okay." He was rocking her back and forth and trying to calm her down. Mia clutched her chest and was still having a hard time breathing. She was going to have a full-fledged panic attack if she didn't get it under control.

"Tell me what to do, sweetheart. What can I do to make it better right now? Do you want some water?"

Mia shook her head. "No. Just don't let go of me for right now."

"Okay. You want to tell me about it?"

Knowing she needed to talk about it she finally said, "They take her. They come in the middle of the night while we are sleeping and take her, and I can't stop them." He knew she had some nightmares about this, but they kept increasing in intensity and frequency.

Derek's grip tightened around her. "That will never happen. I won't let anything happen."

"You can't know that."

Derek sighed. "We can take some steps that can help with that."

Mia had thought about that. Dex had offered to track them down if she wanted, but she didn't really care about that. But would Jack care if he found out about the baby? Would searching for them make things worse? There was so much to consider. "Can we talk about it later?"

"Of course. Whenever you are ready."

Chapter 19

Mia stood in front of the mirror standing sideways staring at her protruding stomach. She could have sworn she'd gained a few pounds from the wedding a couple of days ago.

"Mia," Derek called from the living room.

"I know," she bellowed back.

"We are already a week late with the ultrasound, let's not be late to the appointment, too."

"It's not my fault someone hit snooze one too many times."

"Yeah yeah. You ready?"

"No, but let's do this anyway."

They rushed into the car and Derek interlaced his fingers with hers. "Are you worried?"

Mia's mind had been racing all the night before. What if they found something wrong on the ultrasound? The million little things that she doom-searched on the internet ran through her mind. They called it a miracle having a child, but now it seemed like a miracle if nothing went wrong. "Aren't you?"

"About the baby? No. About you, yes."

"Why me?"

"You're not getting enough sleep. I know the nightmares have been coming a lot lately."

Mia sighed. "Yeah, they have, but it is just the hormones messing with me. Hopefully they will resolve themselves soon."

"Do we need to do something to make them better?"

She knew what he meant. He wanted to at least find out where Jack and Tabitha were. At least then they would know they were far away, or if they were close and should be taking precautions. "Let's just get through this week and then make a decision."

Derek brought her hand up for a kiss. "Okay. But if you change your mind, I can have Grayson and Dex get right on it."

As they entered the doctor's office, they were greeted by an older woman whose cat-eye glasses were nearly falling off of her nose. "Name?"

"Mia Voltaire."

The woman typed into her computer and nodded. "Thank you for filling out your paperwork online. Just the two of you today?"

Mia scrunched her face in confusion. "Yes? People bring more?"

"Honey, last week we had twelve people pushing each other trying to get the best view. We get all kinds, grandparents, aunts, uncles, siblings, friends. I just need to know if I need to send you to the big room or not."

Derek smiled. "I could make a few calls, and I could fill up the big room."

The older woman glared at him. "Nobody likes a smart ass. Smart asses somehow get locked out of the room. Are you a smart ass?"

Mia was trying not to laugh as Derek's eyes widened. "No, ma'am."

"Are you going to be a problem?"

Derek cleared his throat. "No, ma'am."

"Good. Now go sit down until we call you back."

Mia braced herself on the armrests while she lowered herself to the seat. Derek followed shortly and whispered, "Suddenly I am missing my grandma."

"I bet you were a challenge."

"Never. I was the perfect child. Grandma just didn't let me get away with anything. She loved me but also took no shit."

Mia fidgeted trying to get comfortable but ended up just leaning forward to allow Derek to rub her back. Just as she started to relax, a younger woman in scrubs called her name. Within a few minutes she was lying on the examination table feeling the cold gel covering her stomach.

The first moment of relief came when the sound of the heartbeat burst from the speaker. Derek's hand tightened in hers as the screen cleared and showed the profile of the baby. It was amazing. You could clearly see the outline of the head and body.

She heard the technician taking pictures and measurements, and once she stopped, she asked, "We wanted to find out the sex, correct?"

Mia nodded, but Derek quickly spoke up. "Yes, but the results are going to Sweet Dreams Bakery, and only to Phil, not to the owner, Zoey."

The tech reviewed their chart and nodded. "Okay."

Mia noticed her confusion and clarified. "The owner is his best friend, and she wanted to find out with us tonight at dinner. Phil is her assistant."

The woman smiled. "Ah. That makes more sense then. I have worked with Zoey several times for these."

She moved the wand around a few more times and continued with measurements before wiping the gel off of her stomach. As she walked out, she explained that the doctor would be calling with results and that the pictures and video could be picked up as they checked out.

Derek helped Mia off the table and let out a long breath. "That went so fast. It is like all this build up to the appointment and then boom, all done."

Mia looked at the door. "Did she look worried to you? Do you think she saw something bad?"

Derek lifted her chin to look at him. "No. She didn't look worried. Everything is going to be fine, and we get to find out if we are having a boy or girl."

"I hope it's a girl."

"Why?"

"I'm not so sure I could handle a boy who ends up like a mini you."

"Are you kidding? That would be awesome. Think of all the things I could teach him."

"Yeah, after hearing all the stories around town, that's what I'm afraid of."

AFTER WHAT SEEMED LIKE the longest seven hours in his life, Derek was surrounded by family and friends at his house. The original plan was to have dinner first, but Mia couldn't wait any longer. The second the last person arrived she was bouncing on her feet to get started.

Derek held the champagne glass in his hand and Mia had hers. A voice came from his mom's phone. "Mom! Point the phone down. I can only see the top of their heads." It was Ariel. She and Kyle were still enjoying their honeymoon, but didn't want to miss the big reveal.

When Derek told Chase they'd decided to do the blue or pink cake, he had let out a big sigh of relief. "Hey, it's not about the food this time. These gender reveal parties are getting out of hand. Remember last month with the fireworks and backyard fire? Or what about when that Great Dane freaked out from the blue powder and knocked three people over running away? Cake. Cake is safe."

Derek wasn't quite sure what he was hoping for. A little version of Mia all adorable and sweet, but he would have to kill all the overly hormonal teenage boys. Or maybe a boy, all energetic and causing mayhem? Cause let's face it, he was going to be a bit of a bad influence.

Shaking him from his thoughts Mia asked, "Ready?"

Derek nodded and their glasses made it to the bottom. They looked at each other and pulled them away at the same time. He heard the cheers before he even registered the pink color. It was a girl. Holy fuck, it was a girl. As soon as his brain caught up, he turned to Mia and picked her up in a bear hug. Her feet were lifted in the air and he just kept hugging her slightly swaying back and forth. Finally, he whispered, "It's a girl."

He heard her laugh. "Told you so."

Once he put her down, he was surrounded in well wishes and congratulations. He talked to Ariel and Kyle for a couple minutes before they left the call to return to their beach paradise. Kyle had mentioned something about knocking up his sister on the trip, and Derek quickly ended the call.

After dinner was over Zoey and Tyler left first since she had to get up early to open the bakery. As he gave her a hug when she was leaving, he said, "It's going to happen for you too, you know."

Zoey's eyes misted over, and she gave a small smile. "I hope you're right."

"Hey, have I ever steered you wrong before?"

Having the effect he had hoped for she laughed. "Oh, so many times."

All the women were in the living room animatedly talking about babies and stories of pregnancies, with Josie declaring that she'd had it; she had no intentions of wrecking her body for more kids. She had taken guardianship of her siblings' children after they died, and she would tell anyone that would listen that four kids were more than enough. Grayson always seemed to agree with that. With the youngest still wearing diapers it was enough for them.

He was standing with Chase and Grayson as they all watched the women. Chase asked, "You ready for this?"

Derek huffed. "No, but I want this. Even though I know that baby girl isn't biologically mine, I know that she will be mine in every way that matters."

Grayson nodded. "It's kind of funny how that works. Those kids and Josie are my world. The baby will only know me and Josie. The twins and Jessica actually sat us down one day and told us it would be okay if the baby called us Mom and Dad."

Derek looked over at Josie who was laughing and drinking a glass of wine. "Wow, that's huge."

"Yeah. The twins will probably always call us Aunt Josie and Uncle Grayson. Jessica seems torn, though. She still has such clear memories of her parents, but she thinks of us as Mom and Dad, too. She accidentally called Josie Mom one day. Josie stood so still not wanting to make her feel bad, but also partially loving it. It just hurt to see the guilt come over their faces when Jessica slowly corrected to Aunt Josie."

"Damn. That has to be hard."

"It is. But we have left it up to them how to address us. They understand that we are their parents, but at the same time not the same as Mom and Dad. Have the two of you discussed what you would tell the baby?"

Derek peeled the label on the beer bottle. "Not yet. I know we need to, but things have been moving at the speed of light. I want to be the only dad the baby ever knows about, but it doesn't feel right lying to her either."

"I don't think you have to start out saying the whole story. Maybe that Mom was with someone else before she met you and gave the gift of her, but he didn't love her the way you do, and he left before they were born."

"Not bad."

Chase laughed. "Definitely better than the dickhead stole everything and ran away with his fake sister."

Derek shook his head. "Yeah, that little truth nugget would not go over well."

Chase nodded over to Mia. "Seriously, though, how is she doing? Pregnancy going well?"

"Yeah. She is healthy and all the tests keep coming back good. She is just tired all the time."

"Dixie had that too. She fell asleep one time while we were having dinner. One minute she was talking about a wedding that she did earlier that day and then plop! Head first into the pasta."

"Oh, shit."

"She was so mad at me for not catching her. But seriously there was no warning. She just went lights out mid-sentence."

"Well, thankfully, Mia hasn't done anything like that, but those damn nightmares are waking her up every night now."

Grayson frowned. "Is she worried about the baby?"

Derek lifted one shoulder. "Kind of. She has nightmares that her ex and his sister/girlfriend keep stealing the baby. The more she worries about it, the more I worry about it."

"I get it. You not only have to worry about the kidnapping aspect but also the possible legal aspects, too."

Legal? Derek never thought about that. There was no way some judge would grant custody to a thief or probably even visitation. "I don't think the legal part will be an issue."

"It never occurred to us either, but since the family had money, it became an issue."

Chase's eyes drew down. "Did I hear that Jack didn't have any family?"

Derek nodded. "None. Both him and his 'sister' came from foster care."

"Then you should be good to go. He's gotta know that if he shows his face, he will get arrested."

Derek sighed. "I just wish I knew where he was. I would feel better if I knew he was hiding on some Bahamian beach drinking cocktails instead of somewhere close."

"Do you want me to get Dex back on the case?" Grayson asked.

"Maybe. Mia and I were supposed to talk about it, but things have been crazy, and we keep putting it off."

"Just let me know. I think it would put some things at ease if you knew where they were."

LATER THAT NIGHT MIA stood under the hot spray of the shower wanting to relax before going to bed. A few minutes later she heard the door open, and she saw the shadowy figure of Derek taking off his clothes on the other side of the curtain.

"I'm almost done."

The curtain moved aside, and a very naked and aroused Derek joined her. "I came to help."

"To help?"

"Yeah. I can help to wash some of those hard-to-reach places." He wrapped his arms around her from behind and kissed her neck.

"This is not cleaning anything."

"No?" he asked as his hands skimmed lower past her belly to her clit that was throbbing in need.

"No, but maybe... uh... maybe." She wanted to continue but words were escaping her as she leaned against him and his fingers moved in a circle and his other hand found her breast.

Derek's erection grew as she felt it move ever so slightly up and down just above her ass. Her body was so revved up for him. The water was hot, and his touch made her skin tingle. The mix of the two was utter perfection.

As she began to relax Derek thrusted two fingers inside and she let out a sharp gasp.

"That's it, baby. Let go for me. Let your mind clear until all you can do is feel me. No worries, no nightmares. Just you and me. Can you do that, sweetheart?"

She would do anything for this man. Especially at this moment when he had her on the brink of an explosion of tiny nerves in her body. Her hands reached for something to brace herself on. She needed something to keep her from falling over.

He seemed to understand what she was doing, and he switched her around to face him. His lips took hers and tangled while his fingers found their way inside of her again.

She must have cried out his name several times and each time she did he thrust harder and made sure the palm of his hand was hitting her clit. He did as he promised though. She wasn't thinking about anything else. Just the pleasure that he was giving her.

As she finished her climax, he lifted her and growled, "Wrap those fucking legs around me."

If the extra weight she'd put on bothered him, he didn't show it. The amount of strength he had while she wrapped around him was sexy as hell. He backed them up to the tile wall and shifted her until she felt him enter her.

She felt his muscles tighten as he slowly moved in and out of her. With each pull she was eager to move back and get him even deeper. The sounds of their two bodies meeting each other echoed through the room. It only served to make her want more. Her nails dug in on his back and she gave a light bite on his shoulder.

Derek groaned. "That's right, baby. Mark me. Make me yours."

Oh, they were definitely going to have to explore some vampire werewolf play later. But instead of biting again and possibly drawing blood, she tightened her arms around him and whispered, "Harder."

And did that man obey. Her whole body bounced as he thrusted in and out. She felt her walls begin to tighten just as he released inside of her. Her whole body was still rhythmically moving as he was slowing down. When she finally stopped, he pulled out and gently let her down.

Derek cupped her face and kissed her. "You good?"

Mia smiled. "Yeah, but I got dirty again."

Derek reached for the loofah on the hook and said, "I can fix that."

Chapter 20

It had been a couple weeks since the gender reveal, and things had been going really well. Mia had her first few sales on her website for her knitted monsters, and she was setting up at her first farmer's market in Willow Springs. The paperwork to get the business started and learning the ins and outs about sales tax, accounting, and rules at events like these were a nightmare, but she was proud of what she was able to put together.

Her booth was a simple ten-by-ten white canopy tent with a few tables set around the edges and little shelves to display the creations she brought with her. A few other vendors stopped by to welcome the obvious newbie. For the most part they were very kind and offered to help or answer any questions she might have. She wished that she would have met them before she watched over a hundred hours of how-to videos on line. So many of them said the same things but never everything she needed to know.

Derek was there to help her today with set up and sales. She had practiced setting up a few times in Derek's garage so she could take pictures and work out the kinks ahead of time. She was super grateful for that tip from one of the videos she'd watched.

Looking up at the sky Derek said, "Looks like the weather is going to stay nice for the day."

"I know. I am so glad we decided on this week instead of last week."

"Yeah. I had enough rain when I was sitting on Zoey's porch."

"They have that fertilization appointment this week, right?"

"Yup, Thursday. Zoey is a wreck. They say this is the last time. I don't know though. They both want this so bad, and I know Kyle has offered to help if it is only because of the money."

"Did you offer too?"

"I did in the beginning, but she insisted they had this. I think if they needed help, they would feel more comfortable letting Kyle help."

"I didn't realize he had that kind of money."

"He doesn't have obscene money. More like upper middle-class money. Ten or twenty thousand wouldn't put a strain on him, but he couldn't do it too often. He made good money while he was in Philadelphia and lived like a poor person. I can't tell you how many times I would call him and ask what he was doing, and he would tell me watching TV and eating ramen noodles. He won some journalism award once that came with a two-hundred-thousand-dollar prize."

"Wow. What made him come back here?"

"The constant violence. And my sister. But he covered the major stories out there and it just became too overwhelming. He told me once that it was causing depression, and he was worried he wouldn't recover."

Mia placed the last display up and stood back to take a look at her finished set up. "What do you think?"

Derek stood alongside her and nodded. "I think it looks great. Just remember to make eye contact and smile. No hiding in your comfy shell."

Mia sighed. "I know. Friendly people sell stuff. Shy people get avoided."

He kissed her temple. "You're gonna be great. Do you want me to get you some muffins from the bakery stand?"

"Yes, please. And maybe some juice."

"You got it."

Before Derek could return Mia had already had her first sale. She sold a pink glitter monster holding a purple purse. The little girl who got it had squealed in delight when she saw that they had matching purses. While she had sold some of her creations online, this was so much more special. She got to see the smile on her face when she first saw it, and the happiness of taking it home.

Mia loved the market. She met so many new people and nearly everyone had something positive to say about her booth. There were some people who whispered that they could do this too and make it cheaper, but mostly people complimented her. People were patient when there were lines, and it was just a different vibe than shopping at the mall.

Derek had just relieved her a few minutes ago for one of her many potty trips, but he was just down the lane talking to the sauce guys. What was it with men and sauces? Derek must have had twenty different sauces between the opened ones in the fridge and the others in the pantry. Making chicken? There was a special sauce for that. Making chicken but smoking it? Well, that had to have a different sauce. The whole thing mystified her. Just slap on some butter, salt, and pepper and it's good to go.

It was one of the rare times that she didn't have anyone to attend to and she looked around at the other booths and people that she could see. Something caught her eye though. At the end of the lane was a woman with a ponytail through her baseball hat and large sunglasses. She caught the woman barely looking at the merchandise at the booth she was standing by, but instead she kept looking down the way at her. She almost looked like Tabitha for a minute. But it couldn't be. She wouldn't dare.

She might though. Mia squinted her eyes to try and get a better look, but people walked past and blocked her view and then the woman was gone. Mia moved to the end of her booth and looked around wanting to get a second look but nothing, she completely disappeared.

Derek's voice broke through her thoughts, "Look! I got five new flavors."

Mia shook her head. She was being paranoid. They were both long gone. "Really? There are flavors out there you haven't bought already?"

"Sooo many flavors. These guys are from Texas. They are traveling across the states and trying to sell to all forty-eight states."

"What, no Hawaii and Alaska?"

"Right? That's what I said."

"Lazy."

"Downright a travesty."

"Chase and Tyler are wandering around somewhere. I saw them at the funnel cake stand."

"Oooo funnel cakes."

Derek gave a devilish grin. "How is your appetite today?"

"Like my stomach is the ultimate black hole. Why?"

"The local bar is having a hot wing challenge in a few hours. Chase was talking about going. Think you could take him?"

"I will leave the power eating to the big guy."

"There's a five-hundred-dollar prize to the person who can eat thirty the fastest."

Mia's head perked up. Five hundred dollars that she earned on her own and not a handout. "Guess he better be happy with second place."

HOLY SHIT, MIA WAS not kidding. There were six people including Mia on the stage normally reserved for the band and she was inhaling those wings. Some frat guy couldn't handle the spice after three wings and dove for the milk.

A couple other guys were trying to keep pace with Chase, but Mia was sucking the meat clean off the bone like some predator in a cartoon. Chase kept looking over at her half in shock. He had sweat coming off his forehead, but she was chewing like it was a normal lunch for her.

A loud retching sound came from the guy at the end. Another one bit the dust. Mia only had three left; Chase had four maybe five. The cheers came louder, and Derek joined in. "Come on, baby, you got this!"

Mia turned her head to look at the competition and clean off another wing. She was going to have such bad heartburn later.

"Mia! Mia! Mia!" Tyler and Derek started chanting with a few others next to them joining in.

And with a triumphant hand in the air and the other finishing the last wing Mia stood up. The official came over and looked at her mouth, then declared her the winner. The other men put down their last wings and quickly downed the glasses of milk.

Derek half sprinted to her with a wide smile. "You did it!"

"That was fun!"

Looking over at Chase, Derek laughed. The man was sitting extended in the chair looking up at the ceiling. "I think you broke Chase."

Chase groaned while he said, "I lost... to a girl... at a food competition."

Mia put her hand on his shoulder. "To be fair, you lost to two girls. The baby was hungry."

"I want a rematch."

"I don't think now is a good idea."

Chase rolled his eyes. "I want a rematch after the baby is born."

"I don't think I can do that while I am not pregnant."

Chase pointed a finger at her. "Exactly. I need redemption."

Mia held out her hand. "Okay, one year from now at McKenna's."

Chase shook her hand excitedly. "Done. You're going down."

The bar owner greeted them, handed over the check, and asked if she would pose for a picture for their social media. He watched as his girl went back to the stage and posed proudly with the small chicken wing trophy in one hand and the check in the other. She looked so happy it made his chest hurt. It wasn't that long ago she was sitting on a pickle bucket on the balcony in her wedding dress with a tear-streaked face. Maybe someday soon he would see her in another wedding dress and this time there would be a smile on her face.

A short time later they were both sitting on the couch cuddled together watching some movie about a woman being stalked by a murderer. Probably not the best choice with her nightmares but it didn't occur to him until it was too late, and the movie had started.

There was a scene where the women felt like she was being watched and caught a glimpse of someone in a crowd, but they disappeared before she could approach them. Mia played with his fingers laced in hers before she spoke. "I had that happen today."

Derek turned his head to look at her. "Had what happen?"

"I saw a woman watching me at the market. She looked like Tabitha, but when I tried to get a better look, she was gone."

Derek frantically looked for the remote and paused the movie. "What? Why didn't you say something?"

Mia sighed and faced him. "It probably wasn't her. It was probably some woman who just looked like her. She had her hair in a ponytail with a hat and had on large sunglasses."

"Yeah, cause that's not suspicious."

"By itself it really isn't. So many women wore the same thing today, but I couldn't help this nagging feeling that I was being watched. She was way down at the other end, but she kept looking at me and not the other booths that were close by. I tried to get a better look but then she was gone."

"I wish you would have told me then."

"I know, but I'm pretty sure it was just my hormones making me paranoid. I mean, why would they risk coming around here? They have to know I filed a police report."

"When people are desperate, they don't always think straight. Can we talk about hiring Dex now? I think It would put our minds at ease if we knew where they were."

"That's a lot of money."

Derek lifted her chin to look at him. "Please let me take care of this. This isn't about just you anymore. We have that sweet baby girl to think about too."

"What if I am just being crazy and they are living it up out of the country?"

"Then we leave them alone. Let them live their life and we live ours, but if they are here in the states, we call the police and let them go to jail."

"Okay. Go ahead and set it up tomorrow."

Derek kissed her temple. "Thank you. It was killing me not stepping in and taking over."

"I'm so proud of you. You're learning."

"Nobody ever told me how much personal growth could hurt."

IN THE MORNING DEREK drove out to Compass Securities to talk to Grayson and Dex. Mia had changed her mind what seemed like dozens of times about going. Every time she convinced herself to go, she felt nauseous and started to get dizzy. He finally convinced her to rest and knit some more monsters to replenish her stock after the market yesterday.

Walking into the front office he saw the two men already drinking coffee out of the crappy secondhand mugs Grayson kept there. Thinking that some coffee wouldn't be a bad idea he nodded over to the pot and asked, "Mind if I get some, too?"

"Go ahead. You get the mug of shame."

It only took a minute to realize what he was talking about. The only mug left was a pink glitter monstrosity that said, "I'm a Pretty-Pretty Princess." Derek poured the coffee and added the flavored creamer to overpower the cheap grocery coffee. Taking his first sip, he grimaced. "Is this supposed to dissolve the lining of my stomach?"

Dex raised his mug. "Puts hair on your chest."

Grayson laughed. "He waxes that shit off."

Derek glared.

Not being intimidated he just smiled. "Come on, man. We've played basketball together. Ain't no way your chest is that pretty without help."

"Shut up, fucker." There was no way he was going over his grooming habits with these assholes.

"Alright, fine. Let's go over what you need."

"We want to know where Jack and Tabitha are. I want to know what their intentions are. If they are living it up and are far away or if they are a little too close for comfort and might think about coming back for more."

Dex furrowed his brow. "They already took everything that poor girl had. What good would coming back do?"

"A lot, actually," Derek replied. "Mia is pregnant with Jack's baby, and she is with me."

Dex nodded. "Okay, the baby could definitely be cause for alarm, but I don't think the local bar owner is much to come back for."

Grayson extended his hand. "Tell him."

"I am a little more than just a bar owner."

"Aw, fuck. How much more?"

"I have a lot of properties in the state, lots of stocks, and other investments."

"Give me a ball park. A couple million?"

Derek grimaced. "Add a couple zeroes."

"Fuck a damn duck. Is everyone around here swimming in money?"

"Just Josie and him for the most part," Grayson said.

Dex's hand moved quick as he took some notes. "Is there anything new I should know about since we did the field trip to the pawn shops?"

Derek explained to the two men about how Mia thought she saw Tabitha at the market, and how she was having nightmares about the baby being taken away.

"So, what is our end goal at this point?" Dex asked.

"Honestly, I just want Mia safe. If that means they are far away with no intentions of returning, fine. If it seems like they might return to make trouble let the wheels of justice turn. And if that happens, I want to take the steps needed to terminate his rights. Mia doesn't want him in the baby's life, and I don't want to go through what you and Josie did," he said nodding towards Grayson.

"That's fair. That was a fucking nightmare."

"What if it takes some money to get that paperwork signed?"

"Whatever it takes. Mia will balk at first, but I think she'll agree. I can talk to her if it comes to that."

Derek pulled out a piece of paper from his pocket. "This is a list of places that Jack and Tabitha used to talk about for dream vacations. We thought this might give you a place to start."

Looking over the list Dex whistled. "Wow, that's a lot of beaches."

"She put a star by the ones she thought were most likely."

"Alright. Guess I should get packing."

Laughing, Grayson said, "Yeah don't forget that sunscreen for that bald ass head of yours."

"Keep laughing. I am going to dig my toes into the sand while you change diapers."

Later that night Derek was working behind the bar, and Mia was serving a lighter-than-normal crowd. He had discussed what the men had gone over earlier. This might take some time and patience. Their trail was pretty cold, but not impossible. Dex was going to check with the local hotels and B&Bs since she thought she saw Tabitha. He decided earlier that day that he would match their schedules together from now on until things got resolved. Why take any chances?

The singer/guitar player they had earlier at the bar tonight was packing up his gear when a man in a flannel shirt and dirty jeans approached and took the microphone. Mia stood by Derek while they both watched in morbid curiosity. The woman sitting in the booth where he came from covered her eyes in obvious dread of what was going to happen next.

The man cleared his throat and continued bold as could be. "Babe!" She didn't look at him, so he continued. "Babe! Look at me."

She must have decided to give in because she slowly removed her fingers and looked at him with her face flushing bright red. Satisfied with her attention, he dug around in his front pocket and pulled out something small, holding it out between his forefinger and thumb pointed towards her. "Babe, let's get hitched!"

Derek and Mia looked back and forth between the two. "Oh, no," Mia whispered.

Derek studied the woman whose facial features did not match those of a happy woman. Nope, that was disappointment. "She's gonna run."

Everyone in the bar seemed to be focused on the couple wondering what would come next. The slightly drunken Romeo continued, "Babe, come on up here."

Derek saw the woman's lower lip quiver and sure enough she stood, grabbed her purse and sprinted out the front door.

The man dropped the microphone and decided to chase after her.

Mia sighed. "Well, there goes my tip."

"We were so close."

"So close to what?"

"The record for the longest time between train-wreck proposals."

"What's the record?"

"Six months and five days. I think this was month five."

"Just do me a favor, okay?"

"Anything."

"If you ever decide to propose, make it better than that. Not over the top, but please better than that."

Derek leaned over the bar and Mia met him halfway. He gave her a quick kiss and replied, "I promise."

After they had closed and everyone had gone home but them, Derek poured a virgin cocktail for Mia and himself a beer. They sat on the stools of the bar and raised their glasses.

"To never having a dull moment."

Mia laughed. "Today was that for sure."

"Do you think she forgave him?"

"Who, Romeo and Juliet?"

"Yes."

Derek thought for a minute. "I would like to think so. She seemed like she was disappointed. Like she loved him but wanted more than what she got for a proposal."

"There have been a lot of bad proposals here?"

"We have had our fair share. One guy threw up while he was on one knee."

"Oh, no."

"Oh, yeah. Another guy had planned this whole ring in the dessert thing, but he saw a text from his best friend on her phone flash across her screen asking when she was coming over that night."

"Ouch."

"Yeah. We all felt bad for the guy. She tried to deny it, but someone else was here that knew them and just confirmed what he saw. It was a whole thing. Cat fight between the girls broke out and Nicole was the one who broke it up."

"I can believe that. She is kind of scrappy."

"She's really scrappy. Her wife has calmed her down a lot."

"I heard they got approved for their adoption application."

"They did. They are hoping for a baby, but honestly, I think they would be happy with any younger one."

"Did they ever talk about getting a sperm donor?"

"They did. Nicole would have given them the best shot, but she wanted a baby that was part of both of them and if they couldn't have that they wanted to give someone already here a chance."

"I knew a couple who had one carry the baby and used the sperm of the other one's brother, so they still had a biological connection."

"I wonder how they'll handle explaining parentage to the child as they get older."

Mia grew silent and wobbled her glass on the bar top. "Do you worry about that with us?"

Derek shrugged. "A little. I don't feel right lying and saying that I am biologically their dad, but I don't know what kind of impact it would have letting them know that their dad was a criminal."

"I agree about the lying part, but how old is too old to keep that secret from them?"

"What if we made it into a fairy tale what we could tell her at night?"

"What do you mean?"

Derek spun her barstool and interlocked his legs with hers. "I mean, once upon a time there was this beautiful princess who lived in a castle with her grandpa in a magical land."

"That's a very good start to the story."

Derek put his fingers to her lips. "Then let me tell it. Anyway... the princess and her grandpa were very happy together and loved to play games and tell stories each night. But one night the grandpa started to get sick, and this man came to help take care of the grandpa. He seemed like a very nice man and soon the princess started to fall in love with the man. Everything was perfect, but what the princess didn't know was that the man only wanted her for her gold."

Mia laughed. "Oh, no, what happened next?"

"Well, the man introduced her to his sister, and made it seem like they would be one big happy family. This made the princess very happy since the doctors told her that her grandpa may die soon."

"The poor princess."

"Exactly. The poor princess eventually lost her grandpa, but she was going to marry the nice man and start a new family. What the princess didn't know was that her fiancé was actually an evil warlock, and the sister was actually his sorceress girlfriend who was going to help steal everything the princess had."

Derek moved a stray section of Mia's hair and put it behind her ear. "Then on the day of her wedding the evil warlock made all her riches and belongings disappear, and the princess was so sad. Here it was on her wedding day, and she was at her new small home she'd picked out for the two of them and had even managed to get locked out. She had no money, no possessions, just a broken heart."

Mia leaned in close. "I'm on the edge of my seat. What happened next?"

"What the princess didn't know was that she did get the family she always wanted because she was pregnant with a sweet baby girl, who she knew she would love with all her heart. But while she was locked out of her new house, she met the duke who owned the tavern next door. And the duke was instantly in love with her at first sight, tears and all. She was the most beautiful woman he had ever seen, and he knew that he would do anything to ensure she never cried tears of sadness again. He gave the princess a job and became the best of friends with her. Eventually, they found some of her possessions that were guarded by the trolls and started falling in love. It wasn't long after, they found out about the baby and he vowed to love her forever. The duke knew what he had to do. One night after the tavern closed, he dropped to one knee and said…" Derek couldn't believe he was going to do it like this, but the moment was so perfect he wasn't going to let it go by.

Dropping to one knee he looked up into her eyes. "Mia, I didn't plan to do this today, or here, or without the ring, but right now feels right and if I don't ask you to make you mine this very second, I'll regret it for the rest of my life."

Mia's eyes were misting over, and she was biting her lower lip in an attempt not to cry as he continued, "I didn't see you coming. You told me about how your grandparents' relationship was written in the stars, and with each day I can't help but to feel like we were too. So much had to happen to find our way to each other, and if you let me, I will show you every day of our lives that we were meant to be."

Tears were streaming down her face as she nodded her head.

"Wait. I haven't asked you yet."

She gave him a little smile and whispered. "Sorry."

"Mia, will you marry me?"

Jumping off the stool Mia wrapped her arms around him and said, "Yes!"

They kissed passionately with Derek's hands delving through her thick hair and Mia trying to climb him like a tree.

"Can we go home now? I really need to reward you for that amazing proposal," she asked.

"Fuck, yes," he replied as he carried her to the back towards the door.

Chapter 21

Mia woke up and stared at the sparkling ring on her finger. It had been only two days since the proposal, and they had both been hiding out at Derek's house. She had a doctor's appointment yesterday and had been given the good news about the latest test results. The pregnancy was moving along perfectly, and she could feel movements almost regularly now.

Derek came into the room gloriously half naked and wet with a towel wrapped around his waist. "You better get ready. We already did breakfast in bed. We can't do lunch, too."

"But I am happy in our little bedroom cocoon."

He gave her a small kiss. "Rise and shine, butterfly. We have lunch with Mom. If she finds out about the engagement from gossip before we tell her first, she might kill me."

"Drama queen."

"Nope. Just telling it like it is." Derek held out his hand to her to help her off the bed. "Come on."

"Just know I am physically going but my brain is still burrowed under the covers."

"I'll take it. Now move your cute butt."

Within the hour they were pulling into his mom's driveway. Mia clutched the flowers they got for his mom like a lifeline. Why was she so nervous all of a sudden? Amanda had been nothing but kind and accepting since they met. Would she think this was too fast? Was she hoping for something better for her son?

Derek must have noticed her increasing anxiety since he placed his hand over hers holding the flower pot. "You okay?"

"Yes," she said with a squeak.

"It's going to be fine. This is happy news."

"I know, but what if she wants us to wait? What if she thinks it is too fast?"

"You have nothing to worry about. She was more worried about me being single the rest of my life. Trust me. She would order the judge to come over today if that is what we wanted."

Mia shouldn't have worried. As soon as they told her the news, she cried happy tears and just about squeezed the life out of her in a hug. "When do you want to get married? Before or after the baby?"

Derek entwined his fingers into hers and confidently said, "Before. We wanted to ask you if we could just do a small ceremony here."

Amanda tilted her head. "Of course, but you don't want a big wedding?"

"Not really. Ariel had her big fairy tale wedding, and all I care about is whatever makes Mia happy."

Mia nodded. "I don't have any family or really friends from before I moved here. I will invite my parents of course, but they haven't really had interest in my life since I was young."

Amanda reached across the chair to the sofa where Mia was and clasped her hand. "Well, you have a mom now who loves you very much."

Mia's lip quivered, and while she wanted to say so much more all she could muster was, "Thanks."

Amanda cleared her throat and continued. "Okay, so timing. What are we looking at?"

"A month, maybe a month and a half."

"That should give us time to get everything in place and for me to find a dress. While I don't want a big wedding, I still want a beautiful dress and finding the right one while pregnant may take some time to find and alter appropriately."

Amanda thought for a moment and said, "One of the seniors that comes to the center used to be a seamstress. She still does alterations here and there and I bet she would be happy to help, maybe even make a new dress of your dreams."

"That would be amazing. I downloaded some pictures from the internet this weekend of dresses I liked that worked around pregnancy."

"Okay. How many people should we expect?"

Derek winced slightly. "I was thinking maybe around thirty. That keeps it to just a core group friends and family."

Amanda waved her hand in the air. "Thirty is easy. We used to have larger parties than that when you kids were little."

"Great. Tiny is going to be pulling double duty with food and guest. Same for Zoey with the cake and Dixie with pictures. We were thinking a Thursday night so not to interfere with the tourist weddings for Zoey and Dixie."

"Good idea. Have you told everyone yet?"

"Nope. You're the first."

"Look at my smart little boy."

Derek looked to Mia. "See, I told you she would kill me."

Amanda looked confused so Mia clarified, "He said you would kill him if you found out from someone else first."

"He's not wrong."

It was surprising just how quick things got moving after they told everyone else that same day. After Amanda, Derek called his dad to give him the news. When Mia asked why they didn't tell him in person, he just shrugged and said, "A phone call is good enough. Men don't need the in-person treatment."

Mia gave a mental eye roll. She may disagree, but from her understanding this was still good progress for them, and from the parts she could hear on the phone his dad didn't seem to mind and was genuinely happy for Derek.

That night they met up with his friends at the bar where he just dropped the news without warning at the table once everyone was there. "Mia and I are getting married."

It took a second or two for the news to sink in, but once it did, they burst through with excitement and congratulations. The dinner was filled with talk of the wedding and logistical ideas that aligned with everyone's schedule. Ultimately, they decided on having it in seven weeks. This would put Mia at about thirty-two weeks into her pregnancy and it was her hope that she would still be comfortable enough to enjoy it.

The men and Zoey had drifted over to the pool table leaving Mia with Josie, Ariel, and Dixie. Mia looked at Dixie and said, "I wanted to thank you for letting Molly use the equipment to take the pictures for the website."

"Oh, no problem. I'm just thrilled it helps her develop as a professional photographer outside of the weddings she helps me with. I want her to have some exposure to all aspects. Even though there is plenty of work to be done here as a wedding photographer, I want her to know that there are other options."

Josie laughed. "Oh, yeah, there is always picture day at school."

Dixie groaned. "You have no idea how happy I was to pass that off to someone else since I am busy enough at the studio. I kind of felt like the DMV lady just lining them up behind some horrid backdrop and taking five seconds with each kid."

"And why can't the schools just cancel gym that day? I sent the munchkin over with perfectly adorable hair in curls, and they decided she would be first after gym class. She looked like she had fought in some mighty battle and then came straight over for pictures."

"You don't know how many times I suggested that very idea, but I was shot down by the board with the exception of one vote."

"Let me guess all men and one woman."

"Two women, but the one who voted with me was a younger mom. The other woman was older and no kids."

Josie turned to Mia and asked, "How is your business going?"

"It's really good. The farmer's market really outperformed online sales, but I had a lot of people who took my card and said they would order online for some presents, and I did see an increase in website traffic right after the market."

"Being able to see the monsters in person really gives a different experience."

Dixie nodded. "And you can tell they are made well. We got one for Eli and he loves it so much. He carries it around with him everywhere and has chomped on every inch of him."

"Do you think you will be able to do this full time and stop serving?"

Mia thought for a few seconds before responding. "That is the goal. I couldn't live off of this full time on my own, but I have a feeling this pregnancy is going to limit some of my time at work. But I don't want to quit the bar entirely. I actually enjoy the job and interacting with the people. I think even after the baby is born, I may want to work here one day a week or maybe every other week."

The night continued with the girls giving her advice about advertising and some other markets within a couple hours that she could participate in. Mia felt a warmth deep inside as she looked around at the people she was now calling her friends and finally felt that she had truly found her home. If only she could get rid of that little tingle in the back of her brain that she shouldn't get too comfortable, and things could still go horribly wrong.

IN THE COUPLE WEEKS since telling everyone about the engagement, things had been moving at a breakneck speed. She had her first meeting with the seamstress who reminded her of her own grandmother and felt an instant connection to. She was picking her up to travel just outside Willow Springs to a fabric supplier. Just as she got into the car her phone rang through the Bluetooth speakers.

"Hello?"

"Hey, Mia, it's Dex," said the gruff disembodied voice.

"Oh, Dex, hey. Is there any news?"

"There is. They are still here in the states, but down in the Florida Keys."

Mia sucked in a breath. "Not as far as I was hoping."

"I get that."

"What are they doing?"

"I don't really know yet. I found them through some facial recognition by using social media tags from the list of places you gave me. I'm headed out there now. It may take some time to find exactly where they are staying, but is the plan still to call the authorities once I get there?"

"Yeah. Since they weren't dumb enough to leave the country, let's do it."

"Alright, I'll nail down where they are staying and be done with it, then."

Mia thanked Dex and was starting to feel a weight ease off of her shoulders thinking that this whole thing would soon be over.

Chapter 22

Mia was loading her car with boxes when she felt Derek come up behind her and kiss her neck.

"One day until you are officially mine."

Mia giggled. "I am already yours."

Derek's hands drifted up towards her ever-growing and tender breasts. "Think we have time for a little fun?"

His hand stopped at the side of her breast, and he let out a huff of laughter. "Really? Phone boob again?"

"Hey, don't make fun of me. I drop it a lot and bending over has been a challenge lately. These big girls can hold it for me when I am carrying other stuff."

"You can call them big girls and I still can't name them?"

"That is correct. You are not allowed to name them. You tried to give them slutty stripper names."

"No, I didn't. One of them is even from a kid's movie."

"Bambi and Candi are stripper names."

"How would you know? Have you gone to a strip club recently?"

Mia shut the trunk and shook her head. "You're being ridiculous. Go to work."

As she sat and started to shut the door, she heard him shout, "Wait! So, you've been to a strip club? Can we go together?"

Mia rolled down the window. "You're an idiot."

"But I'm your idiot."

"Yes, you are. Go to work."

Derek leaned over and gave her a kiss. "Love you."

"Love you, too."

Shortly after dropping off the packages to the post office, she arrived at her doctor's office for her checkup. Only this time instead of the quiet office she normally saw, the glass door was shattered, and the sheriff's car was parked out front.

Mia gingerly walked around the glass and found Chase talking to the front attendant, nurse, and doctor.

Not sure what to do she carefully walked up to them. "Uh, hi. Should I reschedule?"

The attendant that she saw nearly every time she had come in greeted her warmly but seemed a little shook up. "Hi, I'm so sorry. I was going to call but didn't realize how late it was already. We came in and found it like this."

"Is everyone okay?"

"Yeah. They just took a few things. Probably just some dumb kids thinking maybe we had some drugs they could get high off of here. My file room looks like someone had a temper tantrum."

"I'm so sorry."

"Thanks. We're working with the hospital to move all the appointments there today. Could we move you to five?

We're going to have a room reserved there until we can get this place back together."

"I was going to work tonight but I'm sure I can switch things around or come in later."

The woman gave her thanks and handed her a card to provide for the front desk staff at the hospital. Mia left and nodded her head towards Chase who was still talking to the doctor. He gave a quick wave in acknowledgment and went back to work.

Mia decided to go back home and work on some more monsters until it was time to go to the hospital. After telling Derek what happened, he told her to go ahead and take the whole day off. By the time she would return from the appointment the dinner rush would almost be over. She promised him that she would still check in with him when she got back.

Time moved quickly and before she knew it, it was time to go again. Mia juggled another couple of boxes for orders and her purse. She felt her phone vibrate against her chest and she shook her head. She forgot to take it off of silent from when she went to the doctor's office earlier. Well, whoever it was would have to wait until she got situated in the car.

Mia had just opened the trunk and placed in a box, when a cold chill ran down her spine as she heard a familiar voice call out her name.

Frozen in fear she desperately hoped that this was a figment of her imagination.

"Mia," the woman repeated.

Mia started to turn around but felt something hard pressing against her back. Was that a gun? It felt like one. Not that she had much experience with feeling a gun pressed against her back.

"Tabitha?" she shakily asked in a whisper.

She felt her purse get ripped away from her and tossed aside. "Get in the trunk, Mia."

She was not going to get into the trunk. No fucking way. That was how you died. She had heard all the warnings given to women. Never go to a second location. The chances of you dying increase exponentially if you go with them. "No," she said with as much certainty as she could.

Mia felt the gun press harder and Tabitha growled, "You were always such a bitch."

Mia was thinking about what her best option was, how to fight back, but before she could get an inkling of a plan, she felt a pinch in her neck, and it was almost immediately lights out.

DEREK WAS CLEANING the bar and talking to Chase and Dixie when his cell phone went off. He saw Grayson's name before answering and smiled. He started to say hello, but Grayson immediately cut him off. "Is Mia with you?"

Derek felt his stomach plummet, and he instinctively looked at Chase. "No. She should be at the hospital for her appointment still."

"Thank God. I tried to call her, but she isn't answering her phone."

"What's going on?"

"Tabitha is in the wind. Dex got shot and was unconscious for a couple days. Jack made him and confronted him. They got into a fight and Tabitha shot accidentally killing Jack and getting Dex too."

Derek started to feel the bile rise up in his throat. Don't panic. She's fine. She is probably still at the hospital. "You think she would come here for Mia?"

Chase started snapping his fingers at Derek and started pointing his fingers at the phone. Derek nodded. "I'm here with Chase, let me put you on speaker."

Derek switched the modes and said, "Okay."

Chase spoke up first. "What's going on?"

Grayson repeated what he just told Derek and how Dex suspected Tabitha was coming for Mia. "Dex said she was losing it over Jack getting killed and shot Dex again before he could get up. He had witnessed them earlier fighting about the baby. Her pregnancy was plastered all over the town's social media and they found out about it."

"Grayson, keep calling her. I am going to the hospital to see if she is there."

Chase stood up and nodded to Dixie. "I'm going too."

Dixie's eyes were wide and misting over as she nodded holding the baby closer.

"Check her apartment first before we leave," Chase said.

Derek shouted to Tiny to take care of the bar and that he had to go as they exited through the back door to the alley. The car was gone, so she likely had left for her appointment. Derek sprinted up the stairs with Chase close behind him. He used his key and burst through the door. Nothing was out of place. Everything was as it should be. Not seeing that there were signs of trouble he tried to calm down.

Chase was already leaving down the stairs as Derek started to leave. Memories flooded him as he glanced out the window to the fire escape where he'd first met her. He couldn't lose her. Not like this. She was fine, and they were overreacting. She better be fine. They had a future to build.

They made it to the bottom of the stairs and Derek started running his hands through his hair in frustration. "Fuck."

"Hey, is this Mia's?" Chase asked as he picked up a purse that was against the wall.

Derek reached out his hand and nodded. "Fuck. Yeah." Chase handed it over and opened it, not really sure what he was looking for.

"Is her phone in there?"

"No. Just a bunch of random crap and her wallet."

"You think she might have it on her still?"

Derek thought back and almost went into some type of hysterical laughter. "Shit. It is probably in her fucking bra. She's always carrying the damn thing like that."

Chase let out a breath. "Okay. Do you have a friend locator on her?"

Derek's eyes widened. "Oh, my God." He fumbled to pull his phone out of his pocket and waited for the app to load.

Chase did the same with his and made a call. "Grayson, I need you to stop calling Mia. Do you manage the bar's security?" Grayson must have answered yes as he continued, "Great. I need you to pull the footage of the back alley where

Mia's apartment entrance is. Call us back and let me know what you find."

The app finally pulled up, and he saw Mia's little dot moving down the highway towards a bunch of cabins. He knew the road well. It was also leading to his cabin. "You've gotta be fucking kidding me."

Chase peered over his shoulder to see the dot continuing to move up the winding road. "You know where that is?"

"I think she is going to my fucking cabin. Let's go."

The two men sprinted to Derek's car. As they were leaving Chase made some calls for backup from his deputy and then got a call from Grayson. Chase put it on speaker as the men continued to speed towards Mia.

"Ollie pulled the footage. Looks like Mia was forced into the trunk of her car and given some kind of sedative that knocked her out. The woman definitively had a gun as well. She tossed Mia's purse to the side and took off with the car. You guys are only about forty-five minutes behind them."

Chase let out a breath. "Great. We have location tracking on her from her phone and think they are heading out to Derek's cabin. We think the crazy bitch is using his place to hide out."

They could hear papers shuffling in the background as Grayson asked, "Which cabin? Ollie and I are closer to the cabins and can meet you for backup."

"I think she is going to Fox Den, on the east side."

"Alright. We'll meet you at the clearing just before the turnoff."

Chase looked over as Derek drove faster. "Which one? You have more than one?"

"Yup. I may have a little more money than I let you guys know about."

"Let's just hope the crazy bitch found out about your money and only wants that."

Derek whipped his head over to Chase. "As opposed to what?"

"Just drive."

"What, Chase!"

Chase sighed. "Revenge."

MIA STARTED TO WAKE up, but felt all kinds of wrong. She tried to move her hands down to prop herself up, but they jerked to a stop with a metal clink. Blinking she turned her head up to see her hands handcuffed and tied to the center post of a headboard. Where was she? She started to panic and fiercely pulled trying to free herself.

It was slowly coming back to her. Tabitha. She had surprised her by the car. She had a gun. She wanted her to get in the trunk, but she had refused, and then... then what?

She looked around the room and didn't see Tabitha. She needed to get the hell out of there. She pulled at the spindle of the headboard and tried to move it back and forth hoping to set it free.

She screamed in frustration and started to yell hoping to catch the attention of someone close by. Anyone really. "Help! Please, somebody help!!"

"Jesus, shut up," she heard as another door opened and Tabitha came through. "Nobody is going to hear you. We are miles away from where anyone is going to hear us."

Mia wanted to break down. She wanted to cry for all the things she was going to lose, because she was pretty sure crazy bitch was going to kill her. But she was not going to cry her heart out for her. She wouldn't give her that satisfaction. "Where are we?"

"What, you don't know?"

Mia shook her head.

"This is your fucking boyfriend's place. I figured you guys weren't using it so I would just help myself to it."

"What do you want? You already took all my money."

"Yes, but you took everything else."

"I didn't—"

Tabitha leaned in close and wrapped her hand around Mia's throat, applying enough pressure to hurt, but not to cut off her oxygen supply. "You took Jack from me."

Mia shook her head. "No, I didn't. He left *with* you."

Tabitha pulled her hand away and started pacing the room. "Oh, he did, but then we read about your baby, and he was becoming obsessed with the idea of being a father." She placed her hands on Mia's stomach and lovingly caressed it as Mia tried to squirm away.

"Don't fucking touch me!"

"Oh, I'm not interested in you. We had plans. We were going to wait until his baby was born and come back." Her face twisted into something resembling devastation with rage. "But you, you destroyed everything."

Mia shook her head. "How did I destroy it?"

Tabitha reached over the table and pointed a gun at her. "You killed Jack!"

Oh, God. She was going to die. If Jack was gone, there would be no stopping Tabitha. "I didn't kill him."

"You sent that fucking asshole to follow us."

"Dex?"

Throwing up her hands Tabitha yelled, "I don't know his fucking name. He kept asking questions about us and followed us. Jack confronted him without me." Her pacing quickened, and she started palming her free hand to her temple. "I had to stop him. He was hurting Jack. I told them to stop, but they wouldn't listen." She stopped pacing and looked directly at Mia. "I thought he was going for a gun. I had to stop him. Jack didn't carry a gun. He was always so weak when it came to the hard stuff." Her face contorted and Mia saw her cheeks flush a shade of red. "I had to shoot him. I had to protect him."

Mia's heart raced. Oh, God. Dex. That sweet gruff man who was helping her. "You killed Dex?"

"I had to. But that first shot. That first shot hit Jack too." Tabitha pointed the gun back at Mia. "It's your fault he's gone. He'd still be with me if it wasn't for you."

But it wasn't her fault. She knew that, but saying that might certainly earn her a bullet to the head. "I'm sorry, Tabitha. If you want more money, I'm sure we can work something out. You can disappear. Go to any country you want. Just let me go."

"You think I want your money," she spat.

"I bet we can—"

"I want... the baby. I want the only thing in this world that is left of Jack."

"No!" Mia screamed as she thrashed around trying to free herself. She stopped as she felt the gun held to her temple.

"Do not make me shoot you. I will cut you open to get the baby out, but I don't want to take that risk."

Mia immediately stopped. Tears flowed down her face as she was coming to the realization that she and the baby might die. "It's too early. The baby could die if I deliver now."

"You're the one that fucked that all up. We were going to wait until after it was born, but Jack's dead and plans changed."

Mia started looking around the room as if there could be something that could save them, but then she saw the one thing that would have given her hope. Her phone was on the floor with the screen completely smashed.

Tabitha noticed what she was looking at. "Oh, that. Yeah, I found it while I was carrying you and putting your fat ass in the bed. Don't worry, your boyfriend won't be able to interrupt us."

Mia watched as she placed a backpack on the chair and pulled out an IV bag and needle kit. No. She couldn't let her do this. "Please, don't. It's too early."

Tabitha just carried on preparing the bag and shook her head. "Did you know I worked as a NICU nurse before? I helped care for so many preemie babies. You are at the point where the baby has a ninety percent survival rate. And let's face it. God wouldn't let me lose another person. I mean, he isn't that cruel. I lost my parents, and now I lost Jack. Do you think he's that cruel?"

Mia just watched in horror and couldn't respond. She was crazy.

Tabitha narrowed her eyes. "I asked you a question. Do you think he would be so cruel as to leave me unable to carry a child, lose Jack, and then lose the only thing left of him?"

At this point maybe trying to connect with her would be the best option. "I didn't know you couldn't have a baby."

"Of course not. It's not like you ever really cared about me."

Mia shook her head. "I did care. I was looking forward to having you as my sister."

She slammed down the IV bag and turned to her. "You didn't. All you cared about was Jack. But you know what? He came back to me every day. Even the one time you had sex with him; he came back to me and begged me for my forgiveness."

"And you are the reason he wanted to wait?"

"He was never going to have sex with you. It wasn't supposed to happen. But we had that fight, and he got drunk and then that happened," she said pointing at her stomach.

She must have been done with her tirade because she walked over calmly to the bed and started to insert the needle for the IV. Once it was in, she said, "Pull it out and I'll shoot you in the head and slice you open to get the baby. Do you understand?"

Mia's lip quivered, and she nodded. What else could she do at this point? She helplessly watched as the drug was added and slowly made its way into her system. It was with sad resignation that she watched Tabitha sit in the oversized chair settling in for what could be a long day.

Chapter 23

Derek pulled off to the side of the road where Grayson, Ollie, and another large man were already waiting for them. Chase sprinted out and approached first. Ollie had the trunk opened to what looked like an arsenal. There were several rifles, handguns, and Kevlar vests.

Ollie nodded to the large man. "This is Ian. He's a trained sniper from the Rangers and one of our security detail men."

The man looked over Derek and Chase and said, "Grayson briefed me. I can set up outside once we have a location on the inside."

Chase looked at Derek. "Listen to me. I know you want to go in and get your girl, but you have to let us handle this. My backup is a couple minutes out and Ollie and Ian and I can get her out. But I need you out of this."

Derek wanted to tell him to fuck off, but he hadn't ever really handled a gun before, and he could very well make things worse. "Just promise me you'll bring her back to me."

Chase sucked in a breath. "Derek, I—"

"Just lie to me... Please."

"I'll bring her back. I promise."

He stood back and tried not to let the emptiness he was feeling consume him. This was bad. This was a fear that he never knew before. The ripping noise of the Velcro on the vest and the loading of ammunition was drowning out every other sound of nature surrounding them.

The sound of crunching gravel soon followed, and he turned to see two of the deputies approaching. He had to like these odds a little more. There were now five men going after Mia. Five against one. That had to be good, right?

Grayson stood next to Derek as he watched the men creep up to the cabin. He was dying to join them, but there were no additional vests and going up there might actually get him killed.

"Ollie and I turned off the security."

Derek turned to look at his friend. "What?"

"We turned off the system so that it won't go off in the cabin when everyone approaches."

"God. I didn't think about that."

"You're not trained to. That's what you pay us for."

"I don't understand how she got in to begin with."

"She rented it. We talked to your mom, and she verified that the cabin had been rented for the week. I think she got some sick perversion about using your cabin to take Mia."

"I can't lose her, Grayson."

"You're not going to lose her. If she just wanted to kill her, she would have done so in that alley. She wants something else."

"You think she wants the baby."

"I didn't say that."

Derek looked up to the road feeling certain in his knowledge. "You didn't have to."

The sound of another set of tires had Derek spinning around. It was the county ambulance. Austin was driving with Renna hopping out of the passenger side. "Chase told us to wait here. Is Mia okay?"

Derek shook his head. "We don't fucking know anything yet."

Several minutes passed in deafening silence while the four of them waited for any updates. When a loud crack came through the air, all of them ducked, not quite sure how to respond. Almost immediately another crack sounded and then a third and fourth.

"Fuck this," Derek shouted as he took off for his car with Grayson on his heels to head up to the cabin.

THE IV BAG WAS HALFWAY gone and Mia felt an uncomfortable pressure in her abdomen. Was it supposed to take effect this quickly? Something was wrong. She began to cry out in pain as the pressure increased. "Something's wrong. You need to get me to a hospital."

"Stop your whining. You're fine."

Mia gasped in pain. "But the baby might not be."

"God, shut up. I just gave you a slightly higher dose to speed things along. I can't be staying up with you all night now, can I?"

Mia writhed in pain. This couldn't be normal labor. She'd read about inductions, and it could take hours to start labor. This was all wrong. She cried out again in pain, but

Tabitha came and placed her hand on Mia's cheeks and squeezed them together. "Shut up, shut up, shut up!"

Hot tears fell down as Tabitha's grip tightened. When she finally did release her, Mia looked up at the handcuffs and wished she had the strength to pull the spindle loose. Maybe she could get free and hit the little psychopath in the head with it.

Now she was pacing again and just muttering to herself. She really wanted to know what she was saying but the pain was taking all of her focus and energy. Mia cried out again, and a loud bang thundered through the room. Tabitha used the gun. Did she shoot her?

"Shut up," she screamed.

Before Mia could respond the door burst open and she could see Chase coming into the room. Another loud crack sounded again from what she thought was Tabitha's gun and she watched in horror as Chase fell to the ground. Another deputy was right behind him and just dodged another bullet. Mia turned back to Tabitha worried that she would be next, but before she could do anything she heard another crack, glass breaking and blood bloomed from Tabitha's chest as she fell to the ground.

Was it really over? She tried to pull herself up to get a better look at the woman on the floor, but the restraints prevented her from seeing for certain if she was dead.

She heard the deputy using his radio saying something about getting the bus up here.

"Get me out of here. Please, help me," Mia cried.

The next person she saw through the door was Ollie in a vest and holstering his weapon. He leaned down to Chase who lifted his arm. "I'm fine. Go get Mia."

Ollie looked her up and down and his eyes stopped on the handcuffs.

Mia nodded to the backpack Tabitha used earlier. "Check over there. I think the key might be in there."

Seeing the IV he said, "I'm gonna pull this out first. Can you hold still while I get it out?"

Mia nodded. "Yes, please."

Having it pulled out was a physical relief she hadn't expected. The damage may have already been done, but having that out was like getting a small ray of hope peek through. Just as that hope showed she was instantly reminded that something was still wrong. Her abdomen clinched in pain, and she tried to curl into a ball while her hands were still above her head.

While she was mid-scream Ollie had finally freed her hands. She wrapped her arms around Ollie and cried hysterical tears. She was still clinging in relief of being rescued and the continued pain now also traveling into her back.

She thought she heard someone screaming her name but was still crying and feeling pain radiating from what almost felt like everywhere. "Mia," she heard again.

"Derek?"

"Mia," the panicked voice said again only this time it was right next to her. She let go of Ollie and grasped for Derek.

"You came," she sobbed.

She felt his arms tighten as he held her closer and kissed the top of her head. "Nothing was going to stop me."

The brief break she had got interrupted as pain grabbed hold of her again. She screamed out and heard Derek respond with a yell of his own. "Renna! Renna, help us!"

She heard Renna say something to the other paramedic and then to Derek, but Mia couldn't focus on words. Every ounce of energy was going towards the constant heat and spasm of pain. She felt Derek picking her up and placing her on the gurney. She didn't want to let go, but she heard Renna say, "Mia, you have to let go so I can check you out while we go to the hospital."

Reluctantly, she released the hold she had around Derek's neck. "Please, don't leave me."

She felt his hand capture hers and he squeezed. "I'm not leaving. I'm coming with you."

It was only seconds before they were loading into the ambulance, and Grayson came running up to the door. "Derek, give me your keys and I'll meet you there."

Derek tossed the keys and sat down beside Mia in the ambulance while yet another IV needle was placed into her body. She instinctively pulled her body away, but Renna reassured her. "I need to give you some medicine to try and slow the labor."

"Can you stop it? It's too soon!"

Renna looked at Mia and then back to Derek before responding. "That will be up to the doctor when he examines you. I can only slow things down and we can see what happens."

Mia wasn't sure how long it had been since she was given the medicine, but it felt like hours in the ambulance on the bumpy back road. She heard Derek telling her they were almost there when her chest began a slight burn, and the edges of her vision began to blur.

She noticed Renna frantically pulling items from the cabinets and knew something was going terribly wrong.

"Derek?"

Derek kissed her palm. "Yeah, baby?"

"Don't let our little star fade away." Before she could continue and say that she loved him too, she felt as if she was also fading away.

Chapter 24

Derek watched in horror as Renna used a defibrillator to restart Mia's heart. Her whole body jerked with each attempt. With each thump he clinched his fists as if he could hold her heart and help squeeze it to continue the blood flowing and providing life to what was his whole world.

After the third shock they heard the beeps of life coming through the monitor and they finally came to a stop. Several hospital staff opened the back ambulance doors and assisted with getting Mia inside. Derek followed until a man in scrubs put his hands to Derek's chest to stop him. "Wait here."

Derek was dumbfounded. For the first time, he just mindlessly followed orders and watched as Mia disappeared around the corner to the OR. Derek leaned against the wall and released an agony-filled groan. He found himself almost going into a panic attack. He was barely able to breathe. "Mia." More grasping for breath, and again, "Mia."

He felt someone lead him to a private waiting area he was starting to know all too well. They were here when Zoey got shot and when Dixie had been struck by the car. He was sitting with his head hanging down, arms resting on his knees and looking at his hands folded together, when he finally felt small hands holding his. He lifted his head to see his mom looking at him with tears in her eyes.

He quickly stood to his feet, hugged his mom, and cried into her shoulder. She held him tight like she did when he was young, and even though he towered over her, he felt like he was ten and only his mom could help him.

"It's going to be okay," she softly whispered.

Derek started to shake. "We were losing her on the way here."

"But we didn't. She's strong, and she will beat this."

"What if she doesn't? What if the baby doesn't?"

He finally released his mom and looked around the room. Most of his friends were here now. His eyes locked onto Zoey's and he flashed back to how broken she was when she lost Trevor and then her baby while they were in college. He remembered how much it changed her and how lost she was for years after. Would that be him? A year from now would he be a different person if Mia and the baby were gone?

He saw Zoey was leaning against Tyler, and she gave a silent nod of understanding. She knew the dark thoughts going through his mind. She'd lived them, and he never gave her enough credit for her grace back then. Because he had no grace now. He wanted to tear this room apart. Throw a chair against a window. Smash the television. Something to direct this well of rage overflowing from within.

It wasn't long before Grayson entered the room. Derek didn't want to talk, but he had to know if this was really over. "Tabitha?"

Grayson nodded. "Dead."

"Good," Derek spat.

From the corner of his eye, he saw his mom cover her mouth in shock. He knew that she wouldn't want him to find any kind of happiness in someone else's death but right now, he just didn't fucking care.

"Chase had to stay at the scene, but he said to call him if you need anything. Ollie and Ian are still there as well answering questions."

"Anyone else get hurt?"

"Chase was shot, but the vest took the hit. He is going to have a nasty bruise, and he is pretty pissed off about getting hit at all, but otherwise he's fine."

Derek let out a long breath. "I didn't even ask. I just—"

"Hey, nobody expected you to focus on anything but Mia. We're all good."

"Who got the kill shot?"

"Ian. He sniped her after she took her shots."

Several minutes later a man in scrubs came out and asked for Derek. He stood and braced for whatever was coming. "You have a baby girl. Four pounds and three ounces. She is breathing on her own and is stable, but she is going to have to be in the NICU for a little while. We will be giving her some oxygen and will likely have to feed her through a tube until she is able to feed on her own. We need to maintain her temperature, but you will be able to see her soon."

Still feeling anxiety at not hearing anything about Mia he asked, "And Mia?"

"We had to perform a cesarian and provide medication to offset some of the complications that came with the medication that was given to her to induce labor. She is still in surgery, and we will let you know when she is in recovery. I'll have a nurse take you to the NICU when she is ready. Do you have a name?"

"I know what I think it should be. Can I give you a name temporarily in case when Mia wakes up, we want to change it?"

"Of course."

They had already talked about and agreed that Mia and the baby would take his last name, and he thought of the last words she'd said. Don't let our star fade away. "Star. Star McKenna."

A COUPLE HOURS HAD passed. Mia was resting in the recovery room, and he was sitting in a rocking chair holding the most beautiful little girl. He was doing what the nurses called kangaroo care and holding her skin to skin. She was so tiny, but also so strong.

The nursing staff were very patient with him explaining all the medical care that she was receiving and what milestones she would need to reach to be able to go home. It was so much information. He wished he knew what more of he should be asking, but now all he wanted was to imprint this memory into his psyche.

Within the first few heartbeats together, he started to sing. "Twinkle, twinkle, little star, how I wonder what you are." He finished the song and felt her wiggle a little in discontent when he stopped. It was only then that he truly felt that maybe everything was going to be okay.

A nurse walked in behind him and said, "Hey, Dad. I just wanted to let you know that Mia is doing well and has been transferred to a private room. Your mom said to let you know that she will stay with her while you are here with the little one."

He thanked her and softly whispered, "You hear that, baby girl? Mom is going to be okay, and you will get to see her soon. You are going to just love her. She is kind and funny and loves you sooo much already. So, you focus on getting bigger and stronger so we can all go home, okay?"

She made another attempt at a small movement almost trying to acknowledge him and say, "Okay, Dad, let's go home soon."

MIA BLINKED HER EYES open and felt groggy and pain. So much pain. She wanted to sit up but this stabbing sensation in her stomach stopped her from moving. She felt her hand get squeezed and heard Derek's voice.

"Hey. Welcome back sleeping beauty."

She was still foggy, but a few things were starting to come back. Tabitha, the labor, the shooting. "The baby," she whispered full of dread.

"She's fine. She is in the NICU getting some extra care."

"I want to see her." She tried to sit up again but immediately fell back into the bed.

"Hey, take it easy. You will see her as soon as they clear us to leave your room. They wanted to do a check on you after you woke up. We have to make sure that beautiful heart of yours is going okay."

Mia put her hand to her stomach and winced in pain. "Wha—"

Derek almost instantly pulled her hand away. "Careful. They had to do a c-section to get her out. But she is doing well, and they have every expectation that she's going to be fine."

Mia had so many questions and Derek patiently answered each one. First about their baby and then about what happened at the cabin. It really was over. Jack and Tabitha were dead. Dex was expected to recover from his gunshots and Chase was saved by his vest.

Mia started to cry with all the emotions overwhelming her. She wanted to see her baby. She wanted to be home with Derek in his arms. She wanted this pain to go away. Needing to focus on something happy, she thought about the wedding. "Oh, I think we are going to have to postpone the wedding. I don't think I can make it tomorrow."

Derek let out a small laugh. "We could always bring it here."

Mia shook her head. "Not funny. Don't even think about it." Looking over at the corner where two balloons were floating, one saying It's A Girl, and the other Get Well Soon, Mia sighed. "We never picked out a name."

Derek made a small shrug. "I kind of already gave them one as kind of a placeholder."

"Oh, God. Please don't be some weird girl version of a basketball name."

"Hey, give me some credit. I know better than that."

"Okay what did you come up with?"

"Star."

Mia's heart warmed as she let it settle in. "I love it. It kind of honors my grandparents, too."

"It does, doesn't it? Okay, the wedding won't be tomorrow, but how about the day after tomorrow?"

Mia reached up and grasped his shirt, pulling him closer. "No. Now shut up and kiss me."

And he did. He shut up, kissed her and she melted into the touch of his lips and knew that she found her perfect forever.

Epilogue

Amanda looked around at the happy guests at her home as they celebrated the wedding of her son and Mia. The wedding took place later than they'd originally planned, three months in fact, but everything was perfect. She was eating a piece of delicious cake and holding her granddaughter, and in a surprise turn of events she would be getting another grandchild from Ariel and Kyle in a matter of months.

She was desperately soaking in this moment where everything was right in the world. There was so much new life happening. Her granddaughter, her coming grandchild, and even Zoey and Tyler had finally had a successful in-vitro session.

It had taken almost a month before Derek and Mia were able to bring little Star home from the hospital, but the extra time was needed to ensure that she would thrive. Now, the sweet little girl had no problem telling you when she was happy or very unhappy. Her lungs developed well, and she could be heard in the house next door if she wanted to vocalize her discontent.

Jeremy and Miranda stopped by and he asked to hold Star. She wanted to be stingy with her granddaughter's time, but Jeremy had made so much effort to heal his relationship with Derek, she couldn't deny him. In the couple days before Mia and Derek brought Star home Jeremy and Miranda scrubbed and disinfected the entire house on their own so that Star wouldn't get sick in the new environment. He actually did the work himself and didn't hire anyone to do it for them. She couldn't get him to pick up his dirty clothes when they were married, but whatever.

She gently transferred Star over to him and lightly brushed her hand over her soft head. "You be good for Grandpa. And if you are going to have a blowout, make sure it's when he's holding you."

"Hey," he said offended.

"Yeah. I appreciate you, but you're still my ex-husband. There are some unwritten rules that can't be broken. I can wish minor inconveniences on you and still have karma on my side."

"So mean."

"Eh. Better than the thousand paper cuts and jumping into a pool of lemon juice I used to wish upon you."

Miranda laughed. "That's a good one. I wished a lifetime of always wet socks for my ex. He had a weird thing about his feet."

"Okay, I'm going inside with the baby before you both conspire against me," he said as he walked towards the house.

Miranda followed and said, "Men are such babies."

Nearly everyone was dancing under the twinkle lights and she suddenly felt the need to let go and dance. She roamed her eyes around the yard and found Tiny cleaning up some of the serving dishes from dinner. Walking over with determination she stopped in front of him and put her hand on the edge of the platter gently putting it down. "Dance with me, Timothy."

He blinked at her. She knew that nobody ever called him by his given name, but she felt the nickname was just not suited for him. He was more like a wolf. A fierce predator and protective of his pack. And she would put money on the fact that there was nothing tiny about him... anywhere.

He didn't answer at first. They had danced before, but it was always in a light manner and not with the intensity she was bringing tonight. She wanted to feel more. She needed to feel more. Especially now. Especially before she went Monday and found out about... Stop it. She was going to enjoy tonight and not worry. "Please, Timothy."

His eyes drank her in, and she couldn't help but feel desire burning through her entire body. He didn't respond. He simply finished releasing the platter and took her hand in his. They made their own path to the center of the floor, and she melted into his arms as they swayed.

Occasionally, she saw her son and his new bride gliding around them looking happier than she had ever seen him. She wanted some of that same happiness, but she wasn't sure if she should even try anymore. The only man who had made her feel anything remotely passionate in years had her wrapped in his arms. What if she gave in?

But as soon as those thoughts started to slide in, the song was over and he gave her a hug and said he had to get back to help with the cleanup. Sigh. A hug. She got a hug. She wanted to climb him like a tree, and she got a hug.

She knew the challenges that would face them. She was older. He was an ex-con, and the town didn't always treat him as they should. But she didn't care about that. She had been the focus of town gossip and whispers before. Screw them. But what wasn't fair to him was what she might be facing. No, she needed to know for certain about the road ahead before she could do anything.

A couple hours after everyone left, she was sitting on the back porch enjoying the slight chill in the air. She had been lost in her thoughts when she caught sight of Timothy bringing out a small bowl of food for the stray cat.

He noticed her and nodded. "You good? Do you need anything?"

She needed so many things, but she could only settle on, "I'm good, thanks."

He nodded and started to walk towards the door with his back to her and she thought she heard him say, "Night, Angel."

He paused for a brief second like he didn't mean to say that but chose to ignore it and went inside. She sighed and whispered, "Good night, sweet man."

About the Author

Kate grew up in the suburbs of Cincinnati, Ohio. While attending school, she participated in writing competitions and workshops for young adults. After college, she stayed in Cincinnati and chased her passion of helping others with her work in social services and volunteering in the community.

She moved to Phoenix, Arizona where she again found a love for reading and writing romance books. When she isn't writing new stories she can be found exploring Arizona and reading a good book.

Read more at https://www.katealexanderauthor.com/.

www.ingramcontent.com/pod-product-compliance
Lightning Source LLC
LaVergne TN
LVHW011946060526
838201LV00061B/4220